"When did you try to tell me?" Hank demanded

He took several paces away from Jackie, as though he found her distasteful. "When? I don't remember once in seventeen years."

"Yes," she replied. "I did… That day." She struggled to maintain control, as everything inside her shook with emotion and old pain.

And new pain.

"I tried to explain why I couldn't go with you," she went on, "but you—"

"You said you thought it'd be better if you stayed behind," he interrupted, taking several angry steps back to her. "You never once mentioned—"

"You talked *over* me," she told him quietly. "You didn't give me a chance. Then you stormed away."

"Well, what about the seventeen years since?" he roared at her. "Why didn't you call or write?"

Oh, God, she thought, steeling herself. Anguish squeezed her lungs and made air escape in a painful sound. She had to pull herself together. The hard part was coming.…

Dear Reader,

Some women respond to the dreamer hero in romance novels, while others are attracted to the footloose wanderer. Many have an affinity for bad boys, and some want to make a home for the wounded man in need of a woman with just the right antibiotic.

Personally, I have a thing for the hero with purpose. I like the man who knows what he wants in a woman and goes after her with confidence, determination and just enough vulnerability to leave me wondering whether he'll get her or not. In real life, I'd be offended if my husband behaved as though he had all the answers—particularly because I never seem to have any. Life is a mystery that confounds and confuses me every day. But in my dreams—or in my romantic fantasies—I love to think there's a man out there to whom life is a clear, straight path to the woman he cherishes, and he'll let nothing, including her confusion, get in his way.

This is your introduction to Hank Whitcomb, just such a man.

I wish you all good things.

Muriel

Muriel Jensen
P.O. Box 1168
Astoria, Oregon 97103

Man with a Mission

Muriel Jensen

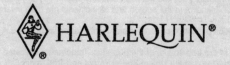

TORONTO • NEW YORK • LONDON
AMSTERDAM • PARIS • SYDNEY • HAMBURG
STOCKHOLM • ATHENS • TOKYO • MILAN • MADRID
PRAGUE • WARSAW • BUDAPEST • AUCKLAND

ISBN 0-373-71033-X

MAN WITH A MISSION

Man with a Mission

CHAPTER ONE

HANK WHITCOMB STARTED backwards down the stairs in his office building, supporting one end of a heavy oak table that served as his desk. Bart Megrath, his brother-in-law, carried the other end.

"Whose idea was it to move your office anyway?" Bart asked. "And why is everything oak? Don't you believe in light, easy-to-clean plastic?"

"The move was my idea." Haley Megrath, Hank's sister, brought up the rear with an old oak chair. "If he's going to bid on City Hall jobs, he may as well conduct business from one of their new rental spaces in the basement instead of in this derelict old mill a mile outside of town."

Hank was counting. Twelve steps—eight to go. "It was my own idea," Hank insisted. Thirteen. Fourteen. "You just agreed that it was a good one."

"I'm the one who told you the City had decided to rent spaces."

"And when you told me, I told *you* that Evelyn Bisset had already called me about it."

"So, the suggestion had more punch coming from Jackie's secretary." Haley's voice took on a deceptively casual but suggestive note. He refused to bite.

He would not discuss Jackie Bourgeois. He'd neither forgotten nor forgiven her. It was unfortunate that she was mayor at this point in time, but she was. Still, there was little chance they'd have to deal with each other. The city manager handled the bids on city hall repairs, so Hank would be doing business with him.

"Hey," Bart said with a grunt. "Let Haley take the credit. Electrical power comes and goes in that ancient building, and the roof leaks. When the time comes that you regret moving Whitcomb's Wonders out of Chandler's Mill and into City Hall, you can blame your little sister."

"Hey!" Haley complained. "How'd you like an oak chair upside your head?"

Hank had reached the bottom of the stairs, but the hallway was too narrow for him to put the table down so they could catch their breath. He turned the bulky piece of furniture onto its side and aimed himself carefully out the door, angling the table so that Bart could follow with the legs at his end.

Snow flurried from a leaden sky, and Hank was instantly assailed by the cold of a western Massachusetts March afternoon, its harshness blunted by the delicious freshness of the air. Old snow crunched underfoot as he headed for the dark green van he'd bought to start his new life.

"Is this going to fit in there?" Bart asked, their pace considerably quickened now that they were outside.

"I measured it." A former engineer for NASA, Hank checked and rechecked even the smallest detail of any project he undertook. He put down his end, climbed into the van, then reached out to pull the table in. He'd removed all the van's seats to make room and now backed his way toward the driver's seat as Bart lifted up on his end and pushed the table under the hatch door.

It was a snug fit. Bart took the chair from Haley and slipped it sideways between the table legs.

"Is this it?" Bart asked. "We've got a little room under the table. What about those files you had in boxes on the floor?"

Hank climbed over the front seat and let himself out the passenger door. Bart and Haley came around the side. "No, I'll take those tomorrow. I've got to clean them out tonight. You guys go back to work and I'll meet you for dinner at seven at the Yankee Inn."

"I told you you don't have to take us out to dinner," Haley protested.

Bart had an arm around her and his thumb, Hank noticed, was unconsciously stroking the curve of her shoulder. In jeans and a fleece sweatshirt, her dark hair in one long braid and her cheeks pink from four hours of helping haul his office furniture up and down stairs, Haley looked about fourteen.

Bart had been good for her, Hank thought, though when he'd sent his friend to get her out of jail last August after a crisis on a space mission prevented Hank from leaving, he'd never imagined that his best friend and his little sister would fall in love. Haley still had the fearlessness that had encouraged her to challenge a crooked mayor and end up behind bars.

The sweetness she'd lost that fateful night five years

ago when she and her fiancé had been attacked by thugs and he'd broken free and ran, abandoning her to her fate, was finally back. Thanks to the timely arrival on the scene of an off-duty policeman, she'd been rescued, though not before she'd lost her faith in men. But Bart had restored it. Hank saw implicit trust in her eyes when she looked into Bart's face—as well as a hot, almost embarrassing passion that made Hank green with envy.

The lack of a personal life was part of the reason Hank had decided to come home to Maple Hill. NASA had hired him right out of the University of Southern California, and he'd spent the next fourteen years devoted to assisting in the exploration of space. One day six months ago, after he'd been up seventy hours when one of their space missions encountered a control problem, then finally landed safely, he realized he had no one to celebrate with. There were co-workers who understood the engineering problem and could share his happiness and relief that the astronauts were safely home. But there was no one who really knew what was in his heart.

He had girlfriends, party friends, who shared the intimacies of a bed without really caring about his thoughts and feelings.

He'd once believed that was freedom. Now he knew it was simply loneliness.

There was no one who knew about the warnings that filled his head—''You're not as good as you think you are. You'll fail just like the rest of us. But your high and mighty attitude will make you fall so far, you'll dig a hole when you land.'' No one who understood that every day was a struggle to live down the sound of his father's words. No one who grasped the depths of his relief every time he proved the voice wrong.

Fortunately, an interest in electricity, which he'd probably inherited from his father, led him to a summer job working with an electrician in high school, and apprenticeship summers while he was in college. When he'd decided to change careers, getting licensed had been a simple thing, and his hobby turned into his livelihood.

''I want to take you out,'' he insisted. ''I couldn't have managed all this in one day without you. Make sure you bring Mike.''

Mike McGee was a fifteen-year-old boy who helped Haley at the *Maple Hill Mirror,* the weekly newspaper she published. She and Bart had acquired custody of him when his mother went to jail.

''He's got an overnight with some friends from the basketball team. The kids are going to have a booth during the Spring Festival. The coach and his wife are hosting them this weekend so they can plan their strategy. Eleven fifteen-year-old boys. Can you imagine?''

He couldn't. Kids in general were not his forte. He liked them fine, he just thought every child deserved more tolerance and understanding than he felt capable of. They were mysterious little beggars, and he'd been an engineer. Specific rules applied to specific situations for specific results.

Even now that he was an electrician, the approach

was the same. There was little mystery involved. If you held on to 120 volts, you fried. It was as simple as that.

"How are you going to unload this when you get to City Hall?" Bart asked, pointing to the table.

"Mom's there, straightening things up for him," Haley said with a grin. "She'll just order the table to get inside on its own power."

Bart laughed. "I can see that happening. But on the chance that doesn't work…"

"Trent promised to stop by and help me," Hank said, pushing the passenger door closed.

"Trent?" Haley asked.

"The plumber I hired yesterday. Seems like an all-right guy."

"And what's his story? Why is he joining your troupe of part-time tradesmen?"

"He's getting his MBA from Amherst, but wants to work part-time. Says school's too cerebral. He needs the hands-on work to stay grounded."

"You're sure you don't want me to do a story on Whitcomb's Wonders?" Haley asked for the fourth or fifth time. "It'd be good for business, and the public would love to know about a service that can fill any need out there at a moment's notice. How many men do you have now?"

"Seven." He didn't have to stop to think. He was surprised himself by how good his part-time help idea was. He'd started the business at the end of September, and by Christmas had employed five men who were surprised and pleased by the notion of working part-time while they pursued other careers, cared for their children, went to school. Evan Braga, a house-painter, signed on in January, and now Cameron Trent rounded out a pretty impressive roster. "We can do wiring, plumbing, landscaping and gardening, furnace repair, janitorial work, insulation and house painting. But I doubt that any of my guys is anxious for publicity."

Haley grinned. "It might get them girls," she cajoled.

He rolled his eyes at Bart. "Why is it they think we have nothing else on our minds?"

"Maybe because trying to guess what they want," Bart replied, "takes so much of our time and concentration."

Haley punched Bart playfully in the stomach. "I've told you over and over. Full-time attention and expensive jewelry."

Her wedding ring of pave diamonds flashed as she punched him, and Hank concluded that Bart must have gotten the message. Or else he loved her so much that what he couldn't say with words, he spoke with diamonds.

"Thanks for the offer, Sis," Hank said, walking around to the driver's side. Bart and Haley followed him. "I'll buy an ad instead to announce the opening of my new office."

"Oh, all right, I'll *give* you the ad." She hugged him tightly. "A good half page in the TV section so it'll be seen every day. Think about what you want in it. A photo of all of you would be good. We don't have to go into details, just let the town see you have a competent force."

"Okay. That sounds like a good idea. I'll see how the men feel about it." Hank shook hands with Bart, then climbed into the van. "See you at dinner. You're sure you wouldn't rather eat at the Old Post Road Inn? The menu's a little more elegant than the Yankee."

Bart opened his mouth, but before he could speak, Haley said, "The Yankee's great. I'm in the mood for their pot roast."

Bart sent him a subtle smirk over her head. She was as transparent as cling wrap. The Yankee Inn had been in Jackie Bourgeois's family for generations. Her father had retired two years ago, leaving her in charge. Haley wanted them to bump into each other.

"The Yankee it is," he said with a cheerful smile, pretending he had no idea what she had in mind. He'd studiously avoided Jackie for the six months he'd been home, afraid she'd see the feelings he couldn't control, even though she'd broken his heart all those years ago. He didn't want to care and never intended to do anything about it. He just couldn't help that he did.

He'd run into her by surprise on only two occasions—once in the dentist's office when he'd been walking out and she'd been walking in with two very grim-looking little girls in tow. He knew they were her daughters. Erica was ten, his mother had told him. And Rachel was six.

The second time was at the grade school when he'd been called in to replace a faulty light switch in the cafeteria. She'd been chatting cheerfully with other mothers who'd gathered there with classroom treats. He'd looked up at the sound of her laughter, startled and weirdly affected by the fact that though everything else about her had matured in the seventeen years since they'd been high-school sweethearts, that hadn't. It was still high-pitched and infectiously youthful.

He'd also noticed her pregnancy. Her stomach was bulbous, her cheeks a little plumper than he remembered. But her strawberry-blond hair had looked like Black Hills gold, her complexion porcelain with a touch of rose.

The moment her eyes had met his, she'd disappeared into the pantry area, the swift turn of her back coldly adult.

She had no use for him. Which was fine with him. He had no feelings left for the woman who had loved him as though he was her whole world one moment, then refused to share her life with him the next. If she was at the Yankee Inn tonight, he was sure she'd be as eager to avoid him as he was to stay clear of her.

Comforted by that thought, he turned the key in the ignition, waved at Haley and Bart, and headed off toward downtown Maple Hill.

He was amazed by how comfortable he'd felt coming home to this quiet little Connecticut River valley after being away for so long. If Jackie Bourgeois didn't live here, he thought, it'd be perfect.

Judging by outward appearances, very little had changed in Maple Hill in over two hundred years. Realizing that its cozy, colonial ambience was its stock-in-trade when tourists visited, the local merchants' association with the aid of City Hall had done everything possible to maintain the flavor.

The road to town was lined with old homes in the classic saltbox and Georgian revival styles and set back on spacious lawns, their trees now naked against the sky. Old barns housed businesses, and old inns had been refurbished.

Houses were built closer to the street as Hank drew nearer to town. Some of the cobblestones were still visible, and the streetlights looked like something out of Old London.

Maple Hill Common, the town square and the heart of commercial downtown, boasted a bronze statue of a Minuteman and a woman in eighteenth-century dress, surrounded by a low stone wall. Around the square were shops that looked much as they had in the 1700s. A 50-star flag and an old colonial flag with its thirteen stars in a circle flew from a pole on the green.

The sight never failed to move him. He felt connected to a historic past here, while bound to a town looking toward the future. You could buy a mochaccino, high-tech software and designer clothing, or sniff oxygen in a bar if you so desired. Maple Hill was quaint, but there was nothing backward about it.

Hank pulled into a parking spot on the City Hall lot, pleasantly surprised that it hadn't already been claimed. The spot next to his held a red Astro van and a sign that read, THE MAYOR PARKS HERE.

He turned off the engine and retrieved his key, annoyed that thoughts of Jackie interrupted his pleasant musings on the good life he lived here. But he'd better get used to it, he thought philosophically. He might not have to deal with her, but he was bound to run into her more often with his office in City Hall.

SUICIDE HAD SO MUCH APPEAL, Jackie Bourgeois thought as she put a hand to the rampaging baby in her womb. She would do it with a dozen Dulce de Leche Häagen-Dazs bars, pots of *caffeinated* coffee and several bottles of Perrier-Jouët champagne—all the things she hadn't been able to touch since she'd found out she was pregnant.

She'd have to wait until the baby was in college, of course. Responsible women simply didn't walk away from their problems. The Yankee ethic wouldn't allow it.

By the time the baby was eighteen, Erica and Rachel would be married and able to provide for him when he came home on school breaks. They wouldn't even miss her. They were all convinced her sole purpose in life was to make them miserable anyway.

Her father loved her, but he'd made his life without her and the girls since her mother died several years ago. He'd bought a place in Miami and often forgot to check in with his family as he embarked on new adventures.

And two of the city councilmen wouldn't miss her, except as someone to accuse of feminine ignorance or heartless female highhandedness, depending upon which complaint best suited their current disagreement. At the moment she was a harpy for renting space in the basement, a capitalist venture they considered beneath the dignity of city government.

Holding on to the railing, Jackie made her way carefully down the basement steps, checking on the city's two new tenants as a way of avoiding the councilmen blustering upstairs.

City Hall was housed in an old colonial mansion that had been built after the Revolutionary War by Robert Bourgeois, an ancestor of Jackie's late husband. City offices were on the first floor, the mayor's office and meeting rooms were upstairs, and local events were hosted in the old ballroom. The basement had been cleaned out and redecorated after a hurricane last summer left it water damaged, and Jackie and Will Dancer, the city planner, had come up with a plan to rent office space there to help support the aging building's many repairs. Will's office had handled the actual rental of space and Jackie had been too busy with other city affairs to find out who'd secured them.

She peered into the first office and found it chaotic, a sort of examining bed, an odd-looking chair, a file cabinet painted lavender and several pieces of brocade furniture clumped in the middle of the room. There were boxes on the floor filled with what was probably the contents of the file cabinet, and several framed landscapes leaned against the wall.

"Hi!"

Jackie almost jumped out of her skin at the high-pitched greeting. She turned to find a tall, slender woman perhaps a few years older than she, dressed in lavender leggings and flats and a long-sleeved lavender T-shirt. A wide purple band circled her carroty hair and was caught above her left ear in an exaggeratedly large bow.

"Mrs. Mayor!" the woman said breathlessly, offering her hand from under a large box she'd apparently just brought in from the side entrance. "How nice to meet you. I'm Parker Peterson."

"Hi." Jackie shook her hand and wanted to try to help her ease the box to the floor, but her pregnancy allowed very little bending at this stage. The woman seemed to have no trouble handling it on her own, a taut line of arm and shoulder muscles revealed by her snug shirt.

She straightened and put one hand on her hip and the other up to fluff her bow. "What a good idea this is! I'll be right in the thick of the stress and strain of business life. These poor nine-to-fivers are my client base, you know."

Jackie looked a little worriedly at the curious couch, the odd chair and Parker Peterson's flamboyant style of dress. She was almost afraid to ask. "What is it you do, Ms. Peterson?"

Parker gave the odd little chair a pat. "I'm a massage therapist. Here. Sit down and put your head right here." She fluffed the small cushion on the funny arm sticking out in front of the chair. "You straddle it like a horse."

Jackie patted her stomach. "We're not very athletic these days."

"It doesn't really take much effort. Here, I'll help you." She steadied Jackie's arm as she spoke and encouraged her to lift her foot to the other side of the stool-like chair.

Jackie would have continued to resist, except that Parker had put her hand to the small of Jackie's back as she spoke and rubbed her fingertips at the base of her spine where the pressure of five or six pounds of baby and fifteen or so pounds of "support" sat twenty-four hours a day. The relief was instant and melted her protests.

"We need to loosen up your back muscles," Parker said. "That's it. Feel that? Gotta prevent that tension or you'll be miserable until you deliver. A couple of weeks?"

"About a month and a half," Jackie replied, unable to believe she was a pile of jelly in this woman's hands after two minutes' acquaintance. She was usually very much aware of her dignity as mayor—not because she was pretentious, but because her council was always looking for something about her to criticize.

And she had to pretend to the town that though her husband had died in the arms of a cocktail waitress after promising Jackie he was rededicating himself to their marriage and their two children, he hadn't humiliated *her,* but embarrassed his own memory. And she liked to think that the pregnancy that had resulted from that promise was a testament to her trust.

The baby stirred as though also appreciating the massage.

Parker's hands went up Jackie's spine and down again with gentle force.

"You have to stop," Jackie said weakly, her voice

altered by her cheek squashed against the pillow and the total relaxation of her now considerable body weight. "I have a meeting in fifteen minutes. You'll have to roll me in on the chair."

Parker laughed as her fingertips worked across Jackie's shoulders. "You'll have to come and see me when you need a break. I'm good, I'm reasonable and I'll give special rates to anyone who works in the building. I'll be here from eight to six."

Parker stopped working and helped Jackie to her feet. "Isn't that better?"

Jackie did feel as though ten pounds had been removed from her stomach.

"Watch that posture," Parker advised. "And drink your milk. You have a husband to give you foot rubs?"

"I wish," Jackie replied, then realized that she didn't really. Foot rubs would be nice, but hardly worth the anguish a husband could inflict otherwise.

"Me, too. So, you're having this baby alone?"

Jackie concluded that Parker had to be new in town. "I was widowed right after I got pregnant. But this is my third, so I kind of know what I'm doing."

"That's nice," Parker said wistfully. "I know all about pregnancies—what to eat, how to exercise, how to massage to relieve strain and pressure. But I've never had the experience. Two husbands but no baby."

"I'm sorry." Men weren't always worth the time devoted to a marriage, but children were. "I'll bring mine by to meet you," Jackie said with a grin. "Then you might think you've had a lucky escape."

Parker walked her to the door of her office.

"My purse is in my…" Jackie began, pointing upstairs.

"That was free of charge," Parker insisted. "Just tell your friends I'm here. I'm taking out an ad in the *Mirror,* but it won't come out until next Thursday."

"I will. And good luck. If you have trouble with heat or plumbing or anything, let us know."

Parker promised that she would, then waved as she went back to the side door, apparently to retrieve more boxes.

Jackie rotated her shoulders as she passed the two dark and empty spaces. She'd have to find a way to work a massage into her daily schedule.

She turned a corner and walked down a small hallway that led to the last office. The hallway was dark, she noted. She would have to see that a light was installed overhead.

She peered into the only office on this side of the building and was stunned to see a figure she knew well standing in the middle of the room and looking around with satisfaction at what appeared to be a well-organized office.

"Adeline!" Jackie exclaimed, walking into the office, her arms open. "What are you doing here?" Adeline Whitcomb was her best friend's mother and the girls' Sunday School teacher.

"Jackie!" The gray-haired woman with a short, stylish cut and bright blue eyes went right into Jackie's arms. "I didn't have a chance to tell you I was moving into City Hall."

Jackie looked around as they drew away from each

other. There were file cabinets against the wall, a map of the city tacked up on one side, a large one of the county on the other. A small portable bar sat under the city map, with a coffeepot on it and a box from the bakery. A low table held a cordless phone atop a phone book. A quilt rack took up considerable space in one corner of the room.

"Are you going into business, Adeline?" Jackie asked, knowing that Addy's skills as a quilter were legendary. She'd made one for each of Jackie's girls when they were born. "Have you found a way to make quilting profitable?"

Adeline looked amused by that suggestion. "As if," she said, then lowered her eyes and looked away for a moment, as though uncomfortable holding Jackie's gaze.

Jackie had a horrible premonition. "This is Hank's office," she guessed.

Adeline smiled and sighed, as though she'd suddenly made up her mind about something. "It is. I'm tidying things up while he moves things in. And the quilt rack is here because I'll be his office staff and help organize all the men."

Jackie's horror was derailed for a moment. "*All* the men? Does he have partners?"

"No. I thought you knew he started Whitcomb's Wonders." Adeline went on to explain about the on-call service of tradesmen and craftsmen Hank had started. If anyone had told her, she hadn't listened. She automatically tuned out when his name was mentioned.

"You know, he's been back in Maple Hill for six

months, Jackie," Addy went on. "It's time you two stopped pretending the other doesn't exist."

Great. The ten pounds Parker's massage had alleviated were now back with a vengeance and, against all anatomical good sense, sitting right in the middle of her shoulders. She started to back toward the door. She would never deliberately hurt Adeline, but she would avoid crossing paths with Hank at all costs.

"It's great that you'll be here," she said diplomatically. "Maybe you and I can have coffee or lunch."

"It's childish and nonproductive," Adeline said, ignoring Jackie's invitation. Exasperation was visible in her eyes. "You're going to be in the same building. You have to come to terms with this."

"We've come to terms with each other, Addy." Jackie put both hands to her back, the pressure there tightening at the very mention of Hank's name. "We like pretending the other doesn't exist. Then we don't have to remember the past or deal with each other in the present."

"You were children when all this happened," Adeline reminded her. "Certainly you can forgive each other for behaving like children."

Jackie closed her eyes tightly against the image her brain tried to form of that time. She didn't want to see it. There'd certainly been grave and very adult consequences for the actions Addy considered childish.

"Just wanted to welcome you to the building," Jackie said, stepping out into the hall and turning to force a smile for Addy. "If there are any problems with the space, please call,"

Addy sighed dispiritedly. "I will, Jackie. Thank you."

Jackie headed back the way she'd come, eager now to get upstairs. With Hank Whitcomb occupying office space in the basement, this would no longer be the place to hide from her councilmen.

In the dark corridor before she made the turn, she collided with something large and hard in the shadows. She knew what it was even before firm hands grabbed her to steady her.

Could this day get any worse? She drew a breath and cloaked herself in mayoral dignity. "Hello, Hank," she said.

CHAPTER TWO

HANK KNEW HE'D COLLIDED with Jackie even before he heard the sound of her voice. Her scent was different, but she was using the same shampoo she'd used seventeen years ago. The collision brought her cap of red-blond hair right under his nose, and the peach and coconut fragrance filled his senses with memories he'd kept a lid on for most of his adult life.

He saw her slender and naked in his arms, her gray eyes looking into his as though he controlled the universe. He saw her laughing, her eyes alight. Then he saw her crying, her eyes drowning in a misery to which he'd hardened his heart.

Why had he done that? he wondered now, as though he'd never considered it before. Then he remembered. Because she'd taken all their dreams and thrown them away.

He felt a curious whisper of movement against his hipbone and suddenly all memories of her as a girl vanished as he realized that her rounded body was pressed against him. For an instant he entertained the thought that if things had gone according to plan all those years ago, this would be his baby.

But the intervening years had taught him not to look back.

Aware that he held her arms, he pushed her a step back from him, waited a moment to make sure she was steady, then lowered his hands.

She hadn't had this imperious manner then, he thought, looking down into her haughty expression.

"Jackie," he said with a quick smile. If she could behave like cool royalty to show him she didn't care about their past, he would be friendly, to prove that he held nothing against her, because it had never really mattered anyway. "How are you? I wanted to talk that day we met at the dentist, but you were in such a hurry."

She looked as though she didn't know what to do for a moment. He liked seeing her confusion. The day he'd left Maple Hill, she'd made him think *he* was wrong, and that had confused him for a long time. Payback was satisfying.

She folded her arms over her stomach, then apparently deciding that looked too domestic, dropped her arms and assumed a duchess-to-peasant stiffness.

"I'm well, thank you," she replied. "I just came to welcome you to City Hall."

"I appreciate that." He smiled again, taking her arm and trying to lead her back toward the office. "Mom's in…"

She yanked her arm away, her duchess demeanor abandoned in a spark of temper. She caught herself and drew another breath. "We've already talked," she said politely. "I told her if you have any problems, to let us know."

"Shall I call you?" he asked, all effusive good nature.

Her eyes reflected distress at the thought, though she didn't bat an eyelash. "No, Will Dancer will be taking care of tenants. Extension 202."

He nodded. "We've been in touch a couple of times about updating the building's wiring with circuit breakers."

"We can't afford to do that," she said.

He shrugged a shoulder. "It'll reduce your insurance on the building. Dancer thinks it's a good idea. And I'm pretty reasonable."

He realized the opening he'd given her the moment the words were out of his mouth.

"Really," she said, old pain furrowing her brow. "That's not the way I remember it."

He didn't understand it. It had been all her fault. So why did the pain on her face hurt him?

She turned and started to walk away.

He followed, determined to maintain the I-don't-care-it-doesn't-matter pose. "I meant," he said calmly, "that I provide a good service at a reasonable price."

"Well, that's what the city would be looking for," she said, steaming around the corner, past the other offices and toward the stairs, "if we could afford to do such a thing. But Will Dancer notwithstanding, we can't."

She turned at the bottom of the stairs to look him in the eye. "I hope you didn't move your office here in the hope of securing City Hall business."

He liked this part. "I *have* City Hall business," he

said, letting himself gloat just a little. "Dancer hired me to replace all the old swag lamps with lighted ceiling fans. He also invited me to submit a bid for rewiring."

She'd always hated to be thwarted. Curiously, he remembered that with more amusement than annoyance.

"Just stay out of my way," she said, all pretense dropped and her finger pointed at his face.

He thought that a curious threat coming from a rather small pregnant woman. It suggested black eyes and broken kneecaps.

He rested a foot on the bottom step, his own temper stirred despite his pose of nonchalance. "I know it's probably difficult to grasp this," he said, "when you've been prom queen, Miss Maple Lake Festival and all-around darling of the community, but you don't control everything. I am free to move about, and if that happens to put me in your way, I'm sorry, but you'll have to deal with it."

Angry color filled her cheeks. "I do run this city hall." Her voice was breathless in her apparent attempt to keep the volume down. "And if you get in my way, I can get your bid ignored so fast you won't know what happened. And I can also see that no other city business comes your way *ever!*"

It was almost comfortable to fight with her again. This was familiar ground. "You're sounding just like the mayor you and my sister helped replace. The one who got too full of his own importance and eventually stole hundreds of thousands from the city and held the two of you at gunpoint? You remember? The one who's still doing *time.*"

She sighed and rolled her eyes. "You don't see me holding anyone at gunpoint, do you? And I don't need anyone else's money."

"You just threatened to arbitrarily deprive me of my livelihood. I'm sure Haley, as the city's watchdog, would have to look into such behavior."

She didn't seem worried. "Your sister is my best friend. I doubt very much that she'd come out on your side."

"She's a reporter before she's a friend, and I am her brother."

Her voice rose to a shout despite all her efforts. "Then keep your distance and don't give me any excuse to get rid of you!"

"You got rid of me," he reminded her, "seventeen years ago."

"Who left whom?" she demanded.

"We were *supposed* to leave together."

For an instant, emotion flashed in her eyes. He tried hard to read it but he was out of practice. Had it been...regret?

"Something unexpected..." she began, and for some reason those words blew the lid off his temper. Probably because they reminded him of what she'd begun to say the night he'd left—alone. *Hank, on second thought, it might be better if you went alone, and I...*

He hadn't let her finish. He remembered that he'd been so sure all along that such a thing would happen, that Jackie Fortin was never going to be his. He was sure she'd find that his father had been right all along and Hank was worthless.

"Yeah, you tried to tell me that then, too," he barked at her. "You expected me to fail, didn't you? And you didn't want to leave all your crowns and tiaras behind to take a chance with me."

IT WOULD BE SO SATISFYING to kick him in the shin, Jackie thought. But Parker and Addy had wandered out into the hallway at the sound of raised voices and now stood a short distance away, looking on worriedly. When Jackie finally did take her revenge on Hank, she didn't want witnesses.

Besides, much as she hated to admit it, even to herself, it hadn't been all his fault. She should have tried to make him listen, insisted that he understand, but she'd been frightened and hurt, too. And brokenhearted.

She was very tired suddenly and her back felt as though sandbags hung from it. "I think you have me confused with your father," she said softly, so that Addy wouldn't hear. "You wouldn't listen to my explanation then, so I doubt you'd want to hear it now. If you'll excuse me, I'll get out of *your* way."

But she couldn't climb the stairs until he moved.

He considered her a moment, his anger seeming to thin, then caught her arm and drew her up on the step beside him. "Come on," he said. "I'll walk you upstairs."

She wanted to tell him that she walked up and down stairs all day long. That was the price of occupying a building that had been constructed before elevators. But he looked as tired of their argument as she felt, so she kept quiet.

With his large hand wrapped around her upper arm, he led the way upstairs. The space was a little tight, but she did her best to ignore him. She didn't realize until they were almost at the top that she wasn't breathing. The baby, apparently convinced he was being strangled, gave her a swift kick in the ribs.

"Aah!" she gasped, stopping to give herself a moment to recover. This baby had Van Damme's skill at *Savate*.

"What?" Hank asked worriedly.

"Just a kick," she said breathlessly, rubbing where she'd felt it.

"Why don't you sit for a minute?" Without waiting for her compliance, he pushed her gently until she was sitting on the stair above them. "Are you sure you should be working in this condition?"

"It's pregnancy," she replied, a little unsettled by what appeared to be genuine, if grudging, concern, "not infirmity. I'm fine."

"You're pale."

"I can't help that," she retorted. "You're very annoying. Preventing myself from punching you is taking its toll."

A reluctant smile crossed his face as he studied hers. "It would be a lot for a woman who wasn't pregnant to run a hotel and a city while raising two children."

He used to do that when they were going together and she remembered that it made her feel very protected. In the middle of a dance or a drive or a game of tennis he would stop to look at her, and always gave her the impression that if he saw something wrong, he would remedy it.

Considering her embattled position as mayor, her ten-year-old having trouble in school, her six-year-old turning into a sometimes fun, but often worrisome wild-child, Jackie enjoyed the momentary fantasy of someone wanting to solve her problems, or at least being willing to help shoulder them.

She saw him note the brief lowering of her defenses and quickly raised them again. She caught the bannister and pulled herself up—or tried to. The baby provided ballast that sometimes refused to move when she did.

Hank took her elbow in one hand and wrapped his other arm around her waist—or where her waist would have been if she'd had one.

"Steady," he cautioned. She felt the muscles of his arm stiffen and was brought to her feet on the step. "Careful until you get turned around."

He held her securely until she faced the right direction, and kept his hold the rest of the way.

At the top of the stairs in a small hallway off the home's original kitchen, which was now the small but comfortable employee lounge, a tall man blocked the doorway and reached a hand down to help Jackie up the last step. He wore jeans and a blue down vest over a red sweatshirt. She'd never seen him before.

"Hi, Hank," he said as he nodded courteously to Jackie, then freed her hand. "I was just coming down to help you with the desk."

"Just in time." Hank cleared the stop of the stairs, and Jackie found herself sandwiched between the two men. "Jackie, I'd like you to meet Cameron Trent," he said. "The newest addition to my staff. He's a plumber. Cam, this is Her Honor, Mayor Bourgeois."

Cameron offered his hand and Jackie took it, liking his direct hazel gaze and his charming confusion. "What do I call you, ma'am?" he asked. "Your Honor? Mrs. Mayor?"

"Ms. Mayor seems to be the preferred greeting in the building. But Jackie will be fine outside. Are you new to Maple Hill?"

"I'm from San Francisco," he replied. "I came here to get my master's at Amherst and to see a little snow."

She laughed lightly. There'd been snow on the ground in Maple Hill since early December. "Are you tired of it yet?"

"No, I'm loving it."

"Good. Well, good luck with your degree." She turned her attention to Hank, unsettled by their meeting and the knowledge that she could run into him at any moment from now on. "Hank," she said, unsure what to add to that. "Welcome to the building."

There was a wry twist to his mouth, as though he suspected she didn't mean that at all. "Thank you, Ms. Mayor. I'll see you around while trying very hard not to get in your way."

She gave him a brief glare, smiled at Cameron Trent, then turned and walked away.

"PRETTY LADY," Cameron said as he followed Hank down the stairs. "Shame about her husband."

When Hank turned at the bottom of the stairs, surprised that a newcomer knew about Ricky Bourgeois, Cameron nodded. "I came in July to find a place to live, and his death was in the paper with a story about how his family helped establish Maple Hill."

Hank remembered Haley sending him the clipping. She'd been discreet about how he'd died, just said that he'd been away on a business trip when he'd suffered a heart attack. He hadn't found out the truth until he'd moved back home.

"You'd think," Cameron went on, "that a man would value a classy lady like that."

Yeah, you would, Hank thought. Cussedness and arbitrary last-minute changes of her mind aside. He led the way out the back door to the parking area where he'd left his van.

"Nice rig," Cameron said. "I used to have one like it, but sold it to help pay my tuition." He pointed across the lot to a decrepit blue camper with a canopy. "That's mine."

"Whatever gets you there and back." Hank opened the rear door of the van. "Give me a minute to get around the side of this thing and push it out to you."

"Right."

They carried the table in without incident, Adeline directing them through the office door to a spot against the wall where she'd hung a map of the city. Hank introduced her to Cameron.

She shook his hand, studying him appraisingly. "Hank, if you're no longer interested in Jackie, maybe we can fix her up with Cameron."

Cameron smiled politely, but Hank saw the panicked glance he turned his way. "Thanks, but I'm a happy bachelor," he said.

"Nonsense," Adeline said. "How can a bachelor be happy?"

"No woman in his life," Hank replied intrepidly, knowing it would earn him retribution. "Yourself excluded, of course, but women just complicate a man's existence."

"Without a woman in your life, it is just that," she argued. "Existence, not life. Though some men never come to appreciate us."

"I like my simple life," Cameron insisted.

And Hank decided he really liked the man.

The telephone rang as Hank placed it on the desk.

"Hey!" he said, reaching for it. "They connected it while I was gone. Whitcomb's Wonders."

"This is the Old Post Road Inn," a panicked female voice said. "The top off one of the kitchen faucets just shot off and I've got water spewing everywhere. *Please* tell me that one of your wonders is a plumber!" Then she shouted to someone at her end of the line, "The cutoff valve! Under the stairs in the basement! The *hot* water one!"

Hank held the phone to his chest and raised an eyebrow at Cameron. "Do I have a plumber? You weren't supposed to start until Tuesday."

"An emergency?" Cameron asked, coming toward him.

"Sure sounds like it. At the Old Post Road Inn. In the kitchen. Top off a faucet, water everywhere."

Cameron headed for the door. "I'm on it."

"We've got a man on the way," Hank said into the phone.

The woman groaned. "I love you," she said, and hung up.

"All right." Hank turned off the phone and reached for the daily log hanging on a hook beside the map. "Business is picking up and we're not even completely moved in." He noted Cam's destination and checked his watch for the time. "Any other calls?" He hung the log back on its hook and turned to his mother.

She pushed a cup of coffee into his hand. "You should have gotten one," she said with an air of disgust. "But you didn't."

He knew the disappointed look meant he'd failed morally, somehow. But she was making some maternal point he wasn't quite getting. He knew he played right into her hands when he asked, "What call?"

"Your wake-up call!" she said emphatically. "What is *wrong* with you? How can you shout at a poor pregnant woman? And the mayor to boot! And the woman you once told me you loved more than your own life?"

He went across the room for his office chair and carried it one-handed to the desk. "She shouted first," he objected, realizing how absurd that sounded even as he said it. "And our love for each other died long ago. She married someone else, had his children..."

"And was miserable every moment."

"I can't help that." He didn't like to think about it, but it wasn't his fault. "She chose to stay."

"Maybe at the time," his mother said more quietly, "she thought she was being wise."

"She had an unhappy marriage." He rummaged through a box for his blotter and the family photos he kept on his desk. "And I had a successful career. Which one of us was right?"

"You can't always judge that by how things come out," she answered.

He looked up from the box to meet her gaze in disbelief. "How do you judge the right or wrong of an action if not by its result?"

"Maybe by the number of people hurt."

"Then her staying should go down as a disaster." The items located, he rose and carried them to the desk.

"Her parents were happy she stayed."

"How could they have been? She went to Boston for two years."

"Well, that wasn't California, where the two of you had planned to go. They had a hope of seeing her once in a while." She came to stand beside him while he centered the blotter on the desktop and placed the photos behind it. There was one of him and Haley and their parents on a trip to Disney World, all of them in Mickey Mouse ears. His father looked grim. He'd never had much of a sense of humor. Then there was Haley's graduation photo, and one of her and Bart on their wedding day. He was supposed to have moved home the day before, but he was still in Florida when the wedding took place, sick as a dog with the flu in an empty apartment. He'd insisted they not hold up the wedding.

"I just think you need to make peace with this," his mother said in the same voice she'd used to talk him out of his sulks when his father had been on him. "It happened. You both made your choices, and for better or worse, you've lived with them. Now you're going to be running into each other on a regular basis and it'll be easier in the long run if you just come to terms with it. And you could be a little nicer."

He remembered clearly how he'd felt that night when he'd had to leave without her. He'd been only eighteen, but there'd been nothing young about his love for her. It had been full and mature with roots she'd ripped right out of him.

"She cut my heart out with a trowel, Mom," he said, hating how theatrical the words sounded. But they did convey the feeling.

Adeline shook her head at him and reached for her coat. "Well, she must have, because you certainly don't seem to have one at the moment. I'm going out for scones."

"Thanks." He handed her a bill from a drawer on the coffee bar. It served as the petty cash safe. "Get one for Cameron in case he checks back in before going home."

She glowered at him and he added as an afterthought, "Please." When that didn't seem to appease her, he tried, "Thank you."

She sighed and walked to the door, turning to say grimly, "Well, at least you learned 'please' and 'thank you.' I'll be right back."

If she were kidnapped by aliens, Lord, he prayed,

falling into his chair to soak up the moment's respite, *friendly ones, you know, that play Bingo and have Ibuprofen and mentholated rubs readily available, I could deal with it. She'd be happy. I'd be happy. No, I know. No such luck. I have to learn to cope with her. And with seeing Jackie regularly, too, I suppose. Fine. But just wait until St. Anthony's needs a microphone for the Blessings Blow-Out auction. See what happens then.*

Hank opened the single drawer in the table to retrieve his Palm Pilot when the room fell into complete darkness.

He sat still, experiencing a sense of foreboding. Faulty ancient wiring, he wondered, or God responding to being threatened?

CHAPTER THREE

JACKIE INSERTED HER KEY in the lock on the front door of her home two blocks from downtown, grateful that her assistant manager had all the night shifts at the inn this week. She anticipated a cozy dinner with the girls and a peaceful evening. That did happen more often than not—at least, it used to—but she knew the moment she opened the door and heard screeching voices that it wasn't going to happen tonight.

She heard the baby-sitter's quiet efforts to calm the girls. They seemed to be having no effect.

With a wistful wish for a different life—any other life, at least for tonight—Jackie dropped her coat and purse on the nearest chair and hurried toward the kitchen, where the melee was taking place.

"I can't *believe* you did that!" Erica was shrieking at Rachel, who faced her down stubbornly, bony arms folded atop a flowered dress Jackie had never seen before. The fabric looked familiar, though. "It was *mine!*" she said, her voice high and shrill and almost hysterical.

Ricky had been a casual father at best, sometimes attentive but more often unaware of his children, caught up with the pressures of his work and his own needs. But the children, of course, had grieved his loss. Erica had turned from a happy, cheerful child to a moody one. Rachel seemed less affected personally, except that she wanted details about death and heaven and didn't seem to be satisfied with Jackie's explanation. "Mom bought it for *me!* You're such a selfish little brat! I *hate* you, *hate* you!" With that Erica flung herself at Rachel.

Jackie ran to intercept her just as Glory Anselmo caught Erica from behind and held her away. Glory was in her second year at Maple Hill Community College's computer classroom program. She played volleyball in her spare time and was built like a rock. A very pretty brunette rock.

"Erica Isabel!" Jackie said, pushing Rachel aside with one hand while catching one of Erica's flailing fists with the other. Erica was dark-featured, tall and slender, built like her father's side of the family. Rachel was petite like Jackie, and blond. Both seemed to have inherited personality traits from some long-lost connection to the Mongol hordes. "Take it back."

"I won't! Look at what she did to my pillowcase!"

"I made it beautiful!" Rachel extended her arms and did an end-of-the-runway turn. That was when Jackie realized she'd cut a hole for her head and two armholes in Erica's pillowcase, the one patterned with cabbage roses and violets, and was wearing it like a dress. She'd added a white silk cord that also looked familiar.

Jackie groaned. Glory, she could see, was having a little difficulty keeping a straight face. It *was* funny,

Jackie had to admit to herself, if you weren't the one required to make peace.

Glory caught Jackie's expression and sobered, still holding on to Erica. "I'm sorry, Mrs. Bourgeois," she said. "I should have checked on Rachel. She was being really quiet."

Rachel, who had brains beyond her years and an almost scary sense of style in everything she did, said, "I was quiet 'cause I was…what's that word for when you get a really good idea and you just have to do it?"

"Inspired?" Jackie guessed.

Rachel smiled widely, delighted that she understood. "That's it!"

"Well, I think you should be inspired to give Erica *your* pillowcase," Jackie ruled. "It's fine to be inspired, but you don't try out your designs using someone else's things."

"Please." Erica clearly loathed the idea. "It has pigs and ducks on it. I think she should clean my room for a year!"

"No way!" Rachel shouted.

"Then she'll pay you the amount of the pillowcase out of her savings," Jackie arbitrated, "so you can buy a new one."

Rachel pouted. She was also frugal.

The tension eased somewhat, Glory freed Erica's arms.

"Now take back the 'I hate you,'" Jackie insisted.

Erica looked her mother in the eye. "But I do hate her."

That cold-blooded admission might have chilled

someone who hadn't seen Erica defend Rachel from the neighborhood bully who'd tried to take Rachel's candy bar just two days ago. The fact that Erica had demanded half the candy bar in payment for her protection didn't really figure into it. Rachel understood commerce.

"No, you don't." Jackie touched Erica's hot cheeks. She was a very physical child and touch usually soothed her. "You're just too young to understand the difference between frustration and hatred. What's our rule about hate?"

Erica gave her a dark look but repeated dutifully, "We can hate things, but not people."

"So?"

"So, I take it back," Erica conceded ungraciously, "but if she messes with my stuff again, even if I don't hate her, I'll..." She hesitated. Jackie also had rules against violence or threats of violence. "I'll let Frankie Morton take all her candy!" Frankie Morton was the bully.

Rachel ran upstairs in tears.

Jackie grinned over Erica's head at Glory. "Want to stay for dinner? Promises to be eventful."

Glory acknowledged the joke with a nod. "Thanks, but I'm meeting a friend."

"It's a guy friend," Erica informed Jackie. "They met at the library. But tonight he's taking her to dinner."

Jackie was happy to hear that. Glory worked so hard

that she seldom had time for dating. "Anyone we know?"

"I don't think so," Glory replied, gathering up her things off one of the kitchen chairs. "His name's Jimmy Elliott. He works for Mr. Whitcomb. He's a fireman and fixes furnaces when he's off."

"Oh." The mention of Hank's name darkened her already precarious mood.

Glory, purse over her shoulder and books in her arms, asked worriedly, "Is that bad?"

"Of course not." Jackie walked her to the door. "He and I just don't get along very well."

"You and Jimmy Elliott?"

"Hank Whitcomb and I. He's just moved his office into City Hall."

"Oh. That's a relief. I really like Jimmy."

"Well, have a wonderful time."

Glory stopped in the doorway. "One more thing," she said, handing Jackie a folded piece of paper, her tone sympathetic. "This is from Erica's teacher. I didn't read it, but Erica says Mrs. Powell picks on her because she's having trouble paying attention."

A note from school completed the destruction of Jackie's flimsy attempt at a good mood.

She went back into the kitchen to ask Erica about it, but Rachel had just returned with her ceramic savings bank shaped like a castle with a blond princess in the tower. She knelt on a chair at the table, her eyes and the tip of her nose red from crying. "How much was the pillowcase, Mom?" she asked.

Jackie sat down opposite her, trying to remember. It

had been part of the package with two sheets and the bedcover. Erica had been feeling blue, she remembered, and objecting to the childish decor of her room, done when she'd been about five. New bedclothes had seemed the simplest and quickest solution.

"It was on sale," Erica said, pulling silverware out of the drawer to set the table, her nightly chore. "The whole set was eighty dollars. I remember 'cause I thought it would be too much. But the lady said it was half price."

Encouraged by Erica's assistance, Jackie asked, "Then how much would you say one pillowcase would be?"

Erica came to the table and sat, the silverware in hand. "The bedspread would probably be half, don't you think?" she asked, her mood lightening fractionally.

"That sounds reasonable."

"So…" Erica closed her eyes, concentrating. "That leaves twenty dollars, and the sheets would probably be three-fourths of that. So…that leaves five dollars for the pillowcases."

Rachel pulled the rubber stopper out of the bottom of her bank and reached in with little fingers to withdraw bills. Change tinkled to the tabletop. She counted four singles, then asked Erica, "Four quarters in a dollar, right?"

"It was two pillowcases for five dollars." Erica fell against the back of her chair in disgust. "You only wrecked one."

The disgust with her sister was a habit, Jackie knew.

But this burgeoning willingness to be fair gave her hope after all.

"What's half of five?" Rachel asked, her expression also brightening somewhat.

"Two-fifty," Jackie replied. "Two dollars and two quarters."

Rachel handed over the money. "I'm sorry."

Erica snatched it from her. "Just leave my stuff alone."

"And?" Jackie encouraged.

"And I won't let Frankie Morton steal your candy."

Jackie's hope wavered. *"And?"* she repeated.

Erica looked at her perplexed, then asked uncertainly, "Thank you?"

"Yes!" Success at last. How often did a mother get to repair an argument and provide a lesson in math and morals all at the same time? "I'm proud of both of you. You fulfilled your responsibilities," she praised, hugging Rachel, "and *you…*" Erica tried to evade her embrace, but Jackie caught her and wrapped her in a fierce hug. "You were generous in victory and didn't gloat."

As Erica hugged back, the baby gave a strong kick.

Erica straightened away from her, brown eyes wide with awe. "It kicked us!" she said, putting a hand with purple fingernails to the spot.

"Probably just wanted in on the hug."

Rachel ran over to touch also, the three of them standing motionless and silent, waiting for another sign of life. It came with another strong kick. They looked up to share a smile.

Without warning, Erica's smile evaporated and she said with a sigh, "Pretty soon there'll be someone else to mess with my stuff."

Jackie refused to let Erica's change of mood dissolve her thrill of success over the pillowcase incident. She made a salad while microwaving spaghetti sauce from the freezer and boiling noodles, and chatted happily over dinner about nothing in particular.

While Rachel related a long and complicated story involving the lizard in the terrarium in her classroom and its shed tail, which someone had put in Mrs. Ferguson's purse, Erica caught Jackie's eye and smiled hesitantly.

Jackie smiled back, sure that before she knew it, Erica would be a teenager and they'd be at loggerheads all the time.

Or she could get lucky. Some mothers did. Evelyn, Jackie's secretary, had three daughters in their early teens, and they seemed to love not only each other, but their mother as well. With her own lively and interesting but contentious girls, Jackie envied Evelyn her family's closeness.

But Jackie was never lucky. She was blessed in many ways, but never lucky. Her victories were all hard-won.

Erica helped Jackie clear the table while Rachel took her bath.

"Are you gonna yell about the note?" Erica lined up three cups next to a stack of plates while Jackie sorted silverware into the dishwasher's basket. She went back to the table without waiting for an answer.

"Difficulty concentrating isn't exactly delinquent or disruptive behavior," Jackie replied, dropping the last spoon in. She didn't look up but felt Erica's glance of surprise. "But it's not very good for grades. Are you thinking about Daddy? It takes a long time to get over the death of someone you love."

Mrs. Powell's note had admitted as much but expressed concern that Erica's inability to concentrate seemed to be worsening rather than improving.

Erica put the butter and the fresh Parmesan in the refrigerator and went back to the table to collect their placemats and take them to the back porch to shake them out.

She returned and set them on the table. "I used to at first, but I don't much anymore." She came back and stood beside Jackie, leaning an elbow on the counter. "I mean, he kind of liked us, I guess, but he didn't really seem to miss us when he was gone, then it seemed like he was always anxious to be gone again after he came home. That's kind of weird for a dad, isn't it?"

"He loved you girls very much." Jackie kept working, afraid that if she stopped and made the discussion too important, Erica would withdraw. "Grandpa Bourgeois never showed Daddy much affection when he was little. The only time he spent with him was to show him around the mill and to teach him how the company worked. Some people have to be shown how to give love, and no one ever did that for him."

"You did," Erica said. "He didn't notice though, did he?"

Jackie was astonished by that perception. "No, I don't think he did." Now she couldn't help but stop, realizing this was important. "But when I came along, your father was an adult. Sometimes adults don't learn as well as children."

"Is that why he was with that lady in Boston when he had the heart attack?"

Erica asked the question so directly that she must have known the truth of her father's death for some time.

Jackie felt shocked, breathless.

"I heard Mrs. Powell and the principal talking about it when I brought in the permission slip so Glory could start picking us up from school."

"You mean…after I became mayor? You've known for that long?"

Erica nodded. "I think everybody knows. A lot of people look at us like something bad's happened. Not just Daddy dying, but something that isn't fair. Like they look at you when you're in a wheelchair. Like they don't want to hurt your feelings and they're pretending they don't notice, but you know they're really glad they're not you."

"You should have told me," Jackie said, touching Erica's arm, waiting for withdrawal and relieved when it didn't come.

"You couldn't fix it," she said sensibly. "He was gone. But why do you think he did it?"

Jackie struggled for the right answers. "I think," she began carefully, "that when someone doesn't love you when you're little, your heart is always empty and looking for love, and sometimes doesn't even recognize it when it gets it. So it keeps looking."

Erica shook her head. "Didn't that hurt you?"

"Well..." Jackie felt curiously embarrassed, as though Erica was judging why she'd stayed in a loveless marriage all those years. "It did hurt me, but maybe not as much as you'd think. Because I understood how he was. And being married to him gave me you and Rachel, and the two of you are absolutely everything to me."

Erica frowned. "And the baby."

The baby. Erica seemed to be ambivalent about the baby, excited over the feel of a kick one moment, then unhappy about its eventual arrival the next.

"What is it you don't like about the baby coming?" Jackie asked directly.

Erica looked guilty.

"You can tell me," Jackie encouraged. "Are you afraid the baby is more important to me than you are?"

Erica shifted her weight, looking down at the floor. "No," she said. It had a convincing sound.

"That it'll get more attention than you?"

"No."

"That it'll change everything?"

Erica heaved a ragged sigh then looked up, her eyes pooled with tears, her lips trembling. "Mom, what if *you* die?"

"What?" Jackie couldn't help the surprised outburst.

"Well, what if you do?" Erica demanded in a tearful

rush. "Nobody expected Daddy to die and he did. And you're at risk!"

Jackie took Erica's hand and led her back to the table, where she pushed two chairs together and lowered her onto one. "What do you mean, 'at risk'? Where did you hear that?"

"Sarah Campbell's mom's a nurse. She was talking about it with Mrs. Powell at the Valentine's Day party at school. Mrs. Campbell brought treats." Erica drew an anxious breath. "All ladies over thirty are at risk of stuff going wrong when they have babies 'cause they're really too old. You should only have babies when you're young."

Caught between the need to calm her daughter and the personal affront at being considered "old" at thirty-four, Jackie focused on soothing Erica.

"Honey, that just means that they take special care of you if you're over thirty. Sometimes there's a problem, but most babies and mothers come through the delivery safe and sound. And I'm not old enough to be that much at risk anyway."

"Are you sure?" Erica looked worried. "You're not as old as Grandpa or Addy Whitcomb, but you're pretty old."

And feeling older by the moment, Jackie thought. She went to the counter for a tissue and brought it back to Erica. "My last checkup at the doctor's proved that the baby is growing perfectly, and I'm healthy as a horse. There is nothing to worry about."

Erica swiped at her eyes and dabbed at her nose.

"We didn't know there was anything to worry about with Daddy."

"That was a heart attack. My heart's fine. My checkup was perfect, remember."

"What would happen to us if you died?"

Jackie accepted that as a legitimate question and was grateful she was prepared for it. "When Daddy died and I found out I was pregnant, I put it in my will that if anything happened to me, you and Rachel and the baby would go and live with Haley."

Erica brightened. Jackie tried not to be offended. "Really? And that's okay with her?"

"Yes. And her new husband, too. She talked about it with him when they got married."

"Wow."

"Yeah. So there's nothing to worry about. Now, you're not going to bump me off so you can go live with Haley, are you?"

Erica smiled—finally. "No. I was just worried. Brenda Harris's dad left when she was little, then her mom died in a car accident, and she's lived at a whole bunch of different places and hasn't liked any of them. All the houses have different rules and new people you don't know. I'd hate that."

"So would I." Jackie leaned forward to wrap her in a hug. "You don't have to worry. I've got everything looked after."

Jackie felt the strength of her daughter's return hug. "Okay. Thanks, Mom."

"Sure."

Erica went upstairs to do her homework and Rachel

came down to report that she was bathed. She stood in footed pink pajamas patterned with black-and-white Dalmatian puppies.

"When I'm grown up," she said, dragging a stool over from the lunch bar that separated the kitchen from the dining room, "I'm going to wear one of those floaty nightgown things with the feathers around the neck and the bottom." She had a predilection for "floaty things" that was fed by Glory's love of old movies from the thirties and forties where the women wore glamorous nightclothes.

"I like those, too," Jackie admitted, closing the door on the dishwasher and setting it to run. "How was your day?" she asked, wiping off the counters.

"Pretty good. Things are kinda dull in first grade. How was your day?"

Jackie rinsed off the sponge, squeezed it dry and propped it up behind the faucet. "Well, things are never dull at City Hall. Some new tenants moved into the basement offices today. One of them is a man the city just hired to take care of our electrical repairs. And his mom is going to work in his office some of the time, and guess who she is?"

"Who?"

"Mrs. Whitcomb."

Rachel smiled. She loved Addy Whitcomb. "Does she do electric stuff?"

"No. She's just going to answer the phones, take messages."

"Erica's not so mad at me anymore," Rachel said, abruptly changing the subject.

"You shouldn't have cut up her pillowcase. But it was good that you paid her for it."

"I just didn't think pigs and ducks would make a neat dress like the roses. Your plain blue ones weren't very good either."

Jackie frowned at the knowledge that one of her pillowcases had been considered.

The chiming clock in the living room sounded seven, time for Rachel's favorite television show about castaway children on a tropical island. She leapt off the stool. "Gotta go, Mom. *Castaway Kids* is on!"

Jackie replaced the stool, looked around her tidy, quiet kitchen, and said a prayer of gratitude that though the evening had begun in crisis, they'd managed to turn it around. Another family miracle.

It was a fact of life, she thought, that raising two little girls was often more difficult than running a city of four thousand.

HANK DROVE HIS MOTHER HOME after dinner at the inn, grateful that Jackie hadn't been working tonight. Running into her once had been all his good humor could handle.

Fortunately the electrical problem he'd encountered at City Hall this afternoon had been simply a blown fuse caused when his massage-therapist neighbor plugged in a faulty microwave. Once he'd found his flashlight, then the fuse box, the problem had been easily solved.

"I've got a girl for you," Adeline said.

The problem of his mother was unfortunately less

easily dealt with than electricity. Unlike other mothers, she didn't beat around the bush or try subterfuge to fix him up with a date. She'd once brought a pizza and the daughter of a friend of hers to his apartment and left them there.

"Doris McIntyre's niece is visiting for a couple of weeks from New York," his mother said, "and she needs someone to show her around Maple Hill."

"Mom, she can see it in a two-hour walk. One hour if she doesn't go to the lake."

"Hank, don't be difficult." She folded her arms and looked pugnaciously out the window at the dark night as they drove down the two-lane road to the lake. "I'm not getting any younger and I have yet to have one grandchild. Not one. Everyone else in the Quincy Quilters has at least one, most of them several. Bedelia Jones has eleven. I have none. Zero. Zilch. Na—"

"I got it, Mom," he interrupted. "But I'm single. Shouldn't you be speaking to Haley and Bart about giving you grandchildren? They've been married six months. Let them give you something to brag about at your quilting sessions."

Adeline made a face. "They're *waiting*." She imbued the word with disappointment.

"For what?"

"They didn't say, I didn't ask."

"So I'm the only one you interrogate?"

"You're my firstborn."

"That means I inherit everything you've got. It doesn't mean you're allowed to harass me."

"Is wanting you to meet a good girl and settle down harassment?"

"No, but trying to pick her for me is."

"I'm not picking her for you," she insisted, apparently affronted that her good intentions were so misunderstood. "I'm helping you find some potential candidates. You don't seem to be working toward it at all."

"I'm building a business."

"I'm going to be seventy in ten years!"

He laughed outright. "Mom, that doesn't have anything to do with anything. Right now you've just turned sixty. And a youthful sixty. Relax. There's lots of time."

There was a moment's silence, then she asked gravely, "What if I told you I was dying?"

His heart thumped against his ribs and he swerved to the side of the road, screeching to a halt. "What?" he demanded.

"Well, I'm not," she said, tugging on her coat collar, clearly feeling guilty for having startled him, "but what if I was? Am I to go to my grave without ever holding a grandbaby in my arms?"

Hank put his left hand to his face and rested the wrist of the other atop the steering wheel. "Mom," he said, "I'm going to drive you to your grave myself if you ever do that to me again!"

"I was trying to make a point," she huffed.

"The point is you sometimes act like a lunatic!" He checked the side mirror and pulled out onto the road again, his pulse dribbling back to normal. "I'm trying to build a business, Mom. Relax about grandchildren, okay?''

"I'm thinking about you.''

"I'm fine.''

"You're alone.''

"I like it that way.''

He turned onto the short road that led to her driveway, and drove up to the house. He pulled to a stop and turned off the engine. He always walked her up the steps and saw her inside.

"I thought you came home because you realized that while you loved your work for NASA, you didn't have a life. It was all future and no present.''

He jumped out of the van, walked around to pull out the step stool he kept for her in the back, then opened her door and placed the stool on the ground. He offered her his hand. "That's true. And I'm enjoying my life here. I just need a little time to get all the parts of it together. Be patient, Mom.''

She stepped carefully onto the stool, then down to the driveway. After tossing the stool into the back of the van, he took her arm to walk her up the drive.

"You're not still trying to prove something to your father with the business, are you?'' she asked. "I mean, you were an engineer at NASA. You don't have anything else to prove. You don't have to expand Whitcomb's Wonders until you have franchises all over the country and appear on the big board.''

He opened his mouth to deny that he was trying to prove anything, but he knew that wouldn't be true.

Every time he did anything, he could imagine his father watching him, finding fault.

"He always tried hard," she said, squeezing his arm, "and he did well, but everything was difficult for him. Then you came along, all brains and personality, and he couldn't help resenting that. I know I've told you that a million times, but I sometimes wonder if you really understand it. He loved you, he just resented that you were smarter than he was, that things would be easy for you."

"I worked liked a dog to end up at NASA."

"I know. But some people work hard all their lives and never get anywhere. He had dreams, too, but he never got out of that little appliance repair shop."

Hank remembered that his father had little rapport with his customers and slaved away in the back room, taking no pleasure in his work.

"Anyway," Adeline said, "sometimes old insecurities can come back to haunt us when we're trying something new, or reaching for something we're not sure we should have. You deserve to be happy, Hank. And if you won't reach for that happiness, I'm going to keep working on it for you. So, when can you see Laural McIntyre?"

Hank drew himself out of moody thoughts about his father to the present and the urgent need to get out of meeting the visitor from New York.

"Actually, I'm meeting Jackie on Saturday," he said, walking his mother up the porch steps.

She brightened instantly. He could see her smile in the porch light. "You are? Where?"

"Perk Avenue Tea Room."

She looked puzzled. "Where?"

"It's a new coffee bar, tearoom, desserty sort of place on the square." She didn't have to know that they'd be "meeting" because Jackie was cutting the ribbon for the grand opening, and he was helping with the wiring for the sign, which wasn't expected to arrive until late Friday night.

His mother studied him suspiciously. "You were fighting the last time I saw you together."

He nodded. "But you didn't see everything. I ran into her later, we talked, and…I'm seeing her next week." A slight rearrangement of the truth, but the truth all the same.

"Well, see now, that wasn't so hard." She gave him a quick hug. "Will you tell me all about it after?"

"The shop, yes," he said. "Jackie, no."

She shrugged, seemingly undisturbed. "I'll just ask the girls at Sunday School. Thanks for dinner, sweetie."

"Sure, Mom." He ran down the steps as she closed and locked the door.

Great. Jackie's girls were in his mother's Sunday School class. She'd mentioned that once, but he'd forgotten.

When he'd been a kid, she'd had spies everywhere. It had been impossible to see a girl, cruise downtown, or sneak a beer without someone reporting him to his mother.

It was annoying that he was thirty-five, and nothing had changed.

CHAPTER FOUR

HE MET HIS MOTHER'S SPIES on Saturday. He'd been working at Perk Avenue for several hours when the crowd began to gather out front for the ceremony. He'd turned the sign on and it glowed brightly, a tall cup of neon mocha complete with a swirl of whipped cream standing beside a fat teapot. Underneath, the name of the shop was written in elegant neon script. The whole sign appeared to sit atop a triangle of neon lace.

The two matrons who owned the shop applauded their approval then wrapped their arms around him.

Hank went back inside as several people in the gathering crowd came forward to congratulate the women. He was collecting his tools when the front door burst open and a little girl in a flared red coat and matching hat ran in. Long straight blond hair fell to her shoulders. In her gray eyes was a desperate look. He recognized her as Jackie's youngest. He studied her one brief moment, realizing that except for a slight difference in the shade of her hair, this was what Jackie had looked like as a child.

"Hi," he said finally, coiling a length of wire. "Lost your mom?"

She shook her head, looking left, then right.

He took another guess. "Bathroom?"

She nodded.

He pointed to the little alcove directly to the right of the door.

"Thank you!" she called as she ran off in that direction.

A moment later, a child he recognized as the little one's older sister walked in wearing a pink coat but no hat. She had thick dark hair caught at the side of her head in a ponytail. This child must take after her father. His mother had told him Jackie's girls were Erica and Rachel. He couldn't recall which was which.

She surveyed the room, then her dark eyes fell on him in concern. A child taught to be wary of strange men. Jackie was doing her job.

He pointed to the alcove behind her. "Your little sister's in the rest room," he said.

She started away, then turned to ask, "How did you know she was my sister?"

"I know your mom," Hank explained. "And I've seen the two of you with her."

"Are you her friend?"

"Ah...not exactly."

"You don't like her?"

Tricky question. "Actually, she doesn't like me very much."

"How come?"

She was beginning to remind him of her mother even if she did look like her father. She had a compulsion for detail.

How did one explain to a child about a bright love

affair that had been halted abruptly by one lover's reluctance to follow the other? You didn't, of course.

"We had an argument a long time ago," he replied, "that we never really fixed."

She frowned at that. "Mom never lets me and Rachel fight without making up."

Aha. This was Erica.

"Adults probably get madder than children," he said. "So quarrels are harder to fix."

The little one ran out of the bathroom, hat slightly askew. Erica straightened it for her. "This is Rachel," she said.

He nodded. "And you're Erica."

She smiled and came forward to shake his hand.

"I'm Hank Whitcomb," he said, thinking her social skills were as polished as her appearance. He wiped his hands on a cloth out of his box before taking hers.

"Our mom's the mayor!" Rachel said with a wide smile, also offering her hand. "We're supposed to smile and be polite!"

Erica gave her a mildly impatient look. "He knows who we are. He's a friend of Mom's."

"I thought Mom just had friends who were other ladies."

WHILE THE WIDE WHITE RIBBON for the ceremony was still being stretched across the front of the shop, Jackie ran in search of her girls. She was sure they were fine, but bathroom runs never took this long. She'd thought a quick trip inside the shop would be the quickest solution to Rachel's second glass of milk that morning.

After all, the café wasn't really open yet and there was no one inside. Erica had followed her sister in.

But a mother's trepidation filled her anyway as she pushed the door open, knowing that safety should never be presumed, that it only took a moment for…

Her heart lurched in her chest at the sight of her girls in conversation with a large man in jeans and a chambray shirt. His clothes were streaked with dirt, his hair…

He looked up at that moment, blue eyes noting her presence. It was Hank. Sudden awareness of him took her by surprise.

She'd never seen him at work before. The other times she'd run into him, he'd been in street clothes. Even the day he'd moved his office into the City Hall basement, he'd worn a respectable sweater.

But he was a little grubby now, work clothes well-fitting but mussed, his dark hair disturbed from its usually neat side part and falling onto his forehead. A longing that was decidedly sexual curled around inside her and embarrassed her with its intensity.

To further confuse her, she saw enjoyment in his eyes, as though her daughters delighted him. That pleased and flattered her and, along with this sudden desire completely inappropriate to a woman in her eighth month of pregnancy, threw her completely off balance.

She was about to scold the girls for speaking to a stranger when Hank interceded.

"They did nothing wrong," he said gently, as though he understood and respected her concern. "Rachel ran in looking for the rest room and there was no one else around. I just told her where it was. Then when Erica came in, I told her where to find her sister."

"And he's not a stranger, Mom," Erica said, going to her. "He's your friend. Even though you guys never made up after the fight."

Jackie opened her mouth to reply to that, wondering just what he'd told them about their relationship, but decided it was all too entangled.

"There's a party here after the ribbon-cutting," Erica said to Hank. "You can sit at our table, so you and Mom can work it out."

Jackie turned to her in astonishment.

"You don't let me and Rachel stay mad," Erica insisted. "And let's face it, Mom. You don't have that many friends."

Jackie couldn't help the gasp of indignation. "I do, too." She ignored the childish sound of her own words. "I have lots of friends."

"But none of them are guys."

"I…" Jackie stopped abruptly when she noticed the amusement in Hank's eyes. "Anyway," she said in a more controlled tone, "Mr. Whitcomb's working. I'm sure he can't—"

"Bridget and Cecilia, the owners of the café, invited me," he interrupted with a slightly smug smile. "I'll be back after I've showered."

Rachel hooked her arm in his. "You can sit next to me if Mom's still mad at you. Are you, Mom?"

Rachel waited for an answer. Hank did, too, his smile expanding.

"I was never angry," she said a little stiffly, forgetting that the girls were listening and focusing only on him. "I was hurt. Crushed, actually."

His amusement vanished. She expected him to accuse her of the same, but apparently unwilling to do so in front of her children, he simply said feelingly, "I understand, believe me."

The front door opened and one of the councilmen stuck his head in. "Ms. Mayor?" he called.

She pushed thoughts of the past aside as she'd done so often throughout her life, and pulled herself together. "Thank you for helping the girls," she said to Hank with stiff courtesy. "We'll see you at the party, then."

It was the usual city function. Two councilmen spoke about the city plan to create a commercial and economic environment that would encourage new business in Maple Hill. The other two spoke about the need to preserve and maintain the area's natural beauty while doing so. The city council was evenly divided on almost every subject.

Jackie's speech centered around Cecilia Proctor and Bridget Malone, sisters-in-law in their early forties who enjoyed each other's company and, now that their children were married or off to college, wanted to spend time together in a profitable endeavor. Each had been involved in community service for many years, so Jackie had the opportunity to praise them for all the time they'd devoted to the city and wish them luck in their commercial venture.

The community college's band played a few rousing numbers, then Jackie cut the ribbon, her daughters on either side of her. There was loud applause and everyone streamed into Perk Avenue.

Bridget caught Jackie's arm and led her to the dessert buffet set up at what would eventually be a long service counter. Jackie turned to make sure the girls were behind her, but saw that they were talking to Haley. Haley shooed Jackie on. "I've got them. Go."

Bridget directed Jackie to the head of the line already reaching out the door.

"If you hadn't fought for us," Bridget said, giving Jackie's shoulders a squeeze, "Brockton would have insisted on holding this spot for 'something that would have put the location to optimum use.'" She was clearly quoting. "Like a chain store or a fast food franchise. So you get to eat first."

John Brockton, one of the councilmen who fought Jackie's every move, had stood at the head of the line until Bridget placed Jackie there. He was short and small and balding, with sharp dark eyes. He smiled continually, but that seemed to contribute to, rather than soften, his poisonous personality. Jackie happened to know that John's brother's Cha-Cha Chicken franchise deal fell through when he learned he'd have to locate it on the highway rather than on the Square, the lifeblood of Maple Hill business.

"You don't mind, do you, Mr. Brockton?" Bridget

asked with feigned innocence, aware of the animosity between them.

"Of course not," he replied for all to hear, then added for Jackie's ears alone when Bridget wandered off, "Ms. Mayor is a privileged person around here and gets whatever she wants."

Jackie could have laughed aloud at that claim, but chose to ignore it instead.

"But we're going to change that." The threat was quietly spoken and chillingly sincere. "You wait and see."

Then Cecilia, who was serving up sampler plates of gooey desserts, handed her one and engaged her in conversation. Jackie was forced to dismiss thoughts of John's retribution and focus on her job as mayor and this event's cheerleader.

Plate in hand, a glass mug of decaf mocha topped with whipped cream in the other, Jackie stepped away from the buffet and looked around for her girls in the small sea of well-wishers.

Then she spotted Rachel, head and shoulders above the crowd—literally. She knew a moment's horror. It would be just like Rachel to stand on a table to find her. Then she realized the child stood too high to be on a table. Jackie headed straight for her.

As she drew closer, she saw that Rachel sat on Hank's shoulders, looking very much as though she owned the world.

"Here, Mom!" she called, waving. "We're here!"

Jackie kept moving toward them, trying to ignore the sexy appeal of the man who held her daughter. He'd changed from his work clothes into casual gray slacks and sweater. His dark hair had been shampooed and combed into order. He looked like the good-twin version of the dangerous-looking man she'd seen that morning.

As Jackie approached, he lifted Rachel off his shoulders and set her down on her feet in the U-shaped booth he'd reserved for them. Rachel nimbly scooted into the middle of the booth, patting the place beside her. "Come on, Mom."

Hank held Jackie's plate for her while she put her mocha down, then he stood aside to let her slide in. He sat at the end of the booth beside Jackie. "Erica's with Haley," he reported. "They told us to hold the booth, that they'll get our plates. But Rachel and I are beginning to wonder if that was wise. Who can be trusted with all this delicious stuff?" He pointed to her plate.

"I can," she said, pretending an ease she didn't feel at all. She offered her plate to Rachel, who chose a little square of cake with lots of cream.

"Yum!" Rachel anticipated her first bite with a gleam in her eye.

"Hank?" Jackie offered him the plate.

After a moment of surprise, he selected a plain tube of a cookie with chocolate inside. "Thank you," he said.

"You're welcome."

They studied each other warily for an instant, then seemed to reach the mutual decision that this moment was meant for peaceful celebration.

He snapped the cookie in half with his teeth and made a sound of approval, then popped the other half into his mouth.

Jackie dipped a plastic fork into a brownie-like concoction covered with a white chocolate mousse and took a bite.

"This is to die for," she said, putting the fork into it again and offering it to Rachel.

It earned another "Yum!"

She scooped up a bit of the mousse, determined to appear unaffected by his nearness. Intending to hand him the handle of the fork, she turned his way. "Bite?" she asked.

His closeness stole her breath. He simply sat beside her, but his large body seemed to block out everything behind him, his arm along the back of the booth hemming her in, tightening her space.

Curiously, it was not an altogether unpleasant sensation.

"Please," he replied without making a move to take the fork. His eyes told her he didn't believe she had the courage to feed him the bite.

Flustered and challenged, she did it before she could think twice.

His strong teeth closed around the little fork as he slipped the morsel off, watching her with mingled surprise and reevaluation.

"Here we are!" Haley appeared with Erica, then stopped in the act of placing their plates on the table, her attention snagged by Jackie, still holding the empty fork to the edge of Hank's lips. She looked from one to the other, obviously confused.

Jackie lowered the fork and turned back to her plate. "All right, you two," she said to Rachel and Hank as though they'd wrested samples from her. "The rest is mine." She dropped the fork on her plate and lowered her hand to her knee, hoping to hide its trembling.

Haley finally distributed plates and slipped into the booth beside Rachel, Erica sitting on the end.

Bridget arrived with a tray bearing a large pot of tea and several cups. "Here we are," she said, handing out cups and a big-handled mug for Hank. She hesitated over Hank's mug as she poured. "Is this going to be all right for you, Hank, or would you prefer something else to drink?"

The aroma of orange and cloves wafted around them from the steaming tea.

"This is fine," he said. "Thank you, Bridget."

"Good. I'll bring tiramisu as soon as it comes out of the kitchen." She picked up her tray, returned a wave to Cecilia across the room and left.

"What is that?" Rachel asked.

Jackie was beginning to feel more like herself, in control again and steady. "It's a cake soaked in Kahlúa, I think, and topped with whipped cream."

"What's Clua?"

She should have guessed that was coming.

"It's Kah-lú-a," she enunciated. "That's a coffee-flavored liqueur. It's alcohol. Sometimes people put it in their coffee or make other drinks with it."

Jackie was not surprised to learn she hadn't answered all her questions.

"If it tastes like coffee," Rachel asked, "why do they put it *in* coffee? Isn't that a lot of coffee?"

"It doesn't seem to be," she replied. "It tastes wonderful." Before Rachel could ask another question, Jackie forestalled her by pointing to a round cookie covered in powdered sugar. "Try that one next," she encouraged. "You'll love it."

Distracted, Rachel was mercifully silent as she ate.

"I love it here, Mom!" Erica held up a macaroon drizzled with chocolate. "Is this one of those coconut cookies?"

At Jackie's nod, she took a careful bite, then apparently finding its taste satisfactory, took a bigger bite. She wriggled in her seat while she chewed, her eyes focused on her mother, obviously about to make a statement.

After finally swallowing, she said eagerly, "When it's my birthday, can we have my party here instead of at the pizza place? My friends and I can all dress up and have pots of tea. I'm going to be eleven, after all."

"That's coming up, isn't it?" Haley asked. "March something?"

"Twentieth," Erica said. "And instead of seeing a movie we could do something more grown-up."

"Like housework?" Jackie teased. "Or go to the library?"

Erica made a face at her. "Funny, Mom. I was thinking maybe go to Boston shopping. Grandpa always sends me money for my birthday. Rachel has that float dress for Easter, but I don't have anything." She made her case to Hank. "I've grown two inches since September."

"Sounds like that requires a shopping trip to me," he agreed. "But when's the baby due?"

"Tax day," Haley replied for Jackie. "April fifteenth." She gave Erica a rueful smile. "I'm afraid your mom's not going to feel like walking all over Boston by that time." Then she turned to Jackie, her eyes bright with an idea. "But I could take Erica and her friends shopping. We could start with a tea party here, then you can go back to bed and I can handle the trip."

"Yeah!" Erica said eagerly. "That would work, wouldn't it, Mom?"

"It would work," Jackie agreed, turning to Haley with a smile, "if you brought along a unit of commandos or Legionnaires. When you're in charge of eight ten-year-old girls, you…"

"I'll be eleven then," Erica corrected.

"Eleven-year-old girls," Jackie continued, "you should have seasoned veterans with you, skilled in hand-to-hand combat."

"She can take Bart along," Hank suggested.

"Excellent idea." Haley slapped her hand on the table. "That's settled."

The crockery shook and everyone reached out to steady their cups.

"Sis, come on," Hank chided. "Let's not break the crockery on their first day of business."

"Sorry." She looked guilty and embarrassed. "I was overcome with enthusiasm."

They finished their treats, went through a second pot of tea, then Haley shooed Erica out of the booth. "Okay, we're off. I'm taking the girls back to the paper with me," she said. "I have some inserts to fold for the next edition, and they can be a lot of help to me. Don't worry about their good clothes. I'll put them in aprons. Hank, can you get Jackie home? She and the girls rode in with me."

Jackie frowned at her. "I thought we were all going shopping and to lunch?"

Haley shook her head, gathering up her things. "I couldn't possibly eat now, I'm stuffed!"

"I'll get her home," Hank said.

"But…" Jackie tried to protest the sudden turn of events, sensing a set-up. It was Saturday. She always spent her weekends with the girls.

Hank slipped out of the booth and stood helplessly by while she squirmed her considerable bulk sideways toward the edge of the booth. He tried to offer her a hand, but she waved him aside. "It's slow work, but I can do it," she said, already weary from the effort. "It's like getting the first pickle out of the jar."

Once she reached the end, he caught her arm to help her laboriously to her feet.

She finally stood, the energy expended draining her. "When did you all decide this?" Jackie asked.

"While we were in line." Haley wrapped an arm around each of the girls.

Jackie couldn't dispel the notion that there was some sort of plot underway here.

"Erica told me that the two of you met here to patch up your old quarrel." Haley looked into Jackie's eyes as she spoke, but seemed to be carefully avoiding her brother's. "We're just going to get out of the way so that can happen. I'm sure it'll be healthier for both of you to put that behind you." Haley consulted her watch. "It's ten-thirty. I'll have the girls home by one. Can you reestablish productive communication in two and a half hours?"

Neither Jackie nor Hank answered.

"Good," Haley said. "See you then. Come on, girls."

The three went off giggling, apparently pleased with their collusion.

"Since your sister solved her own problems and found love," Jackie said to Hank, "she's almost intolerable."

Hank placed an arm around her shoulders as a new influx of patrons pushed past them, headed for the buffet line. "She's always been intolerable," he said. "It was just never directed at you before. There's Bridget. Let's say our goodbyes."

He led her across the room, shielding her with an occasional body block to prevent her being jostled by the cheerful group.

Bridget wrapped her in a hug, then embraced Hank. "Are you two seeing each other?" she asked, looking from one to the other with new interest. She had to shout over the crowd to be heard.

Jackie leaned closer. "We were in high school together."

"Oh!" She seemed to like that notion. "Sweethearts who've rediscovered each other. I love that!"

Jackie wished her luck, thanked her for the VIP treatment, and promised to be back.

"Please do," she said. "We have a special dessert for lovers. Comes on one plate and requires two forks. Have a great day, you two. Thanks for coming."

Hank got them through the crowd, then outside. Jackie drew in a deep gulp of air. Her breath was visible on the cold air.

"I hate to leave the aroma of that place behind," she said, turning up her collar. "But I'm grateful for a little room to breathe. If they're that busy every day, they should be able to retire next year."

Hank studied her, his eyes knowing, and she realized he wasn't going to be sidetracked from a discussion of their past by her business predictions.

HANK SAW THE RELUCTANCE in her eyes and wondered if reverse psychology would work on her. As he remembered, nothing ever really "worked" on Jackie. Either she was in agreement with what he wanted to do about something, or she wasn't. If she was, her help brightened and simplified any project or pursuit. If she wasn't, she could be coolly detached while he struggled on, or deliberately obstructive, depending on how strongly she felt about the issue.

But he'd always believed that risking nothing got you nothing. So he tried it.

"Shall I take you home?" he asked. "The fact that Haley and the girls set this all up doesn't mean we have to cooperate. It was our decision to spend the rest of our lives disliking each other. We're entitled to that."

Her eyes had been focused somewhere over his shoulder while he spoke, but suddenly met his with the force of a clang he swore he heard.

She frowned. "Dislike." She repeated the word, seeming to analyze it while she lifted her shoulders and stretched her back as though it hurt. "You dislike me?"

Score! he thought, careful not to appear satisfied. "So, you *do* want to talk about it?" he asked, keeping all urgency out of his voice.

"No," she admitted with a deepening of the frown. "But I live with two little busybodies who'll ask questions, and I never lie to them. I also try to practice what I preach, and I never let them quarrel without trying to make it up as soon as possible." She gave him a disapproving look. "This never would have happened if you hadn't told them we'd fought all those years ago."

He accepted that responsibility. "I'm sorry. Your daughter was interrogating me and I couldn't lie to her either. She asked me if I was your friend, and I didn't think you'd want me to say I was. So when I explained why I wasn't, I kept it simple by just saying we'd quarreled."

She gave him an understanding nod. "Nothing's simple with children. You want to come to my house?"

"Sure," he replied casually, leading her toward his van.

He hauled out the stool he used to help his mother.

"Thank you," she said in pleased surprise. "I wondered how I was going to do this."

Yeah, me, too, he thought, silently congratulating himself on his brilliant tactics.

He had to know more about the impulse that had prompted her to feed him a bite of that brownie-white chocolate thing. He'd never thought of food as particularly erotic, but that moment had been electric. In the years they'd been apart, he'd thought of her often, even fantasized that she'd come looking for him one day. Then anger over how much she'd hurt him would set in and he'd put those thoughts aside.

But he'd seen sexual interest in her when she'd fed him the dessert. She'd spent all the time after that pretending it hadn't happened, but she didn't know the man he'd become.

In his days with NASA, he'd outwitted weather and gone head-to-head with the rules of science. He was going to find out what was brewing in Jackie Fortin's heart.

CHAPTER FIVE

JACKIE'S HOME LOOKED just as he'd imagined it would. She lived in an old Victorian just a couple of blocks from town. It was painted soft yellow with pale blue trim and dark blue accents—the insides of the window frames, the fancy shingles, the front door. It had a full front porch with window boxes filled with ornamental cabbage—the only green that survived the winter in this part of the country.

Inside, one formal room flowed into the other. A front room, a parlor, a dining room, a sort of study she seemed to be using as an office. Though the rooms were set up formally with tall windows, bay windows and fireplaces, the furnishings were covered in floral chintzes, with lace and fresh flowers everywhere. It was definitely feminine and like a throwback to another time, but he was curiously comfortable in it.

In the study she pointed him to a light blue brocade settee. She removed the dark green wool jacket she wore to reveal the round-necked, long-sleeved dress in the same shade.

She went to the chair that matched the settee, kicked off her shoes and sat down, propping her feet on the matching ottoman. She let both arms fall over the sides of the chair and expelled an "Ahhhh!" whose relief he could feel himself.

He sat on the settee and angled one foot on the other knee.

"No, I don't dislike you," he answered, as though fifteen minutes had not elapsed since she asked the question.

"You said we'd decided to spend the rest of our lives disliking each other," she reminded him.

"We had," he interrupted. "And I did for quite a while. But I don't anymore."

"Why not?" she asked candidly, a wry smile in place. "I still have dreams of murdering you."

He wasn't sure he could analyze that. When he'd spoken to her the day he'd moved his office into City Hall after not having exchanged a word with her in seventeen years, his anger had come right back—hot and resentful. But despite his anger, he knew that the old feelings had survived. He hadn't wanted them so alive then, but now he understood that love that enduring deserved a future. And he had an agenda.

"I guess," he finally replied, "because I realize that it was all so long ago and we were so young. In relation to all that's gone on since, it hardly matters. You've been married and had children, and I've spent all that time in the rarified atmosphere of space research. We're not even the same people we were then."

"No. We're not." There was a note of sadness in her voice, as though she regretted that. It came as no surprise. She was now alone in the world with two children, a baby due in six weeks and the lingering scandal of her unfaithful husband.

"My mother's organizing a group of women at church to help you for a couple of weeks when the baby comes." That was really none of his business, but he felt called upon to tell her something cheerful.

She smiled fondly. "I know. She's been wonderful to me. She's the girls' Sunday School teacher, you know."

He smiled, too. "I know. She intends to use them to spy on our conversations. I told her we were seeing each other today, even though we weren't intending to actually speak."

When she raised an eyebrow, he went on to explain. "She's always trying to set me up with someone. This time it's the niece of a friend."

She looked amusedly concerned. "You shouldn't give her hope that something will develop between us because then she won't leave either of us alone."

"Hey," he said, unrepentant. "If I have to suffer through this, so do you. You're the one who changed your mind."

He hadn't intended that to come out. The mild censure had begun lightheartedly, but apparently traces of anger lingered.

She bristled instantly, sitting up and swinging her feet to the floor. "And you're the one who wouldn't let me speak. Maybe I had a reason for changing my mind. But you wouldn't know that, would you, because you never heard it."

Anger sparked in her eyes and he felt the answering

anger within himself. But he'd just claimed to have magnanimously put the past aside because they were both more mature now. This was going to take more than simple determination. He would have to be clever and patient.

He swallowed the anger and asked quietly, "Do you want to tell me now?"

Her anger seemed to have collapsed also. "It hardly matters anymore, does it?"

"We're supposed to be making things right," he reminded her. "Haley and your girls will question you. I hate to tell you what she might do to me if I don't make an effort here."

JACKIE GROPED for a reasonable response. She hadn't wanted this to happen. She hadn't wanted to try to mend fences, to become friends again. Because then she'd have to explain, and she couldn't. At least, not so he'd ever understand.

Still, she'd always felt connected to Hank in a way that couldn't be denied. Despite her sexual response to him, their relationship could never be romantic again, but she wanted to right the past. What happened after he left couldn't be fixed, but he didn't know about that. And this was now. Perhaps they could forgive each other for the way they'd parted and just move on. It would be such a relief not to feel panic every time she saw him.

So she had to make something up, because the reason she'd chosen to stay behind was connected to what had happened later, and he couldn't know that.

She tried desperately to think of a good excuse that wouldn't make her seem like the shallow, selfish person he'd thought wouldn't leave her comfortable surroundings.

But nothing came to mind, and he was already looking at her with puzzlement.

"You were absolutely right," she said, eager to be able to say something, anything. "My parents were indulgent, people knew my name, I'd been accepted to Boston College. Even though I thought I loved you, I couldn't see myself giving all that up. I told myself you had a better chance of fulfilling your dreams on your own, and I believe I meant that sincerely, but I know I was also thinking of myself."

She waited for the scorn, possibly even an explosion of anger.

Instead, he simply nodded, a tolerant smile in place. "And you were probably right. My college years were a struggle. A marriage might not have survived them. I've resented your choice all this time because as a kid, I interpreted it as a decision against me, rather than one of common sense. And it hurt so much that even as an adult it's taken me a long time to come to terms with it."

He stood, seeming to feel restless, and walked around the beautiful room with its floor-to-ceiling books, elegant but comfortable furnishings, long, lace-covered window looking out onto snow falling on a small yard and a bare hawthorn tree.

"Two years after I graduated, I could have bought you a mansion," he said, "but I couldn't have lived in it with you. I was at work day and night most of the time, and when I finally had free time, I spent it with other engineers and all we talked about was space anyway. You got your comfort and security. You did the right thing.''

It was generous of him, she thought, to forgive that youthful attitude. Yet she couldn't help a niggle of annoyance that he'd been forced to live without her for all those years and could say in an even voice, ''You did the right thing.''

''You said a lot of nasty things then,'' she reminded him with mild pique, standing in her stockinged feet because his restlessness seemed to be catching.

He stopped his perusal of the room and turned to look at her.

''I know,'' he said. ''I'm sorry.''

''They hurt,'' she insisted, her annoyance building.

He hesitated a moment, a pleat forming between his eyebrows. But his voice remained calm. ''I'm sure they did. I'm sorry.''

''Yeah, well, that didn't help when you walked away without even listening to me.'' She went to the window, hearing herself in disbelief. He'd just forgiven her, and though her explanation was fictitious, he was generous to do so all the same. There could be peace now. They could meet each other without acrimony. His mother and his sister would be happy. Her girls would be happy.

So what was she doing?

''Pardon me,'' he said. There was an edge to his quiet voice now. ''But didn't you just admit to shredding my heart out of pure selfishness? I'm willing to let all that go, and now you're going to batter me because I got angry about it at the time?''

She hadn't understood the strange tension building in her, until she remembered one of the details of her lie. The one detail in all she'd said that was true.

She padded toward him across the blue, burgundy and white Persian carpet, emotion that had been capped all this time bursting its way out of her.

''Well, I'm mad about it now!'' she shouted at him. ''I let you go so that you could live your dreams, so you would be free to have everything you wanted, and what did you do?''

He was looking at her as though she was a madwoman.

''What?'' she demanded. ''What did you do?''

She saw him scan his mind for an answer. ''I accomplished my goals. I did live my dreams.''

''Yeah,'' she said, as though that wasn't the point. ''Then you came back! I was lonely and went through hell with a husband who could never find the real me, and look what you did—you gave up and came *back!* So my life was all for nothing?''

He folded his arms and stared at her, probably thinking that if he studied her long enough, he'd be able to make sense of what she was saying.

''I did not give up,'' he said reasonably. He had done that even when they'd been kids, she remembered—always grown calmer in the face of her irrational behavior. ''I'd done everything I wanted to, then realized that I'd done nothing for myself personally. I thought I explained that. In no way does that equate to giving up. I'm simply starting over. And anyway, you just said that selfishness was at the heart of your decision. You stayed because you wanted to remain comfortable.''

She put both hands to her face, baffled by her own logic. "Things would have been a lot easier for both of us if you'd started over somewhere else."

HANK HAD NO IDEA what was going on here, but he was beginning to believe that her distress was more related to the fact that she cared about him now than the fact that she'd been angry at him then. He could see it in her eyes, love overlaid with anger and frustration. And they weren't old feelings. This was something fresh and new, something that might have begun in the past but now had a very present identity. He was careful not to betray his satisfaction.

"I'm sorry I'm not making sense," she said, dropping her hands and slipping on her shoes. Her feet were puffy and she was having difficulty.

"Sit down," he said. "I'll help you."

She tried to fend him off but he pushed her gently back into the chair. The shoes slipped on with a little effort.

"At least you've escaped having to deal with an unglamorous and moody pregnant woman," she said.

"That seems to be what I'm doing," he countered, then added with an apologetic smile, "except for the unglamorous part, of course. You're very beautiful."

That stopped her cold. She looked at him as though

he was insane, then stood. He got to his feet. She led the way to the door.

"What're you going to tell my mother and Haley and the girls?" he asked.

"Me?" She looked flustered.

"Just tell them we made up," she said, turning the knob.

He placed his hand over hers to hold the door closed. "They'll want proof."

She frowned. "What kind of proof?"

"You have to invite me to dinner or we have to make a date. Something definite to give them so they'll be satisfied and leave us alone." He wasn't leaving here without a plan in motion.

She didn't know what to make of that suggestion. Of course, she didn't know, either, that her eyes revealed the same lingering traces of love for him that had reignited within him for her. He'd botched it as a boy, but he'd grown into a smarter man.

She shook her head. "That's a bad idea."

He fell back on the old it-doesn't-really-matter tactic. "Okay. Just thought you might want to be prepared. I'll refer all questions about this discussion to you."

He pulled the door open, but she caught his arm before he could pass through. Beyond the porch, snow fell in silent beauty, making all the big old homes in the neighborhood look like a Christmas card.

"Okay. Next weekend? I have a really busy few days coming up."

He knew about that; everyone at City Hall was talking about it. The Massachusetts Board for the Homeless Foundation would be visiting all week. They were being escorted around western Massachusetts, and a tea and a reception were scheduled at City Hall.

"Next weekend is fine," he said.

She leaned against the door frame and rubbed her arms against the chill. "Thank you. I apologize for shouting at you. I was very upset all those years ago, and every time I think about it, it happens all over again. But you're right, of course. We're not even the same people who hurt each other, so we should just put it away."

He offered his hand. "I'm willing."

She took it. "Then, that's done. I'll see you next weekend."

"All right. Get back inside before you get chilled." He ran down the steps to his van without turning back.

He drove home while snow drifted down onto Maple Hill. Calls to Whitcomb's Wonders would be forwarded to his home over the weekend.

So she still cared, he thought as the pace of traffic slowed through town. She wouldn't get so angry if she didn't care. She wouldn't want to hurt him if it didn't matter.

Memories of the past created images of the two of them as kids. He saw himself holding her on a balmy night at the lake, astonished by the depth of his feelings for her, confused by and yet accepting of the soft puddle she'd created in the center of his being where— like the other guys his age—he'd been trying to grow rock.

She was beautiful, seductive, and smart, and she had

a way of turning to him, of leaning into him, that made him feel as though he had potential even he wasn't aware of.

She made him feel invincible.

It was ironic, he thought, accelerating as the traffic began to move, that it had been the strength she'd given him that eventually made him leave Maple Hill even when she wouldn't follow.

He'd lived a challenging and exciting life, but in the quiet hours of night, he'd thought about her, wondered if she'd regretted her decision. He certainly did.

But there was no time for regrets now. He couldn't change the past, but he could certainly do something about the future—starting now.

He was going to get her back.

CHAPTER SIX

JACKIE FUSSED around the table set up in what used to be a ballroom but was now used to host various social events at City Hall. The Massachusetts Board for the Homeless Foundation, a group made up of government officials and representatives of contributing charities, was expected in an hour to celebrate the building of a shelter for the homeless on a piece of property donated by Alfred Warren, one of Maple Hill's prominent citizens.

Jackie had become mayor when the man who'd held office before her was found guilty of trying to abscond with the funds provided by the board. At the time, Jackie had been a junior councilwoman, but had lived in Maple Hill longer than the others. She'd been considered the person most likely to help the city recover from the embarrassing situation.

She wanted this reception to go without a hitch so that the board would be impressed with Maple Hill's rebound from near disaster, and more likely to contribute to their program in the future.

Half an hour into the proceedings, she realized she should have known better than to think anything would go the way she wanted it. She was talking to Jeremy

Logan, who chaired the board, explaining that during the January blizzard that had paralyzed New England, Maple Hill had sheltered their homeless in its three churches. The two of them had been sipping coffee and eating fudge gateau catered by Perk Avenue when the lights flickered.

Jeremy looked up at the Hancock chandelier.

"Please don't worry," Jackie said with more confidence than she felt. "It happens all the time. The furnace probably kicked on and that makes everything else flicker. Old buildings, you know."

He nodded appreciatively. "This is quite a place." Then he returned to their discussion. "I didn't realize such a small town would have so many homeless."

"More families are homeless now than ever before," she said, wondering why he didn't know that as head of the board. "And our program is better than the surrounding cities, so their homeless come here."

"I see. I'm new to the position and still learning. Then how do you…?"

Before he could pose his question, the lights went out. They didn't flicker, they didn't dim, they went out, leaving the room black except for the faint glow from a streetlight beyond a corner window.

There was an instant of silence, then something crashed to the floor, followed by a shriek and the sound of excited voices.

Jackie knew she had to do something quickly.

"Do you have a lighter, Mr. Logan?" she asked.

She heard the rustle of fabric, then a small blue flame

at the tip of the man's lighter pierced the darkness around them.

"May I borrow it, please?" she asked.

"Of course." He handed his cup and plate to the person beside him, then took her plate and passed her his lighter. The room fell silent.

Jackie pointed to her half-eaten gateau. "This better be the same size when I return, Mr. Logan," she teased.

The man smiled and there was a titter of laughter around them.

She went to the wall behind the buffet, the lighter guiding her way, people stepping back to let her pass. She lit the candles always kept in the sconces on either side of the fireplace.

There was an aah! of approval as that part of the room took on a golden glow. She lit two other sets of sconces in the room and was relieved that people could at least find the buffet table and see who they were speaking with.

"This is a disaster!" John Brockton whispered behind her as he followed her to the double doors that led to the corridor. "We should be investing money in this rattletrap of a building rather than building something to shelter those who contribute nothing to this community."

"It makes it clear that we don't waste our money on opulent surroundings, doesn't it?" She pushed the door open. "Or is that what you'd prefer?"

"Don't get sanctimonious with me, Ms. Mayor. You know what I mean. There isn't that much money in

Maple Hill that we can waste any of it on those who don't produce. And by the way, a lot of good having an electrician in the basement office is doing us.''

She was speechless for a moment, astonished by his attitude. ''Where did you learn that method of governing? *Mein Kampf*? Civilization is judged by how it treats its weakest members. And Hank isn't our maintenance man. He's been hired to replace the ugly old swags, that's all.''

He made a scornful sound. ''I'm not for mowing the homeless down, I just don't think they need a building. And Whitcomb says he's replacing the swags in order and my office is last. Me! A councilman!''

She sighed. ''What did you do to him first, John? And we have the money for the building for the homeless already, so there's not much you can do about it. Why don't you do *your* job as a representative of the city and go keep our guests entertained. Get out of my way, please.''

He moved away from the doors and she pushed them open, stepping out into the hall and closing them behind her.

Holding the lighter flame in front of her, she took her cell phone out of the small bag on her shoulder and punched number 13 on her speed dial. She prayed that Hank was still in his office, or at least within reach. She closed her eyes, wondering how to ask for his help when she'd been so adamant that he leave her alone.

''I'm on it, Jackie,'' he answered. ''Lights are out on the main floor also. Caterers probably plugged in too many warmers or something. We've got fuses fried all over the place.''

"Can you fix it?"

"Give me ten minutes."

There was silence on the line, then she added sincerely, "I'm grateful you were still here. I had visions of having to make torches out of the cattail arrangement in the gallery and leading people with them down the stairs to their cars."

He laughed. "Primitive but resourceful. Hang on. Lights will be on in a minute. Only one of the fuse boxes is beyond repair, but that's for the back stairs. Make sure nobody leaves that way later."

"Thanks, Hank."

"Sure."

Jackie went back to the ballroom, certain that Hank would do precisely as he'd promised.

"According to our new resident electrician," she told the crowd that turned her way, "the lights will be on in ten minutes."

"Who is it?" someone asked.

Before she could reply, someone else said, "Hank Whitcomb."

She heard a low rumble of relief. "They'll be on in five," another voice said.

And they were right. Jeremy Logan had just provided Jackie with a fresh piece of gateau and was telling her that he'd spent the last few minutes speaking to the editor of the *Maple Hill Mirror,* when the room was suddenly flooded with light.

There was laughter and applause directed at Jackie.

She took a modest bow, thinking guiltily that the restored light was all due to Hank at work in the basement after an already long day in his office.

"And what did she tell you?" Jackie asked.

"That you've accomplished a lot despite a divided council and animosity toward you personally. That you and she are the ones who caught the old mayor who tried to abscond with our money."

"We did."

He nodded thoughtfully. "You know," he said finally. "I have a friend on the Historic Buildings Restoration Board. You should hit them up for funds."

"We did last year." She shrugged regretfully. "We didn't qualify, mostly, I think, because our mayor was already under investigation for the money for the homeless shelter."

"Then you should try again. You've shown that you keep a careful eye on your funds and I'll put in a good word for you. I don't think they'll turn you down again."

"That's very kind of you," she said, knowing that hardly expressed her gratitude. "I can't begin..."

He stopped her with a shake of his head. "Civil servants who are truly serving their communities need the funds with which to work. I'll do everything I can for you."

Jackie felt as though she'd made a valuable friend for Maple Hill.

When the evening was over, she walked the visiting board members to their cars, then returned to the main doors to find Hank in the middle of a cluster of men who'd attended the reception. Amid their suits and ties, he stood out in his uniform of jeans and chambray shirt. But they were all laughing heartily, with good-natured pushing and shoving, as though they were twelve years old.

Ricky had never been like that, she remembered. But then, all his friends had been privileged, jaded men like him. They hadn't taken pleasure in anything, as she recalled. Except women they weren't married to.

As Jackie approached the steps, Hank broke out of the group and the other men disbanded to head off in different directions across the parking lot.

Hank took her arm to help her up the steps. "Where's your coat?" he asked. "And why are you wandering around an icy parking lot in your condition?"

"In my office," she replied, unused to being interrogated but not entirely unhappy about it. With her father in Miami, it wasn't often that she had a man concerned for her welfare. "And because this is America, I can walk across an icy parking lot if I want to."

He ignored that smart sally. "When does your leave of absence start?"

"The day the baby's born."

"Don't you have to prepare?"

"I've done this before," she replied as he pulled the doors open. She went inside. "I already have a bag packed. I've made plans to take the girls to Haley and Bart's. Everything's handled."

He smiled. "No wonder you run a tight city. You going home?"

"As soon as I go upstairs to get my coat and purse."

"I'm going downstairs to close up my office. I'll walk you out to your car. Wait for me here."

"I'll be fi—"

"Wait for me," he repeated, then loped off toward the basement stairs.

He was back in time to help her on with her coat. "Where are the girls tonight?" he asked.

"I have a regular baby-sitter," she said as he stood aside while she locked the ballroom door. "She's at the house when they get home from school and helps me when I have nighttime obligations or weekend duties." The door locked, she took his arm and started for the main door. "In fact, she's dating someone who works for you. He repairs furnaces, I think."

"Oh, right. Jimmy Elliott. Good man. She's a smart girl."

"She really is. My girls love her."

"Is she going to be able to take care of the baby, too?"

"She's willing to try, but we'll have to see how it goes. I'm going to take a four-week leave. If I had any other kind of job, I could take longer, but it's not as though I can count on someone else to do my work."

He stopped them in the middle of the parking lot. There were only two cars there—his van and her spiffy red Astro.

She held on to him as they walked toward it over a wide patch of ice.

"Extended model," he noted of her van. "Useful with the children."

"I sometimes pick up guests of the inn at the airport. It's nice to have the room. Hank?"

"Yeah?"

"Thank you for acting so quickly tonight. You saved the evening."

"It's all in a day's work for one of Whitcomb's Wonders." He patted the hand she held on his arm. "You're welcome."

She felt that touch so deeply that even the baby moved. The simple affection in it reminded her of the richness of the friendship they'd shared as teenagers, and how it had subtly developed into feelings that changed her from girl to woman—and eventually ruined their relationship. The lover in Hank had been angry when she'd tried to explain why she had to stay, but if he'd still been her friend, he would have listened.

"Why didn't you ever get married?" she asked. They'd reached her car, but she made no move to unlock it. The cold night air swirled with their breath, but she felt warm because they could finally talk peacefully. "No time?"

He nodded. "Also, no inclination. Until I decided to come back home. I feel as though my professional life was a success, but my personal life never really started."

"Marriage doesn't define your personal life," she said with a wry expression. "If I'd judged myself on mine, I'd have given up long ago."

"Then what do you think defines it?"

She knew the answer to that. "How much you're

willing to love. How long you're willing to hold on in hope.''

''But you held on to Ricky for fourteen years, and ultimately it didn't matter, did it?''

''No, it didn't,'' she replied.

But she hadn't been talking about Ricky.

He couldn't know that, of course. Probably didn't care. They'd planned to meet again to make their families happy, and because they wanted to do the civilized thing and be friends again.

She wanted that. But right now, leaning against the car, with his body blocking the wind, his eyes smiling down on her, his easy presence offering a comfort she hadn't felt in years, she wanted more.

But she couldn't have it. She straightened up, unlocked the door with her remote and let Hank reach around her to open it.

''I'll follow you home,'' he said.

''It's only three blocks. Look,'' she said, catching the sleeve of his jacket as he would have turned away. He had to understand this. She had to put him at a distance in order that the friendship, at least, might live. ''You don't have to look out for me. All the time I was married to Ricky, I pretty much took care of myself and the girls. I'm smart and I'm competent and I don't need a man to look after me.''

He considered her a moment with that possessive look that once made her feel so special, then put one hand on the top of the door and the other on the roof of the car, trapping her in between.

''Every woman needs a man to care about her,'' he

said softly. "It's a law of nature. Just as every man thrives on the attention of a woman."

She had to say it. He wasn't getting the message.

"We're not going to have that kind of relationship," she said firmly, folding her arms on the mound of her stomach. She was sure it made her look more ridiculous than determined.

"Says who?" he asked with smiling belligerence.

"Says me. We can be friends, but nothing more."

"There's already more than that in your eyes," he said mercilessly. "And please don't dictate to me. I didn't like it when I was a kid, and I'm even worse about it now."

She lowered her lashes and tried to turn away from him, but it was impossible. He had her backed into a corner. Her only choice was to brazen it out.

"You see memories," she insisted. "Not feelings."

She wished she hadn't said that, because now he looked more deeply into her eyes. She prayed her soul wasn't visible.

"The hell I do," he denied.

"I'm the mother of a ten-year-old!" she said desperately. "And I'm eight months pregnant, for God's sake! My face is puffy, my ankles swell and I waddle!"

He put a hand to her chin, turning her face toward the street light illuminating the parking lot. "I don't see much of a difference from the young woman I remember."

She put a hand to his chest. "Hank! I'm not a woman anymore!"

She heard her loud declaration on the cold night air

and felt as though the words formed into icicles and hung right over her head.

He blinked, clearly amused. "What?"

She sighed, wishing she'd told him she had to work late and had avoided this whole conversation. "I'm a mother, an innkeeper, an elected official. And I'm tired and disillusioned. There's nothing in me of the girl you remember. Maybe you want there to be, but there isn't. Trust me."

She was beginning to think she'd finally gotten through. He listened to her with a frown between his eyebrows, his eyes roaming her face, the frown continuing as though he saw what she'd told him.

Then he caught her in his arms and pulled her to him, pressing her close as though there wasn't seven-plus months' worth of baby between them. One of his hands caught her hair and tipped her head back.

He looked into her eyes and she tried hard to hide from him everything she felt. She tried to be the woman she'd been before she'd met him the afternoon he'd moved in.

But she could tell it wasn't working. The desire she felt must show in her eyes, and the ticking his touch caused in the heart of her womanhood, pregnant though she was, must be lighting her face because there was a small smile on his lips.

His head came down, his mouth opened over hers and made a bald-faced lie of everything she'd told him.

She tried not to respond, but it had been years since she'd been kissed with genuine passion. Even when the baby she carried was conceived, Ricky had made love to her with the purpose of recommitting himself to their marriage, but it had been done with more desire than affection, more need on his part than sharing.

But this was all about her. Hank kissed her tenderly but without the gentle uncertainty of a first embrace. This said he knew her, and inexplicably, in spite of everything, he treasured what he knew. The kiss praised her, revered her, and when she responded, every neglected emotion of the last ten years of her life clamoring to be noticed, he deepened the kiss and she kept pace. Their tongues warred, explored, his hands wandered over her body and managed to make her feel naked despite a wool overcoat.

His palm settled on her backside. She fidgeted a little, sure it was now broad as a barn, but his fingers closed over her, pressing her even closer. The baby stirred between them until Hank finally drew back laughing. "A kiss shared with three is an odd feeling."

She couldn't agree with him, primarily because she couldn't speak. Astonishment clogged her throat. The woman in her not only lived, it was jumping up and down.

"I'll follow you home," he said again. "And when we meet this weekend, I don't want to hear any more of this you're-not-a-woman idiocy."

He held her arm while she got in behind the wheel, now a very tight fit, then he closed her door and walked across the parking lot to his van.

Oh, God! Oh, God! Oh, God! she thought. *This can't happen. I can't let it happen. He'll find out and then I'll lose him again!*

But he wasn't that easily dismissed, and she could still feel his hands all over her, remember how it felt to be worshiped with a kiss. For a woman who hadn't known such things since the last time they'd made love all those years ago, it was impossible to walk away a second time.

"YOU KNOW," Bart Megrath said, his breath puffing out ahead of him as he and his companions ran around the high-school track, "you can do this indoors now, on machines!" He pulled his hat farther down over his ears as they rounded a turn in ragged formation. Cameron Trent, in the outside lane, ran a little faster to keep abreast.

"Yeah!" Cam said. "We could be doing this *in*doors!"

Hank frowned at Bart on his left, then at Cam on his right. He'd run the high-school track before breakfast since he'd moved back to Maple Hill.

"You know, it was your idea to join me," he reminded them. "You don't *have* to be here."

"We *wouldn't* have to be here," Bart corrected, "if you hadn't volunteered us for the city basketball league. I was happy being a couch potato."

"You're starting to get a gut."

Bart made a horrified sound. "I am not!"

"You are, too. This is good for you. You spend ten hours a day in your office chair. It's nice that Maple Hill has a good lawyer, but we don't want to have to point at you and laugh and call you 'fatty' behind your back."

Bart gave Hank a shove. "Haley's told me stories about your brutal persecution of her when you were kids, but I thought she was exaggerating. I'll have to reconsider."

"We're going to the bakery after this, right?" Cam asked, keeping up as they rounded the far end of the loop.

"No, we're going to Heart's Haven Health Bar for breakfast. An all-white omelette and fruit."

Bart made a scornful sound. "Yeah, right. Like that's going to happen."

"Food eaten after exercise," Cam contributed, "is burned more quickly."

"Well, that's an argument for sugar if I ever heard one." Bart picked up speed, but instead of turning for another lap around the track, he went straight toward the sidewalk and freedom. "Follow me, Cam!" he shouted over his shoulder.

Cam took off in his tracks.

"Hey!" Hank called, but with the speed they'd picked up, his voice floated back to him, unheard. And with it, a whiff of sweet aroma from the bakery several blocks away. All right. A cruller did have more appeal than an omelette with egg whites. Chucking health considerations aside, he followed them.

"You're already in good shape," Bart said to Hank as the two of them settled into opposite sides of a corner booth at the French Maid Bakery. Cam sat beside Hank. "We helped you cut firewood yesterday, we installed new cabinets in your kitchen the day before that. We could probably enter the Olympics in the shotput competition. What is this compulsion for physical exercise?''

''Unlike you, garbage gut,'' Hank replied, taking a large bite of cruller, chewing and swallowing, ''I have some standards when it comes to appearance.''

Unoffended, Bart ripped a maple bar in half. ''I have a wife. They feed you. And if you compliment the food, there are rewards beyond imagining.''

''That's Hank's problem.'' Cam tore open a packet of non-dairy creamer and poured it into his coffee. ''Not the wife, but the need for 'rewards beyond imagining.''' He underlined the last three words with a lascivious lift of his eyebrow.

Hank gave Cam a dark look. In the brief amount of time that he'd known him, he'd proven to be a loyal, hardworking employee and seemed determined to be a good friend. But he was also insightful and intuitive, and Hank hated being read by anyone—particularly if that person was right. Since he'd walked back into Jackie's life he thought about her all the time, memories of the old days vividly clear. He couldn't help but wonder what making love to her would be like now that they were adults. ''A psychologist as well as a plumber?'' he grumbled.

''Anyone can see that you have strong feelings for the very pretty and very pregnant Ms. Mayor. And that her cool demeanor and advanced pregnancy and the months ahead of no physical contact even if you *can* warm her up are making you crazy. Am I right?''

''Ah,'' Bart said with a pleased smile. ''So Haley

wasn't just indulging in wishful thinking when she said she was sure there was something between you.''

Hank made a palms-up, noncommittal gesture. "I'm determined there will be. She's as determined there won't."

"She said there was a look in Jackie's eyes as well as in yours. And the high-school sweetheart relationship is strong stuff."

"I know. But we caused each other a lot of pain. That can be hard to get past."

Cam spread a cube of butter on a cream cheese Danish. "But you were kids."

"Things hurt more when you're kids," Bart said. "They last longer. But you went on to be a great success, Hank. And she had a rotten husband, but her children are great and the whole community seems to love her. Isn't it time to put the old stuff away?"

Hank leaned into the corner of the booth and sipped at his coffee. "I took her home the day of the ribbon cutting at Perk Avenue and she said she was angry because I came back. Not simply because I'm here, but because she decided not to leave with me when we were kids so that I could live my dreams unencumbered. And then I came back. She let me go, had a rotten marriage, and now after her great sacrifice, I've given up and come home."

Bart frowned. "You didn't 'give up.'"

"I know. I explained that. She's just not rational about it."

"Then maybe that isn't the truth. Maybe she doesn't know why she's angry with you, and she just said that to try to explain it." Cam turned toward him, clearly warming to his theory. "So, that's a good sign. Because in my experience, when a woman is angry at you and not making sense, that's usually because she has feelings for you, and just can't accept them for one reason or another."

"If Jackie has feelings for me she can't accept, why is that a good sign?" Hank asked impatiently.

Bart shook his head as though Hank were simple. "Because feelings always win out. Don't you know *anything* about women?"

Hank rolled his eyes and finished his coffee. "I thought I did, but maybe I don't. Sometimes I'm sure there's something there, then the next minute she seems to hate me. Still, I'm working on it."

"You can get to her," Cam advised, pointing his plastic fork at him, "through her children. Make friends with them, and you've got it made."

"And you know this how?" Hank demanded. "You have no loving wife with children in tow that I've seen?"

"Just passing on what I've observed," Cam replied. "My brother did it. He fell in love at first sight with his dentist, but she had four little boys and wouldn't give him the time of day because she thought he could never be serious about a woman with that much responsibility. So, when the oldest one's baseball coach got sick, Jake saw his opportunity. He volunteered to coach the team, got Sandi to help him set up a pizza party after the games, and watched the boys for her one night when she had an emergency with an abscessed bicuspid.''

"You're a step ahead already, Hank," Bart said, folding his empty paper plate in half. "We baby-sat the girls the other night when Jackie had a meeting and her baby-sitter was busy. All they could talk about was you. Had quite a conversation with you the day of the ribbon-cutting, apparently."

Hank explained what he'd told the girls.

"Well, you must have made a good impression. Erica is very interested in whether or not her mother's getting any kissing action."

Cam leaned an elbow on the back of the booth. "So am I. Is she?"

Hank slapped his elbow off its perch, then gave him a teasing shove out of the booth. "None of your business. Come on. We have work to do."

"Isn't that employee abuse?" Cam asked Bart, who threw their trash away and followed them out the door. "Do I have a case?"

"I'll look it up for you," Bart promised unconvincingly as they all loped back to the cars they'd left at the high school.

THE GOOD COUNCILMEN looked skeptical. The bad councilmen looked hostile. Jackie couldn't help that they lined themselves up in her mind under categories of good and evil.

"It's going to cost us a fortune," John Brockton said with controlled anger. "And we've spent one already with all the man-hours devoted to the homeless shelter and the refurbishing of the basement for commercial enterprise—a project far outside the city's mission, if you ask me.'' He happily ticked off the changes Jackie had implemented. He'd opposed every one. Fortunately, she and the good councilmen were sometimes able to sway him.

"I thought you told me the night we lost power that you wanted something done about the wiring," Jackie challenged.

"If we repair what's in place," John said. "I don't think it's necessary to rewire."

"All I'm asking for," she said reasonably, "is that we call for estimates."

"Why don't we just ask Whitcomb to do it?" Alan Dartford asked. "We all know his work and respect his ethics. He'll do a good job for us."

"We have to put the work up for bid," John said.

"Technically, we don't," Paul Balducci corrected. "We have to put bids out county-wide. Besides Whitcomb, that leaves Dover Electric, and there's a suit against them for the Connecticut River Lumber fire, so we don't have to consider them. And Brogan and Brogan closed out everything but their retail shop when Patrick Brogan died last month."

John Brockton looked thwarted. "Under the circumstances, we should be able to look beyond the county for an electrician."

Alan rolled his eyes. "Why would we want to do that?"

John exchanged a glance with Russ Benedict, who usually supported his opposition to Jackie's every move. He owned a construction firm that would have put up Brockton's brother's fast food franchise on the highway if the deal hadn't fallen through.

"Because," John said finally, "I think it's bad enough that she advances every plan or program that squanders employee man-hours and wastes taxpayers' money. I don't see why we should also have to employ her paramours, further wasting…"

The gasp of indignation was still caught in Jackie's throat when John Brockton was suddenly yanked out of his chair, his shirt front caught in a fist. Hank's fist. Jackie had invited him to stop by City Hall to give her an estimate she could pass on to the councilmen.

Russ Benedict, a short, rotund man with glasses and a shiny black suit, got to his feet. Neither Alan, nor Paul stirred, simply watched the proceedings with interest.

"Hank!" Jackie said in astonishment.

"That's assault, Whitcomb!" Russ shouted, his voice high and raspy. "Leave him alone!"

Hank ignored him. "You owe the mayor an apology," he said quietly to John. Brockton managed to swallow, though his head was tipped backward and both his hands on Hank's wrist failed to dislodge it from his shirt. John's face took on a purple tinge. "Now would be nice."

Evelyn, taking notes at the end of the table, looked on in wide-eyed disbelief.

Ross Benedict turned to his fellow councilmen. "Are you just going to sit there?"

Paul Balducci smiled. "Yes," he replied.

Jackie stood and came around the table to Hank's side. "Let him go," she ordered firmly.

"When he apologizes," he said, applying a little more pressure.

"No-o!" John whispered brokenly.

"How much air does he have, Baldy?" Hank asked Paul Balducci. "You're an EMT."

"Five to seven minutes," Paul replied, his hands laced comfortably over his stomach. He was in his middle thirties, a widower with three children. "Of course, with Brockton it'd be difficult to assess brain damage since he starts out with an advanced—"

"That's enough!" Jackie decided it was time to get tough. She frowned at Paul. "Nice professional behavior on your part. And you!" She glared at Hank and tugged at his wrist. "Let him go."

"I will. The moment he apologizes."

"You will do it now!"

"I'm going to call the police!" Russ shrieked.

Alan Dartford grabbed his arm and yanked him down into his chair. "Shut up, Russ."

"Hank!" Jackie warned.

A small squeak of sound emitted from John's mouth.

Hank leaned closer. "What was that?" he asked amiably.

The room fell still.

"I'm...sorry!" came out just above a whisper.

"That's more like it." Hank lowered his hand and eased a gasping Brockton back into his chair. "Now, I know you give Mrs. Bourgeois trouble all the time about city affairs, but I also know she's smart enough to deal with you. But when you impugn her honor as a woman, or as a public servant, you'll have to deal with me. Are we clear on that?''

John had a coughing fit, then glared at Hank. ''You *were* lovers!'' he said in that pained whisper.

''That was seventeen years ago.'' Hank's voice was dangerously quiet. ''When we were kids. You have no reason to suspect her of impropriety, either with me personally, or in the matter of this bid, except in your own small mind.'' He looked at the other councilmen.

''Of course not,'' Alan agreed.

Paul shook his head. ''We know better.''

Russ's jowls quivered. ''Well...I thought it looked as though she might have, you know...maybe could have...um...'' As Hank's expression pinned him to his chair, he grew paler. ''John said...well, obviously he was wrong. I mean, it's clear that she...didn't...''

''I'd like to adjourn this meeting,'' Jackie said, going back to her chair before she fell down. There was a great pressure in her stomach and her back, and her nerves were shot. ''It's clear nothing positive will be accomplished after...''

''If I might interrupt, Ms. Mayor,'' Hank said, taking an empty chair beside Alan Dartford, ''I'd like to give you this formal bid for consideration before you close the meeting.'' He picked up a folder he'd apparently placed on the table unnoticed when he'd come into the room. He passed it to Alan, who passed it to Paul Balducci, who gave it to Jackie.

She opened it to register the bid in the minutes of the meeting. Scanning it, she saw that it included new wiring throughout done in phases so that the daily operations at City Hall would not be interrupted. The entire system would be converted to circuit breakers, outlets would be added, and all the computers in the building would be connected on special dedicated lines.

Thinking it sounded like everything the building required but could not afford, Jackie checked the total and saw a zero.

She looked up at Hank in surprise. "There is no total," she said.

He nodded, seeming to enjoy her perplexity. "Zero *is* the total."

She stared at him a moment, then said blankly, as though repeating it would help her understand, "Zero is the total."

"That's right. I'd like to donate my work to the city."

"What?" three councilmen asked simultaneously. John Brockton simply stared suspiciously, one hand soothing his throat.

"I'm volunteering to donate my work to the city," Hank said again. "Switching to circuit breakers will improve safety and efficiency, and it'll also reduce your insurance on the building. With my plan, you won't have any more embarrassing situations like the night of the Board for the Homeless Foundation reception."

"But…without charge?" Balducci asked, obviously shocked.

Hank shrugged. "Right now the city can't afford it and I can. I'm not ashamed to admit that I'll benefit with public relations perks."

"Damn right you will," Alan Dartford said. "I'll tell everyone I know. I move that we hire Hank Whitcomb to rewire City Hall."

"I second the motion," Russ Benedict said before Paul Balducci could do it.

Jackie still couldn't quite believe it. "You're sure?" she asked Hank.

"I am," he replied.

She blinked at him, then looked at the small group assembled around the table. "It's been moved and seconded that we contract Hank Whitcomb to rewire City Hall. All those in favor?"

There were three Ayes.

"All opposed?"

"No," John Brockton whispered.

"Motion carried," Jackie said. She turned to Evelyn. "Let the minutes record the bid to show that Hank Whitcomb is hired. Meeting adjourned."

Hank stood to shake hands with Paul and Alan while John Benedict rushed from the room with Russ in pursuit.

"Mr. Whitcomb!" Jackie said from the head of the table.

He looked up. "Yes, Ms. Mayor?"

"Would you stay for a moment please?"

Paul, Alan and Evelyn left and Hank moved to take the chair at a right angle to Jackie.

The moment the door closed behind the good councilmen, she punched Hank angrily on the arm. "What is wrong with you!" she demanded.

CHAPTER SEVEN

DESPITE THE COOL MANNER in which Jackie had taken the vote then ended the meeting, she was flustered. He liked that.

He rubbed his arm. "A broken bone, quite possibly."

"Don't get smart with me," she threatened, on her feet with exasperation, "or I'll punch you in the other one! What's wrong with you?"

"For a mayor," he said gravely, "your PR skills lack a certain one-of-the-people kind of sty—"

"That's exactly my point!" she shouted, trying to lean her hands on the table, but the baby got in her way. Further frustrated, she came around the table to growl right over him. "When I'm being the mayor, I'm not the woman you're trying to charm into dating you! I'm...I'm one-of-the-people, as you put it. You don't come to the defense of my honor with physical violence!"

"I don't care what role you're assuming," he retorted calmly, but with the very conviction he'd felt when he'd walked into the room and heard Brockton accuse her of showing favoritism to her paramours, "you're a woman above all else, and when you're dating me, the safety of your person and your honor are my responsibility!''

''That's antiquated!'' she accused.

He shrugged. ''That's me.''

''I'm not dating you.''

''We have a date for tomorrow.''

''That's a one-time thing!''

He sighed and shook his head at her. ''Jackie,'' he admonished gently. ''Stop kidding yourself. It's all still there. Everything we felt as kids and more. Accept it.''

She opened her mouth to speak, but nothing came out. She put a hand to her back and rubbed. He caught her around the waist and pulled her into his lap.

She struggled for a moment, but then it must have felt so good to be off her feet that she stopped. He rubbed gently where she'd rubbed, and uttering a small groan, she closed her eyes.

''Damn it, Hank,'' she complained.

''Yeah, I know.'' He kept rubbing.

''I'm pregnant!''

''It's not like I haven't noticed.''

''Who in their right mind wants to take up a relationship with a pregnant woman?''

''A man who never got over the woman who just happens to be pregnant.''

''You got over me,'' she said, leaning her forearm on his shoulder. He felt her weight relax against him. It was the best feeling he'd had in months. Maybe years. ''You became a great success.''

''At first,'' he said, massaging up her spinal column, ''I think I was trying to prove something to myself. Or my father. I'm never entirely sure who's behind my efforts to accomplish things. Then I loved the work. Until it took too much of me and I had to find my life again.''

"Yeah," she breathed quietly. "I understand that. My marriage took so much effort, I sort of lost myself for a while. Do you think," she asked with a worried frown, "that seeing each other again made us need to…what? Recapture the past? Find ourselves again?''

"Possibly. Or what we had just reignited. It was pretty hot stuff, remember?''

There was a pained look in her eye for a moment, then she did something totally unexpected. She leaned her head on his shoulder and seemed to abandon the moment to his care.

"I never meant to hurt you so much," she whispered.

The soft, tearful sound tore at him. "I had no intention of hurting you. Can we just forgive each other and move on from here?''

There was a moment's silence, then she lifted her head, her cheeks pink, her eyes moist, and asked anxiously, "Do you think that can happen?''

"If that's what we want," he asked, "why can't it?''

Her face crumpled and she wrapped her arms around his neck. "Trouble is, I don't know what I want," she said, small sobs moving her and the baby against him in tantalizing tremors. "Can we just be friends again for now?''

He held her to him, a little disappointed but ready to accept whatever she could offer. "Friendship's good,'' he said. And it was a foundation for building his plan.

She sat with him another moment, then pushed herself to her feet, swiping her hands across her eyes and visibly pulling herself together.

"Thank you,'' she said, smoothing the skirt of her blue jumper. ''I'd better get back to work before someone finds the mayor in tears and reports to Brockton that the sky is falling on Maple Hill.''

"Right. I've got things to do, too.'' He took his cue from her suddenly brisk mood. ''About dinner tomorrow.''

"Yes?'' Her expression was concerned. She didn't want him to cancel. That was hopeful.

"Your place,'' he said, remembering Cam's advice about winning over her children. ''Six o'clock. I'll bring everything.''

"Uh...okay.'' She seemed taken aback by the suggestion. ''You cook?''

"No, I get take-out. Shall I rent a kids' movie?''

"Yes. Sure.''

"Anything particular they haven't seen or wouldn't mind seeing again?''

She still appeared confused. ''I can take a poll and call you.''

"Good idea. See you tomorrow.''

SHE WAS WEARING the same look the following evening when she answered his knock on the door. She wore overalls over a long-sleeved red shirt, and the dramatic color made her gray eyes even more silver and her short cap of curls like pale copper.

She pulled the door wider to let him in and he was immediately assailed by her daughters. Erica took one of the bags from his arms, and Rachel, who appeared to be wearing a pillowcase, jumped up and down beside him as he followed Erica to the kitchen. Cam had apparently had the right idea.

"What are we gonna eat?" Rachel wanted to know, pulling a stool up beside him as he placed the bags on the counter. She climbed up to peer into them.

"Chicken noodle casserole from the Maple Market Deli," he said. There was immediate and enthusiastic acceptance. Haley had given him the tip. "Salad, cheese bread and chocolate cake with ice cream."

"Can we have that first?" Rachel dug into the bag and pulled out a half-gallon of vanilla ice cream with both hands.

He laughed. "Someday when you eat at my house, we can have dessert first," he said. "But your mom's probably more traditional. Would you put that in the freezer, please?"

Rachel put the ice cream down, leapt off the stool, then carried the carton to a tall, cream-colored side-by-side.

"Erica, can you set the oven on warm, please?" he asked.

She hurried to comply. He took the still-hot foil container out of a bag, but held it away from her when she tried to take it from him.

"It's too hot," he said.

She opened the oven door for him, then hovered at his elbow as he put in the container. She closed the door and both girls followed him to the counter.

He removed the flat package of foil-wrapped cheese bread and put it in the oven, too. The girls followed him back and forth across the kitchen like faithful retainers.

He took out the makings of a salad. Without being asked, Erica retrieved a large stainless steel bowl from under the counter and handed it to him. Then she brought him a cutting board.

He handed her a plastic bag of chopped and washed greens.

She found kitchen shears, cut open the bag, and emptied it into the bowl while he chopped green onions, radishes, and red and yellow peppers.

"Rachel doesn't like onions," Erica advised him. "You have to put her salad in her bowl before you add the onions."

"Got it," he said. He pulled three bottles of dressing out of the bag. "Want to put those on the table, please?"

"Yeah. Did you bring salad sprinkles?"

And he was sure he'd thought of everything. "What's that?"

"It's okay." She pointed to the shelf above his head. "They're in there on the turny thing."

He opened the cupboard and found a lazy Susan full of spices. Taller than everything else was a plastic bottle half-full of what the label said was salad topping containing soy nuts and other flavorful ingredients.

He handed the bottle to Erica, who hurried to put it on the table already set for four.

While he worked, Hank saw Jackie putting out wine-glasses. She poured milk into them. She also placed a single brass candlestick with a purple candle in the middle of the table and lit it.

She looked up from her task and caught his eye, a curiously serene expression in hers. He wondered if she was thinking, as he was, that this was the way their lives were supposed to be, had they been a little more mature, a little less volatile.

"Want us to taste the cake?" Rachel asked, atop her stool once more. She pointed to the plastic dome in the bottom.

He was about to put her off again, then Erica stood on tiptoe to look into the bag. She smiled at him. "To make sure it isn't poison, you know? Somebody should check."

"Now, would I invite myself to dinner," he asked playfully, knowing he was being worked, "and bring poison?"

Jackie came to stand on the other side of the lunch bar that separated the kitchen from the dining room. "It's a game we play," she explained, leaning her fore-arms on the bar. "Sometimes to get them to eat their dinner, I let them preview dessert to make sure they eat their liver, or vegetables, or whatever nutritious food I'm promoting at the time."

"Ah." He pulled the container out of the bag. "In-sidious," he praised. He removed the lid, cut a sliver, divided it into three pieces and offered them on a napkin Jackie provided.

The girls were enthusiastic.

"You can bring take-out to us anytime," Jackie said, savoring the fudgy frosting.

"Mom said you were gonna bring a movie." Rachel wrapped both arms around his large one. "Which one did you bring?"

He remembered with a spark of amusement his mother's puzzled expression when he returned to the office after a run to Hill Hardware for supplies.

"I have a message for you from Jackie," she'd said.

"Yeah?"

"It's weird."

"What isn't? What'd she say?"

"She said to tell you, *'Toy Story II.'*"

"Great. Thanks." He carried a box of supplies to the cabinet in the back.

She came to stand behind him and swatted the back of his head. "You don't think you're going to get away without explaining that."

He explained.

She raised her eyes heavenward. "Thank you, God. You inserted his brain at last!"

"Toy Story II," he said now to Rachel.

She looked into the empty bag. "Where is it? Can we put it in the VCR? I know how to get by all the commercials so when it's time to watch, the movie will start."

He pointed to the hall closet where Jackie had placed the jacket she'd taken from him. "It's in my pocket."

Rachel leapt off the stool and ran to the closet.

Erica shook her head at her sister's youthful foibles. "I'm glad you're here," she said. "Everybody else's mother has a husband or a boyfriend except ours."

"Really." He heard Jackie's groan as he sliced tomatoes. He looked up to grin at her.

"Nobody ever takes Mom anyplace. Except Grandpa, when he's around. But he's in Miami. Can you put the tomatoes *in* the salad? They don't look as pretty, but the salad tastes better."

"Sure." He stacked the slices and chopped them up. "Where would your mother like to go?"

"She always says…" Erica closed her eyes and cleared her throat, apparently preparing to impersonate Jackie. Jackie, fortunately, had gone to the closet to help Rachel.

"God," Erica said, making a hand gesture Jackie used unconsciously while talking. "I could use a month in Bermuda."

She had Jackie's voice down pat, complete with a note of end-of-the-rope exasperation. She opened her eyes again. "Your mom says she'd watch us if our mom can ever get anybody to take her."

He nodded, scooping the tomatoes onto the blade of the knife and dropping them into the salad. "It's nice that part of her wish is taken care of."

"Yeah. You have to do the other part."

"I see."

"And she doesn't like to fly, so you'd probably have to take a cruise."

"I'll look into that."

"Look into what?" Jackie had reappeared while Rachel, videotape secured, set up the VCR.

Erica opened her mouth to explain, but Hank wisely placed his hand over it. "Let's let it be our secret," he said into her ear.

Erica beamed and lowered his hand. "She loves surprises!"

Jackie looked from one to the other worriedly. "Can we clarify that I only like *good* surprises?"

"This is a *great* one!" Erica said.

Hank handed her the salad bowl and she carried it to the table. He removed the cheese bread from the oven and passed it to Jackie, potholder and all.

"What were you talking about?" Jackie whispered.

"A surprise," he whispered back.

"Vegetable or mineral?"

He thought about cruising with her under the stars. "Celestial," he replied, turning to fold a tea towel to get the chicken dish out of the oven. Jackie was still standing there when he went to take the dish to the table.

"Celestial?"

"Yeah."

"Erica talked you into taking me to an observatory?" She was teasing, but she was closer to the truth than she knew.

He walked past her with the chicken. "In a manner of speaking, yes. Anything missing?" He put the chicken down on the tea towel and checked the table.

"The chocolate cake," Rachel teased.

Hank couldn't remember when he'd enjoyed a din-

ner so much. The chicken noodle dish was pretty pass-
able, and the girls had seconds. Jackie had lots of salad
and three pieces of cheese bread. Hank drank his milk
and took in the scene. The plan was working.

The Bourgeois women were a beautiful bunch. They
talked playfully about hiring him on in a sort of nanny-
maid capacity because of his ability to provide good
food without any of them having to cook it.

"Then, what would we do with Glory?" Jackie
asked.

"She's gonna marry the man who works for Hank,"
Rachel said.

"She *hopes* she's going to," Erica amended. "And
anyway, even if she gets married, she'll still have to
have a job."

Rachel pointed her index finger in the air. "I know.
Glory can watch the baby, and Hank can watch us."

"Hmm," Jackie considered with a sidelong glance
of amusement in Hank's direction. "Two nannies.
That's going to cost us quite a bit."

"But Hank's going to bring all the food, so we won't
have to buy any!"

Erica looked at her in complete disgust. "If Mom's
paying him to take care of us and bring the food, she's
paying for everything anyway."

Undaunted, Rachel kept thinking. Her face brightened suddenly and she said, as though wondering why
it hadn't occurred to her before, "Maybe if we asked
his mom, she'd just *give* him to us. Then we wouldn't
have to pay him, but he'd be here all the time. And
he'd bring the food."

As Erica laughed hysterically and Jackie, maintaining a straight face, explained the dark qualities of slavery, Hank studied Rachel as she listened intently to her mother. He wouldn't be surprised, he thought, if she became CEO of her own company one day—a brilliant product making her the talk of Wall Street. That little brain never stopped working. He had to remember to ask Jackie about the pillowcase Rachel wore.

Erica and Rachel cleared the table and served dessert.

"Is Erica okay with a knife?" Hank asked softly.

"We have a serrated cake server," Jackie replied. "And she's careful."

"What about Rachel's pillowcase?"

Jackie put a hand up to hide a smile. "It's her own design. I think she's looking toward a career in fashion. Unfortunately, the pillowcase was Erica's. We came very close to bloodletting. Rachel paid Erica for the pillowcase, and Erica gave her a deal on it since we'd gotten it on sale. So—all's well that ends well."

That was a philosophy he could endorse—if he was sure this plan to win Jackie over would pay off. The more time he spent with her, the deeper his feelings ran. And the more he saw of her children, the more he thought a lifetime with them could be a very good thing.

But Jackie wasn't ready for more than friendship. That was okay, he told himself. Time—and her children—were on his side.

THEY SAT ON THE SOFA to watch television, Hank and Jackie side by side, Erica on the other side of Jackie, and Rachel in Hank's lap. They reached the mutual agreement that they were all too full for popcorn.

Hank was surprised to enjoy the movie almost as much as the children did. The girls' laughter was infectious, and even Jackie's sense of silly was sparked by the combined efforts of the toys.

After the movie, Erica went upstairs to do her homework, and Rachel went to bed without protest. Jackie had walked halfway up the stairs to tuck her in when the telephone rang. She turned to come down.

"I'll answer it," Hank shouted to her. "Take your time on the stairs." He picked up the kitchen phone. "The Bourgeois residence."

"Um…hi?" a young, uncertain male voice said. "This is the Yankee Inn. May I speak to Jackie, please? It's important."

"Hold on," he replied. "She'll be right here."

Jackie waddled toward him from the stairs, a hand to the small of her back. "Who is it?" she whispered.

"The inn," he replied. "Something important, he says."

"Hey!" a demanding voice shouted from upstairs. "Aren't you gonna tuck me in, Mom?"

Jackie closed her eyes in a bid for patience. "In a minute, Rachel," she called as she took the phone.

"I'll go," Hank said. He pulled the stool up for her. "Sit down. I'll make coffee when I come down."

He took the stairs two at a time as Jackie's voice soothed the young man on the other end of the line.

He found Rachel sitting up in bed, waiting expectantly. The moment he appeared, she fell back against her pillows with a giggle.

"Your mom got a call from the inn," he explained, "so I volunteered to do the tucking. How did your dad handle this? Do I do the feet first?"

"He was always at work," she said, head tipped up to watch him. "You can do my feet first."

"Okay." He made a snug bundle of her feet, then tucked the blankets in at her waist and at her shoulders. She giggled again. "Can you breathe?" he asked, sitting on the edge of the bed beside her.

"Yeah." She beamed at him, apparently happy in her inability to move. "You did a good job. Now you have to read me something."

"The *Wall Street Journal*?" he teased. "The works of Shakespeare?"

She giggled again and turned her head toward her bedside table, where a thick book with gold-tipped pages rested. "We're reading *The Mouse Chronicles*. There's a red ribbon on the page."

He reached for the book, found the ribbon and flipped it open.

"The part where Mama Mouse goes to fix dinner and doesn't have any food." She wriggled a little in her tight confinement, clearly anticipating.

He read in a high falsetto, "'What shall I do? My babies are hungry and the cupboard is bare. And the cat's asleep under the table!'" Rachel giggled at his voice, but stared with rapt attention.

Erica wandered in in white flannel pajamas patterned in large red hearts. "How come *you're* reading?" she asked, walking around the bed to sit beside Rachel, who slid over to make room for her.

"Mom's on the phone, so Hank's tucking me in."

"I think that makes you a boyfriend," Erica said. "Officially."

He was scoring points here right and left. "I don't think it's official until your mom says so."

"Keep reading," Erica prompted, "and we'll report on whether or not you did a good job."

"Fair enough." He turned the page and read on, feeling smug.

JACKIE GOT AS FAR as Rachel's bedroom door and stopped, touched by the scene. The girls lay side by side, Rachel under the covers and Erica atop them in the pj's Jackie had given her for Valentine's Day. Hank sat on the edge of the bed, leaning back on an elbow and reading from the book he'd propped against Rachel's feet.

The three of them seemed to be sharing the pleasure of each other's company and enjoyment of the story. The tale was one of Rachel's favorites. It was about a mother mouse and her two babies and their struggle to get through the winter. They worked together to insulate their little floorboard hole by weaving hairs from the household's dog and cat. They made forays into the kitchen at night for crumbs on the table or the counter, and replaced the bows in their hair with threads taken from the frayed edges of the tablecloth.

Every time Jackie read it, she related it to their struggle to get on with their lives.

When Hank finished and closed the book, Rachel sat up in bed. "That's just like Mom and Erica and me," she said.

Erica smiled. "Except for the part about weaving dog and cat hair." She seemed in a mellow mood and made the correction with humor, not malice. "And you bought the food. We didn't have to fight a cat for it."

Rachel seemed to understand the difference. "And me and Erica have to work together to help Mom with stuff even though Erica hates me most of the time."

"I don't hate you," Erica corrected. "I just think you're weird." To Hank, she added, "She made that weird pillowcase dress out of *my* pillowcase, you know."

"I asked your mom about that," he admitted, still relaxed. "That was a pretty clever notion, Rachel. But you probably should have used your own pillowcase."

"The design on hers was better." She reached back to grab her pillow and hold it so close to his face that he crossed his eyes exaggeratedly. Both girls giggled. "See!" Rachel exclaimed. "It has baby animals. I wanted a grown-up dress."

Erica rolled her eyes. "Grown-ups can't usually fit into a pillowcase."

Rachel swatted her with the pillowcase. Thanks to Erica's mellow mood, laughter ensued rather than mayhem. She snatched the pillow from Rachel and whopped her with it. When Hank tried to intervene, he was whopped as well.

In a moment they were a chaotic tangle of flannel-clad limbs flailing the air amid shouts and high-pitched squeals of battle.

Jackie was just about to intervene when Hank rose to his feet, a child caught under each arm.

"Mom!" Rachel screeched with laughter. "Help us!"

"I saw the whole thing." Jackie walked into the room feeling a happiness she'd thought she'd stopped believing in. Ricky had seldom played with the girls like this. And it had been years since a look into Ricky's eyes made her feel the palpitations she felt now as Hank looked at her, his eyes filled with laughter. "You two started it," she said breathlessly.

Erica, still dangling from his arm, glanced up at her, her dark hair half covering her face. "We want you to make him official."

"Official?"

"Your official boyfriend. We want him to be, but he says it isn't official until you say so."

She hedged. "He's my official friend. How's that for now?"

Both girls frowned at her, then Erica brightened. "And he's a boy, so…so…what's a word for something that's true, even though it isn't official?"

Jackie couldn't think. She loved the sight of him with his arms full of her girls.

"Technically," Hank suggested.

"That's it. So, if he's a friend and a boy, technically, he's your boyfriend."

"Yeah!" Rachel shouted as he dropped her onto the bed.

"Look at what you did to my great tucking-in job," Hank said, easing Erica to her feet also. Both girls reached up to hug him. He bent down to accommodate them. "Everybody's untucked. I guess I'll have to leave it to your mother after all."

Jackie went to cover Rachel, then realized she held the cordless phone in her hands. *That's right,* she thought, a little alarmed by her forgetfulness. *I came up here to give him the phone.*

"Here," she said, thrusting it into his hand and pointing Rachel back to her bed when she would have climbed out again. "I picked up your mom on call waiting. There's some kind of power problem at the church, and they're having a deacons meeting tonight."

He groaned and was stabbing out the number as he walked into the hallway. "You'd think," he said, "that a place with so many candles would be able to cope."

Erica tried to follow him, but Jackie pulled her back. "That's a business call, Erica," she admonished gently. "He'll need privacy."

"I wish he lived here," Rachel said. "I really like him."

Erica nodded. "I think," she whispered, "that he likes us more than Daddy did."

"Your father loved both of you very much." Jackie was sure that was true, though Ricky had never understood how to show his love. She was always trying to make sure they knew he cared.

Erica nodded wisely. "I know, but he didn't really like it when we hung around him. Hank does."

"You can't base a decision like that on one dinner and a movie," Jackie said.

Erica looked at her as though she was surprised to understand something her mother didn't grasp. "Yes," she insisted. "You can."

Once Rachel was securely tucked in, Jackie hugged her, then turned out her light.

"If we could vote," Rachel whispered loudly as Jackie and Erica walked toward the door, "it would be two against one, Mom!"

"But this is a monarchy," Jackie turned to explain. "Not a democracy."

"What does that mean?"

"It means I'm the queen, and you do as I say."

She pulled the door partially closed on Rachel's protest.

In the hallway, Hank was grinning. He'd clearly heard her remark. "All of us?" he asked.

She fought an answering grin, but lost. "Just my loyal subjects," she clarified.

"What about your neighboring..." he groped for the right word to continue the role-playing.

"Kingdom?" she asked, thinking she really had to get him out of the house before she got too comfortable with his easy presence. "You, of course, are free to do as you please."

He made a low, sweeping bow. "Then I must be away, your highness. I am beseeched to relight the torches at the...vicarage." He frowned. "Vicarage is the wrong period, isn't it?"

She nodded. "I think so. What would it be? Abbey?"

"I think that's it."

"*What* are you guys talking about?" Erica asked, looking from one to the other in puzzlement.

Hank pinched her nose. "That's how adults play—when the guy isn't the official boyfriend—with words. Good night." He started to back away. "I'll call you."

As much as Jackie had wished he would leave for her peace of mind, now that he was going, she wanted to hold on to him.

"I'll walk you out," she said, then added to Erica, "I'll be right back, sweetie."

"Take your time, Mom," she said. "I'm still finishing my math homework. Bye, Hank."

"Bye, Erica."

He waved and started away, then Rachel called through her half-open door, "By-ye!"

"Bye, Rachel!" he returned.

Jackie caught his arm and walked him to the stairs. "Go, before they try to follow you."

"I have a great place at the lake," he said as they made their way down the stairway. "You'll have to bring them by sometime. I'll bet they'd love it."

"On the far side," she said. "Just about opposite your mother's. She pointed your lights out to me one night when she baby-sat for me at her house."

He laughed as they reached the bottom. "Hoping you'd wander over on your own, no doubt, and we'd make peace and provide her with a horde of grandchildren."

Jackie stopped at the hall closet, tugged his jacket off a hanger and held it open for him. "Yes. She's about as subtle as my daughters."

He shrugged lightly. "Don't worry about it. We're still two independent people free to do as we please. We've had the obligatory date, so whatever happens now is completely up to us."

She nodded, turning away from him to open the door. That was a pretty cut-and-dried assessment of their situation, and suddenly she didn't feel quite that independent. It felt so right to have him in this house, sitting at her table, reading to her children.

And the date hadn't been *that* obligatory, had it? Or maybe it had. Maybe that was why he'd chosen to bring dinner here rather than take her out somewhere. He hadn't wanted to be seen dating an elephant.

But he'd argued for the date, hadn't he? She couldn't quite determine how much of this warm and wonderful evening had really happened, or how much was in her imagination.

Then he pinched her chin in a sweet, affectionate gesture, gave her a quick, chaste kiss and ran down the porch steps to his van.

"Bye!" she called—probably a little too eagerly. She sounded like one of her children.

"I'll call you this weekend," he promised, climbing into the van.

It wasn't until he'd driven away with a tap of his horn that she remembered with great disappointment that the girls were going on a Sunday School fun trip this weekend with Adeline chaperoning. And Jackie had promised to cover the desk at the inn.

Doesn't matter, she thought dispiritedly as she tidied up the kitchen. *This can't possibly work out.*

No way at all.

Guilt was already beginning to nibble at her insides, telling her that he should know.

She'd done what she thought was right at the time. But he wouldn't think so.

So what did she do now? Her girls thought he was wonderful, and she was just beginning to remember what a very special boy he'd been. And what a thoughtful, kind and deliciously sexy man he'd become.

God. The church wasn't the only place in this town that needed light!

CHAPTER EIGHT

ON FRIDAY NIGHT, Jackie imagined what she would do with her weekend if she had only herself to think about. March was a quiet month for guests at the inn, and she dusted the old leaded glass lamp on the front desk as she thought.

The girls had left with Adeline and the rest of their class two hours ago, there was no pressing city business left undone, and the house was clean. Hank had said he'd call, but she'd had no word from him so far. That was probably for the best. She needed time to herself.

She would eat ice cream out of the carton when she got home sometime after midnight. She would watch a movie with love scenes in it because she never did that with the girls around and her mind seemed preoccupied lately with how long it had been since she'd had sex. She would take a shower uninterrupted by ''Where are my shoes?'' ''Can I have a banana?'' or ''Erica won't let me have the remote!''

She would spritz herself with White Diamonds and wear the black lace negligee she'd bought just before Ricky died and never got to wear. She would pretend that she was a cool career woman with the world on a string, rather than a mother and a civil servant who did indeed look like two women rolled into one.

The front door opened to the ring of a melodic little bell and Jackie raised her head with the smile of greeting she demanded of all desk clerks. And then she noticed her father, six feet, two inches of handsome male in brown pants and jacket over a mossy green turtleneck. Adam Fortin had a thick thatch of pure white hair, and a white beard and mustache with touches of gray in it. He was just beginning to get a little thick around the middle.

"Dad!" Jackie exclaimed, delighted to see him. He hadn't been home since the previous fall.

She'd started walking around the desk to welcome him when she realized there was something else wrapped around him that was not clothing.

It was a woman. At least, she thought it was; she'd never seen a form quite that perfect, and for a moment wasn't convinced she was alive. But she had to be. She was walking, although she was holding on to Jackie's father so tightly, she could be getting her propulsion from him.

When Jackie reached him, he wrapped his free arm around her, his other arm still caught in the woman's. He smelled of something masculine and herbal, not the fresh Old Spice he'd always preferred. But his grip was strong and reassuring, and Jackie was delighted that he was back.

"You look as though you're going to deliver that baby tonight!" he said, holding her away from him. "I thought you were due in April."

"I am." She drew one hand away to pat her water-melon-sized middle. "It's just a particularly healthy little guy."

"It would be such a relief to have a boy in this family. Here. Let me introduce you to Sabrina Bingley." He drew the beautiful woman forward. "Bree, my daughter Jackie Bourgeois."

Sabrina offered her hand, her knuckles directed upward almost as though she expected Jackie to kiss them. She gave Jackie's hand the barest of squeezes.

Jackie disliked her. She knew it was impulsive and unreasonable to form an opinion so soon, but she couldn't help it. The feeling had begun the moment she'd laid eyes on the woman, and grew stronger as she offered Jackie a cool smile.

Sabrina was almost as tall as Adam, and wearing an off-white wool outfit with clinging pants, a long top belted at a waist that was certainly no more than twenty-two inches around. A fringe wool wrap in an oatmeal color draped her shoulders, making her look like something off a Paris runway.

Short dark hair framed a very beautiful, unfreckled face. Dark blue eyes were assessingly frank. *You look like Dumbo,* they said.

Quickly dismissing Jackie, she looked around the inn. "Beautiful old place," she said. "Maine oak bannisters."

Jackie wondered how she knew that. Bree apparently read her mind.

"I'm a decorator in South Beach," she explained. "I could do a lot with this place."

Jackie had mixed feelings of horror and relief. Horror because she loved this old place just as it was with its old wood, worn floors, fieldstone fireplace discolored from 260 years of keeping family and guests warm, the patina of age sitting on everything like gray in an old woman's hair. In her two years as manager, she'd struggled to restore the old fixtures and furnishings rather than replace them. She didn't want "a lot" done with them.

But she'd feel better if her father had brought the woman here as an employee rather than as the... companion she appeared to be.

"You're on vacation, Bree," Adam said, wrapping his arms around her shoulders. "And Jackie won't let you touch a thing. She connects with her ancestors here, or something. She loves its age."

"Well, I do, too," Bree said, fixing Jackie with a condescending smile. "I was just talking about a little freshening up. If guests think a place is being neglected, they won't come back."

"Our repeat business," Jackie said with a forced smile, "is about seventy percent."

Sabrina patted Jackie's arm. "I suppose this area doesn't have that much to offer, does it? Adam, I'm dead on my feet. Can we retire?"

Jackie struggled to remember that her father had brought this patronizing snob.

"Why don't you two sit in the parlor for half an hour?" she suggested. "I'll bring you a brandy and have Honorine tidy up your suite." Home for Jackie's father was a suite of rooms on the third floor.

Adam took her chin in his hand and kissed her cheek, completely unaware of the tension. "No need. I'm sure it's fine. I'll open a few windows, shake out the blankets. Come on, Bree."

He caught Sabrina's hand and tugged her along toward the elevators. "John's bringing our things in," he said. John was the night bellman. "Would you ask him to park the Caddy in my spot when he's finished? And tell him to be careful. It's a rental."

"Sure."

She wanted to follow him, plead, "Tell me you're not serious about this woman!" But he put an arm around Sabrina as they waited for the elevator and she leaned into him like a kitten.

"Oh, God!" Jackie groaned to herself.

She was distracted from her concerns for a few moments by a call for reservations, followed by a call from Haley. She was at work, she said, and wanted a comment on John Brockton's plan to impeach Jackie.

"What?" Jackie demanded.

Haley was silent for a moment. "You didn't know," she asked finally, "that Brockton and Benedict are mounting a campaign to have you impeached?"

"No, I didn't."

"Something to do with assigning business favors to your lover." Haley sounded more intrigued by the reason than upset. "Are you and my brother finally…?"

"No!" Jackie shouted at her. When John, pushing a luggage rack stacked with seven or eight beige and green tapestry bags, stopped to look at her inquiringly, she shook her head to assure him that she was fine and that he could continue to the elevators. Then she lowered her voice and wrapped her hand around the rim of the mouthpiece. "I am so pregnant I have neither the desire, nor probably even the ability, to accommodate a man!" That wasn't entirely true. She did certainly have the desire, but she was determined no one would know that but her. "And your brother and I have decided that we can be friends. Friends! That's all! Brockton's just being hateful. Can he even do this?"

"Yes," Haley replied. "I checked the city's charter. All it takes is two councilmen to form a recall committee. But the decision on whether or not to proceed is made by a judge. Brockton's out to get you, and Benedict's going along because he doesn't want to lose his business."

"I know."

"So, what's your statement?"

"I'll save it until the hearing. Then I'll have a lot to say." Actually, she had a lot to say now, but none of it was printable. Jackie put a hand to her suddenly aching head. Another line began to ring. "I'm sorry, Haley, I've got to get that."

"Okay. Talk to you later. And you know I'll give you all the support you need."

"I know. Thanks. Bye." She drew a breath and answered cheerfully, "Front desk."

"Jackie, this is Sabrina." The tone was clipped and superior—guest to peon. And it suggested a major problem.

"Hello, Sabrina," Jackie said pleasantly.

"The heat light in the bathroom doesn't work." That

news was delivered in the same way a doctor might tell a patient, "You have three months to live." "I have been on a plane for twelve hours and I was about to take a quick shower. Fortunately, I flipped on the heat lamp first, otherwise I'd now be wrapped in a towel and freezing to death."

And that would be bad? Jackie asked herself.

"I'll send someone up to change the bulb," she promised.

When John returned with the luggage cart, she handed him a replacement bulb she'd retrieved from the supply closet. He was twenty and taking drama classes at Amherst. He got on his knees in front of her. "Please don't make me go up there again! She made me hang her suit bags in the closet, put her train case in the bathroom, place all her other cases in the middle of the bed, and then open them. She sent me for ice, then asked me to call the restaurant and place her room service order. And she stared at me the whole time, ordering me around like a field general. Please, Mrs. Bourgeois. And there was something weirdly sexual about it—like ordering me around was arousing her." He clutched her hands theatrically. "I think she's a succubus."

Jackie giggled, then frowned at him, urging him to get to his feet. "We're it tonight, John. Do you really want to see me on top of a ladder?"

He wrapped his arms around her. "I'll put you on a pedestal if you'll hire someone else for an hour to go up there."

"I've changed thousands of these in my career as

innkeeper,'' a deeper male voice said. Jackie and John turned in surprise. Adam stood there, apparently having heard everything. Or at least John's last plea.

"Mr. Fortin!" John said, standing straighter, his complexion going pale. "I...I..."

"Not a problem." Adam took the corrugated box containing the bulb from Jackie and started back toward the elevators. "I would have given you a big tip, though, John," he added with a grin over his shoulder. "Can you have breakfast with me in the morning, Jackie?" he asked as he punched the up button.

There went her sleeping-in plans, but she'd happily abandon them to find out what on earth her father was doing with such a dragon. "Sure, Dad. I'd love to."

"Good. I'll pick you up and we'll go somewhere that won't remind you of work." The elevator doors parted and he stepped aboard.

As the doors closed again, John turned to Jackie with a look of dread. "Am I fired? Do you think I'm fired?"

Jackie shook her head. "I own the inn now, John, and you're not fired. I think she's a pill, too, but we have to be courteous, okay? She's a guest."

He closed his eyes, drew a breath of relief and nodded. "Thank you. I'll give you a kidney, my liver, anything. Just say the word."

"I'd settle for a mocha."

"Right away." John hurried off in the direction of the restaurant.

He hadn't even delivered the mocha when Sabrina called again. "It isn't the bulb," she said, the b's in the last word enunciated with royal displeasure. "Your father has put it in and taken it out several times and there is still no warmth in the bathroom.''

Jackie wondered if it had occurred to Sabrina that her presence in the room was providing too much chill for a simple bulb to counter. Aloud, she said, ''Can you live without it tonight, and I'll have it looked at in the morning?''

''I'd prefer not to,'' Sabrina replied simply.

Jackie drew a breath for patience. ''Then I'll see what I can do. I'll be in touch.''

She dialed Hank's number, happy to have an excuse. Time alone be damned.

''Whitcomb,'' he replied.

She explained the problem. ''I'm sorry,'' she added. ''I know you probably thought you were finished for the week and could finally relax, then along comes...''

''An opportunity to see you,'' he filled in for her. ''That's a good break whatever time it is. I'll be right there.''

She hung up the phone, a ray of light invading the grimness of Sabrina's arrival and Haley's phone call. Hank sounded as though he wanted to see her.

And she was a little horrified by how much she wanted to see him.

HANK RECOGNIZED A DRAGON when he saw one, even if it was wearing an ivory peignoir. Jackie had told him simply that the warming light in the bathroom of her father's suite wasn't working, changing the bulb hadn't helped and that housekeeping had brought up a ladder for him. But John Granger, her night bellman, had shared the elevator with him. He'd warned Hank about Jackie's father's guest.

Sabrina opened the door to him, yards of flimsy fabric hanging from the arm that held it open. She looked him up and down with an expression that reflected disdain for his chambray shirt and jeans, mingled with interest for what might be underneath.

Then Adam Fortin appeared behind her with a surprised greeting and her interest was quickly banked.

"Hank!" Adam said, pumping Hank's hand. "It's great to see you. What are you doing here? Last I heard you were responsible for bringing Traveler Two down safely."

Hank began to explain but Sabrina interrupted by giving Adam a long-suffering smile. "Could you two talk while he works? I need my shower."

"Sorry. Of course." Adam led Hank into the old-style but sumptuous bathroom. As Jackie had promised, a ladder stood in place right under the light.

Hank flipped off the light and examined it closely. It took only a moment to determine that the problem was simply a loose connection. While he set about fixing it, Adam sat on the rim of the tub, continuing their conversation.

Hank told Adam about his sudden realization that he had nothing in his life but his work and his very occasional trips home.

He described his business and the men who worked for him part-time.

Holding a hand down to Adam, he asked, "Would you pass me the light, please?"

Adam handed up the new one. Hank installed it, then Adam went to flip the switch. Brightness and warmth instantly filled the room.

"Thank goodness," Adam said, helping Hank fold the ladder. "If Sabrina had had to wait any longer for her shower, I'd have never heard the end of it."

Hank couldn't imagine loving a woman who made a man accountable for things he couldn't control. But every man to his own taste.

"Well, now you're safe." Hank carried the ladder out into the living room.

"You're finished?" Sabrina sat in the middle of a blue and orange chintz sofa, reading a magazine. She looked up in surprise, eyelashes fluttering.

"It was easily fixed," Hank replied politely.

"Thank you," she said, grabbing a robe that lay on the sofa beside her and hurrying off for her delayed shower.

"You're welcome," Hank said to Adam. "I'll take the ladder down to housekeeping."

"You don't have to do that."

"I'm going down anyway."

Adam opened the door for him. "Have you and Jackie…you know…"

"We've agreed to be friends," he said, then he grinned. "Well, *she's* agreed to be friends. I have other plans."

Adam looked vaguely troubled. "Have you… talked?"

"Yes." He nodded wryly. "We just don't agree

about the direction of our relationship, so I'm letting
her believe friendship's good enough for now.''

"I'm pulling for you. I always thought you'd be
good for each other." Adam shook hands with him.

With a wave goodbye, Hank headed toward the elevator with the ladder. After meeting the dragon, he
wasn't sure he should trust Adam's opinion on who
would be good for whom.

He found John behind the front desk.

"Mrs. Bourgeois is taking a break," he said. "Just
prop the ladder up against the wall there, and I'll take
it back to the supply closet."

"Mrs. Bourgeois go to the restaurant?"

"No. She put her coat on and went outside. Said she
needed some air."

Hank took his tool box out to his van, which was
parked around the side, and scanned the grounds for a
sign of Jackie. The night was crisp and cold, the ground
covered with snow that crunched underfoot.

His tools stowed, he walked under a pergola at the
side of the inn. It was covered with the naked vines of
a clematis that would have beautiful pink flowers in
the summer. Moonlight gleamed on the snow-covered
lawn, which eventually sloped to a spring that ran
along the back of the property. He could hear its mu-
sical movement as it rushed along, a beautiful sound
in the night-time quiet.

That was where he found Jackie, standing at the top
of the slope. A decorative little bridge crossed the
stream, but he guessed she didn't dare risk slipping on
it.

"Jackie," he said quietly, afraid of alarming her in the dark. But she was apparently deep in thought and he had to say her name again before she heard him.

She turned to him, only the contours of her cheeks visible. She wore a big, dark coat, her hands buried deeply in its pockets. She looked almost pitiful for a moment, then he saw the brilliance of her smile as he approached.

"Hank," she said. There was a sort of sudden, desperate relief in her voice, as though she truly was glad to see him. It was all he could do to play it cool. Eagerness, he was sure, would send her running.

"Hi." He went to stand beside her, arms folded against the cold—and to prevent him from reaching for her. "Thought you might like to know the light's fixed."

"Bless you," she said. "What was the problem?"

"Just a loose connection. I only get to bill you for the minimum."

She sighed. Her breath puffed out around them, a white mist in the darkness. "You could name your price for this one. If I'd had to listen to her complain one more moment, I'd have been forced to slap her. She should pay you, too, for saving her from bodily harm."

"I'll bill her," he teased, "and see what happens. What's your father doing with her anyway?"

"Haven't a clue. They just came back tonight and I haven't had a chance to talk to him yet. But he's picking me up for breakfast tomorrow. I can't imagine what he sees in her."

He pointed out the obvious. "She's a young, beautiful woman with a great body."

"But my mother was a sweet, gentle woman. This one's a...a..."

"Dragon?" he helped.

"Yes! So what's the appeal?"

"He's getting older," Hank speculated. "Maybe she's visible proof that he's still got it—if he thinks he's in danger of losing it."

"That's such a cliché."

"Life's full of them. And try as we do to be unique, we all succumb to the same fears and foibles."

"You didn't. You went off to make your mark, and you did it."

"Yeah. Then I got lonesome and came home. That's an old story, too."

"Still, all I did was become notorious. The woman whose husband died in another woman's arms. The mayor they tried to impeach."

"What?" he demanded.

"Brockton wants me recalled for giving city business to someone with whom I'm having intimate relations."

"No one will believe that."

She turned and took several steps away from him. "I know. I just worry about the girls. They've been subjected to so much junk this past year...."

Her voice sounded high and strained.

He reached her in one stride and turned her to face him. There were no tears on her cheeks, but he could see them in the misery in her eyes, just a breath away.

He wrapped her in his arms, tucking her sideways so that he could draw her closer. "It's all right," he told her, stroking her hair. It was cold and silky under his hand. "You're entitled to be tired and discouraged and sick of all you've had to put up with. You want to shoot at tin cans or something? Break crockery? I remember you used to like to stomp around when you were angry."

She sniffed, apparently refusing to let the tears fall. "I was seventeen then. If I stomped now, the ground would shake in Connecticut. And you might find yourself delivering a baby."

"Oh, please." He laughed lightly and kissed her forehead. "I guess it's just another kind of engineering skill, but I don't have it. Why don't I hang around until you're off, then I'll take you to my place where you can get a different perspective on things? I know your girls are with my mother this weekend."

Her eyes, still glossed with unshed tears, looked at him with uncertainty. "I can't just..."

"Why not?"

"Because we'd be proving just what Brockton suspects."

"I doubt that he's out and about at this hour. I'll take you home whenever you're ready to go. At 1:00 a.m., or after breakfast tomorrow."

A charmingly embarrassed look crossed her face. "Hank, I can't..."

"I didn't think we'd make mad passionate love in your condition," he interrupted to assure her. "But I have four bedrooms, each with a view of the lake. Two of them have a fireplace, and one of them has a fire-place between the bedroom and the bath so that you can sit in the tub and watch the firelight.''

She sighed longingly. ''That's the one I'd want.''

He laughed. ''Good choice. That one's mine.''

She shoved him in exasperation. He laughed and caught her hands. ''I was teasing. I thought I'd cook for you, let you rest awhile, then take you home.''

He could see that she found the idea tempting, so he stopped pressing.

''I'd have to bring my beeper,'' she warned.

''That's not a problem.''

''Something to eat,'' she bargained, ''a look at the lake, then you'd have to take me home.''

''Okay.''

''You won't try to coax me to stay?''

''I won't say a word.''

''I'm off at eleven.''

He glanced at his watch. It was 9:42. ''I'll pick up some groceries,'' he said. ''And be back for you at eleven o'clock. Come on. I'll walk you back. The path is slippery.''

CHAPTER NINE

THE FIRST THING Jackie noticed about Hank's property was the quiet. There were fewer homes on the far side of the lake where his sprawling two-storey split-level was located. The darkness seemed to amplify the silence.

The second thing she noticed was the fragrance. There was little vegetation in early March, but the sharp freshness of winter filled her nostrils and the smell of woodsmoke lingered in the air.

"A couple from Washington, D.C., built this two years ago," she told him, "as a refuge from their hectic life. He was a senator from the southwest, I think. They weren't here very long."

"New Mexico," he said, "according to my Realtor. He lost big when tech stocks dropped, so they had to sell."

He took her arm to help her up six steps that led to a broad deck. He pointed to a bare corner of the deck. "First thing I did when I moved in was buy a huge gas grill that goes right there, and a long table with chairs and a big umbrella. Unfortunately, business got really good almost right away, so I didn't have many opportunities to use them before the snow set in. I'm looking forward to spring and summer."

"I'd love to cook outside," Jackie said, huddling into her coat as he unlocked a large front door with a leaded glass window in it. "But our back yard is so small, I have to barbecue on the porch. Since there's no room to sit there, the girls and I have to run up and down with the plates and the food. Ricky had no patience for it."

"This deck runs all around the house," he said, pushing open the door. "And I own five acres on each side of it. Lots of room to eat on the deck while the girls are running around the property, playing with the dog."

"My girls?" she asked in confusion.

"Of course," he replied.

"But we don't have a dog."

"I know. You should, though."

She was used to reciting her arguments to the girls. "No one's home during the day. It wouldn't be fair. And I couldn't expect Glory to look after them and a dog."

"Does she like dogs?"

She hesitated. "I'm not sure. It's never come up."

"Just wondering," he said, pushing her gently into the house. "Jimmy raises Black Labs."

Whatever Jackie might have replied to that was blocked by a gasp of astonishment when Hank flipped on a light. He walked her into a huge room with hardwood floors and a vaulted ceiling. The walls were painted a warm off-white, and a deep fieldstone fireplace dominated one side of the room. The stone hearth was strewn with colorful cushions and potted plants.

Large sectionals in an oversize green-and-beige check formed a conversation area around the fireplace. Farther into the room, several overstuffed chairs in co-ordinating fabrics were clustered around a rough-hewn coffee table, and there was a padded oak bench and two chairs that matched it filling up another space by one of a series of long windows.

"The Senate could meet *here!*" she whispered.

"Yeah." He took her coat, then pointed her to the sofa in front of the fireplace. "The corner of the sofa reclines," he said, putting her coat on a hook near the door, then crossing the room to the brass wood box on the hearth. "Make yourself comfortable. I'll get a fire going and find you something to eat."

"I had a mocha at the inn," she said. Then she made a face. "Decaf, of course. The first thing I'm going to do when this baby is born is drink an entire pot of caffeinated coffee."

He laughed. "I've got to have the real thing myself. Didn't you have anything to eat?"

She sat in the corner of the deep sofa and reached to the outside of it for the handle to make it recline. There was none.

"How does this…?" she began, but Hank was already there, reaching between her and the sofa arm for the control hidden beside the cushion. His hand brushed her hip as he found the handle and tugged. She was tipped slightly backward and her feet came up, propped comfortably against the elevated bottom of the seat.

For an instant she was in a complete dither. The spot

on her hip where his knuckles had brushed felt hot, as though someone held a match to it.

I'm going insane, she thought, in a state of mild panic. *It must be hormones. Or maybe the stress of my life is turning me into a sexual deviant. It is deviant, isn't it, to think about sex all the time when you're almost eight months pregnant?*

"What?" he asked worriedly, frowning over the dismay that must be showing in her face. "Is that uncomfortable?"

"No, no," she denied quickly, forcing a smile and wriggling into the enveloping upholstery. "It just surprised me. It's very comfortable."

He appeared unconvinced. Still frowning, he put the back of his hand to her cheek. "You're flushed," he observed. "You probably shouldn't be doing so much this late in your pregnancy."

She swatted his hand away. "I'm fine. This is my first weekend as a bachelor girl in…well, ever! At work, I was thinking about going home to eat ice cream out of the carton and watch Jay Leno while I had a bubble bath."

He laughed lightly. "Sorry, but that's not going to happen here. No ice cream, and no bubbles."

She sighed deeply, pretending disappointment. "I thought you went shopping."

He laughed again. "I guess my ideal staples are different from yours."

"All right, what do you have?"

"Ah…" He reached to the back of the sofa for a fleece blanket with which he covered her. "I can fix you a cold sandwich, a grilled sandwich, soup, chili, stew, fruit, Oreos, bacon.'' He looked inspired suddenly. ''How about a BLT? You always used to order those when we were dating.''

A bacon, lettuce and tomato sandwich. She hadn't had one in ages. ''I'd love that. Can I have another choice, too?''

He straightened and smiled teasingly down on her. ''You want chili with it?''

''No. An Oreo.''

''Sure. What to drink? I don't have decaf coffee, but I have some herbal tea Parker gave me.''

She blinked in surprise. ''Our Parker? The massage therapist?''

''Yeah. It's chamomile and something. I haven't had the nerve to try it. Shall I brew a pot?''

''Yes, please.''

''Okay. You relax, I'll get the fire going, then make your sandwich.''

She watched him kneel before the grate, jeans encasing his neat backside. He'd been leaner when they were kids, she remembered, but even then he'd had an athletic, beautifully formed body. She'd loved watching him, clothed or naked.

Their physical relationship had been a development of the last half of their senior year. Hank's father had died in April, and Hank had mourned their wasted relationship. He'd wept, and Jackie had tried to offer comfort. In his grief and her helplessness, comfort had come in the only sure way either could communicate true feelings.

Lovemaking had become as much a revelation as a pleasure. It had been a shock to both of them to see how deeply they loved and understood one another.

Or so they'd thought.

She remembered suddenly how he'd refused to listen to her reasons why she couldn't leave Maple Hill with him as they'd planned, and the shock she'd felt that he could hurt her that way.

Then she remembered, too, the truth she'd never told him. They were probably even. In the light of adulthood and all that had happened since, refusing to listen to reason seemed like such a paltry offense.

She closed her eyes against the sight of him, reminded of how impossible her desire for him was. She felt tears form under her eyelids, but held them back. She'd once cried enough tears to flood the lake, and that hadn't changed anything. She had two beautiful daughters, work she enjoyed, a comfortable living and good friends. She had no right to whine simply because she'd really only loved one man in her lifetime and the fates decreed that she couldn't have him.

She heard flames crackle as Hank's fire apparently took, then felt warmth emanate from it. Resigned to what must be, she felt consciousness drift away.

THE FIRE BRIGHT, Hank went to the sofa to ask Jackie if she wanted fruit or chips with her sandwich and saw that she'd fallen asleep. Filled with tenderness, he leaned over her to readjust the blanket and stopped when he saw the tears on her cheeks.

He could have sworn that a moment ago they hadn't

been there. Had she been holding them back and sleep released them? She did have a lot to worry about—her father's demanding girlfriend and the threat of impeachment the two latest worries in the life of a single mother who was also a public official.

He wished he could keep her here and protect her from everything that could hurt her. But she'd never stand for that. He'd just have to do the best he could for her tonight. He went into the kitchen to make her sandwich.

He'd put mayonnaise, lettuce and tomato on toasted wheat bread and was draining the bacon for two sandwiches on paper towels when Jackie walked into the kitchen ten minutes later. She had the blanket wrapped around her, her cheeks pink, her eyes still heavy.

"I fell asleep," she said apologetically. "Is there anything I can do?"

The tears had dried on her cheeks, he noted, leaving faint tracks of mascara. There was something charming about it that touched him, but he knew she wouldn't appreciate having it brought to her attention.

"Everything's ready." He put the bacon on the sandwiches and handed her the plates. "You want to take those back to the fire, and I'll bring the tea."

She smiled at him over her shoulder. "Don't forget the Oreos."

He took the bag off the tray and held them up. She smiled her approval and disappeared into the living room.

He poured boiling water over the teabags in the simple brown pot and caught a whiff of something medicinal and unappealing. He put the lid on the pot and consoled himself with the thought that Jackie might like it.

And apparently she did. She was on her second cup, her sandwich almost finished, when she reached into the open bag of cookies and took one.

She watched him note the action. "I know," she said, taking a bite. She chewed, put a hand to her chest as she moaned in approval, then swallowed. "I'm not finished with my sandwich, but I'm taking advantage of the girls being gone to live recklessly."

He arched an eyebrow. "This is reckless? A cookie before your dinner's finished?"

She smiled and nodded. "I guess to someone who sends men hundreds of thousands of miles into space, that doesn't seem reckless, but when you're a mom, any flouting of the rules is reckless. And you never risk it when there's a possibility the kids will see you. But mine are miles away tonight."

"You seem to enjoy being a mom." He topped up her teacup. He'd be able to do that a few more times, because his remained untouched after the first sip. Whatever curative properties it might have, chamomile was vile-tasting stuff in his opinion. "Will it still be fun with three?"

"Oh, sure," she said with the casual confidence of experience. "When I had Rachel, I was shocked by how much more work two children were than one, then you fall into the rhythm of who needs what and when and what makes them happy, and somehow it's all pro-grammed into your brain and you no longer notice the effort. It doesn't diminish the way you worry about them and their safety, but you're just no longer aware of what it costs you to keep them happy. I'm sure three will be no different.''

"Of course, you'll still be mayor."

"Right. But my baby-sitter will stay on, hopefully, and your mother and the ladies at church will be helping me in the beginning. It'll all come together."

His sandwich finished, he leaned on his elbow and watched her snag another cookie. She talked bravely, he thought, but she looked desperately as though she needed rescue. Or at least help. "What are you going to do to sustain *you?*"

She cast him an amused smile and bit into the cookie. "I just don't think about it. Most mothers don't think about it. Somehow, keeping your children happy and functioning sustains you."

"Maybe the mother part, but what about the person? The woman?"

She opened her mouth to reply, but he interrupted quickly with, "And don't tell me she doesn't exist. I've kissed her."

"There's just no time for her," she said with a shrug. "I never liked her much anyway. Nothing she ever did turned out quite right."

"She was going to go away with me," he reminded her quietly. "That would have turned out. We might have struggled, but it would have turned out. We'd have had the kind of marriage where you support and sustain each other, rather than what you had with Ricky."

She looked suddenly weary. "Let's not go there to-night, Hank."

"I'm trying," he insisted intrepidly, "to make you see yourself. There's a whole part of you you're ignoring. That's not good for you."

She dropped the half-eaten cookie on her plate and picked up the rest of her sandwich. "You've been gone too long to know what's good for me," she said with more conviction than anger. "And how would you know, anyway? You came home because you didn't have a life? That suggests a whole part of your own life was ignored."

"True. But at least I recognized the problem."

"Yeah, well, for me it's not a problem. I didn't like being married, so it doesn't really matter if the woman in me ever finds another man. I don't intend to get married again."

The words seemed ludicrous coming from such a beautiful woman ripe with pregnancy. And they weren't helping his cause at all.

"Oh, don't look so surprised," she snapped, suddenly impatient. She dropped the sandwich to her plate, put the plate aside and pushed herself laboriously to her feet. "I know you kissed me and I reacted. Sex is great, living with a man just to get it wouldn't be."

Hank sprang to his feet, following her to the hook where he'd hung her coat. "Do you think that's all marriage has to offer?"

"No," she said, yanking her coat down. "In my experience, it has nothing to offer. I just thought you might think I'd want to be married for the sex. But I don't. I *don't.*"

SHE WAS PROTESTING TOO MUCH. She could hear it in her own voice. Instead of being convincing, she came off sounding like a frustrated old maid who said she didn't want any because she couldn't get it.

Which was just about true at the moment. She'd felt all softened and vulnerable in this warm and wonderful house, enjoying his sandwich and his cookies and the attentive way he covered her with a blanket. But it didn't change what was. Nothing would ever change that. And she was impatient with herself that she kept forgetting.

Then she caught sight of her reflection in the mirror near the door and gasped at the sight of her mussed mascara. The tears she'd thought she'd suppressed had fallen when she was asleep.

Hank turned her to him, framing her face in his hands and running his thumbs over her cheeks. "What hurts so much," he asked, "that you cry in your sleep?"

She wanted to pull his hands away, but his touch did something to her, made her want to believe that nature and fate could be thwarted, that there was some way they could be happy together.

"I'm pregnant," she said in a suddenly frail voice. "I feel like crying about everything." Tears crowded her eyes now and she drew a ragged breath, trying to hold them back.

He put a gentle hand to her shoulder and rubbed

down to her elbow. "Maybe you'd feel better if you indulge that feeling once in a while. While you're awake and can enjoy the release."

She took a step backward, out of his reach. "No. I'm a mother. I'm a mayor. I have to keep it together."

He took a step toward her. "Everyone has to let go once in a while."

She shook her head firmly, the threat of tears making her voice raspy and frail. "I have to go."

"Why?" he asked gently. "The kids are gone. Why don't you spend the night here?"

"You promised you wouldn't try to make me stay."

"I'm not trying to make you stay. I think you *want* to stay. I'm just trying to make you admit it."

She put a hand back to the doorknob. "I have to meet my father for breakfast."

"I'll drive you in in time," he promised.

"No, no!" she shouted, her voice gaining sudden power in her need to escape before she fell apart. Then she remembered that she couldn't escape. Her car was in the inn's parking lot. Hank had driven her here. "Just…just drive me back to the inn and don't say anything."

"Nothing at all? Not 'fasten your seat belt,' or 'are you warm enough?' or…"

She pointed a threatening finger at him. "Hank. If you say one more word, I won't be responsible for what happens to you."

He seemed willing to accept that with equanimity. "I've always faced up to the consequences of my actions." He waggled his fingers at her in a come-and-get-me gesture. "Come on. Do your best. Because I'm going to keep talking. I'm going to tell you that you want to stay with me because all the feelings we had for each other as kids are still alive. They've lain dormant all these years, but now that I'm back, you're going to have to stop pretending that you're fine, that your life is just the way you want it."

"Hank," she said, tears streaming down her face at the utter injustice of having to deal with this all over again. "Believe me when I tell you it can't be."

He shook his head at her. "Sorry. I believed you seventeen years ago when you told me it'd be better if you didn't come with me. This time I'm going with what I think is best. We are meant to be together. I'm going to make you love me again."

She closed her eyes so that he couldn't see that she already did. Had never stopped.

He was reaching for his jacket, about to comply with her plea that he take her home, when the baby gave her a firm and punitive kick to her spine.

"Ow!" she complained before she could stop herself, putting a hand to her back and the other to Hank's arm.

He wrapped his arm around her and drew her back to the sofa. "What?" he demanded. "Pain? Contraction? You want me to call your doctor?"

The baby kicked again, this time to the front. She winced and leaned back against the pillows. "No," she groaned. "It's just kicking, I think, but geez! The baby must be in a temper."

Hank sat beside her, putting a gentle hand to her

belly. "Well, no wonder. He's fighting for space amid all your suppressed stress and emotion." He grinned. "And he knows what's going on inside you. He knows you're fibbing when you say you don't want it to work out between us."

"I didn't say I don't want it to work, I said I'm sure that it can't. I've been another man's wife, I have two children, and as angelic as they were when you brought dinner over, they can be that devilish when things aren't going their way." She sighed and finished wearily, "Seventeen years is a long time. We've grown in different directions."

"If that was true," he said, putting a pillow against the arm of the sofa and lifting her feet so that she lay the length of the cushions, "we wouldn't find ourselves in the same place, comfortable together despite the past."

"You're comfortable?" she asked doubtfully as he pulled off her shoes and spread the blanket over her.

"I am," he confirmed. "And you are too. You just don't want to admit it to yourself and let it be. Baby settled down?"

She put a hand to her stomach, where all was quiet for the moment. Her back hurt and her ribs felt as though someone was wedging them apart, but she was getting used to that.

"Yes."

"Good. You stay here where I can keep an eye on you, then I'll take you to meet your dad in the morning."

He flipped the lights out so that all she saw was

firelight. It danced cheerfully and silhouetted Hank's figure as he knelt before it to add another log.

All the stress and tension of the evening left her. She thought that strange in light of the fact that nothing had changed; all her problems remained in place.

She closed her eyes and listened to the sound of Hank stirring the fire, his footsteps across the room as he locked the door, then into the kitchen, where he probably checked the back door and made sure the stove was turned off.

A little wave of comfort stroked across her body, seemed to pat her shoulder and tell her to relax.

She heard a sound nearby and opened her heavy eyelids to see Hank sitting on the end of the sofa beyond her feet.

"Go to sleep," he ordered gently, draping an arm over her ankles and catching a blanketed foot in his hand. "Everything's all right."

"For the moment, anyway," she qualified, closing her eyes with a sigh.

"That's all we have." His voice came to her through a long tunnel as her awareness began to drift. "Moment to moment."

HANK AWOKE TO DARKNESS and a definite chill in the air. The fire had gone out and the furnace had turned automatically to a lower nighttime setting. He pressed the winding stem on his watch for illumination and saw that it was 3:17.

Jackie was curled up under the blanket into as tight

a ball as she could achieve. She needed another blanket, and he could use one himself.

He reset the furnace, then got the fire going again to take the chill away until the furnace warmed up the air. Then he sprinted upstairs to the linen closet for blankets. He was opening one out over Jackie when she said his name.

The plaintive sound of it in the darkness made his pulse accelerate.

"I'm right here," he said, adding the second blanket.

She caught his hand as he tucked the blanket around her.

"I'm cold," she complained. "Really cold."

"I just got the fire going again," he said, trying to free his hand to give her the third blanket, but she seemed unwilling to part with it.

"Cold," she said again.

"Okay. Can you sit up?"

She didn't sound entirely awake, but he could feel her shuddering under the blanket.

"Sleepy," she said, "and cold."

Smiling in the darkness, he reached under her to lift her upper body, heavy with her pregnancy. He sat under her, wrapped the third blanket around his shoulders, then tugged her toward him. Her bulk made it awkward, but the moment she realized that his arms promised warmth, she propped herself up and literally fell into his arms and turned her face into his chest.

"Mmm," she said with a heavy sigh.

"Mmm," he thought, enfolding her in the wings of

his blanket and smiling again at her little moan of approval.

He wasn't giving up, he thought, until they were curled up in the darkness together every night.

CHAPTER TEN

HANK AWOKE to pale daylight and found Jackie still in his arms, watching him. She looked warm and rumpled, and there was something in her expression from the old days—love, admiration, affection. But there was a curious sadness there, too, that confused and worried him.

He gazed into her eyes, trying to assess the strength of this enemy to their happiness. There were dark layers in the depths of the soft gray—pain, he guessed. The pain he'd caused her? he wondered.

No. He didn't think so. He wouldn't see love and affection there too, would he, if he'd caused the sadness?

She put an index finger to his lips and smiled. "You still smile in your sleep."

He caught her fingertip and kissed it. "Because I had you in my arms."

To his complete surprise, she leaned forward to plant a light kiss on his lips. "That was the best night's sleep I've had," she said, "since Erica was born. Thank you."

If he was calculating the amount of time spent sleeping, it was the worst night's sleep he'd had since he helped bring the astronauts home last August. But discounting that, it was the most delicious six hours he'd spent since he'd left her and Maple Hill all those years ago.

"My pleasure," he said softly. "I intend to do this for you every night."

She smiled, but that sadness filled her eyes again and she pushed her hands against his chest and tried to lever herself to her feet. It was a job for two. Hank slipped out from under her, and catching her hands, pulled her to a standing position.

She groaned with the effort, then the sound turned to one of exasperation. "Next time I decide to have a baby at this age," she teased, looking carefully away from him as she searched for her purse, "remind me that it makes me move like a Buick without wheels."

He went to the hearth where she'd left the large leather pouch and handed it to her. "Next time you decide to have a baby," he returned, "I'll be involved enough to do that."

She scolded him with a look.

He spread his arms helplessly. "What do you want from me? It's not going to go away. We have to deal with it. *You* have to deal with it."

"Hank, don't start," she admonished quietly. "Do you know where my shoes are?"

He pointed to the floor in front of her.

She looked down at them in dismay, then put her arms out for balance as she tried to push her feet into them. But her feet had swollen overnight and the task was impossible. She couldn't even bend over to retrieve them, and she looked up at him pleadingly.

He folded his arms and stood his ground. "You tell me what the sadness is about," he said, "and I'll get you your shoes."

She pretended surprise. "What sadness?"

He didn't fall for it. He put a hand to the side of her face and traced the delicate skin under her eye with his thumb.

"The sadness right here, under the smile and the strength. That's what's keeping us apart, isn't it? Not the fact that I left and you stayed."

For an instant, he saw horror in her expression that he'd read that much. Then the old resolve to do what she had to do took over and that glimpse of vulnerability was lost.

"You agreed that we'd be friends," she said judiciously, "and friends don't torture each other." She walked to the other end of the sofa where his Romeos lay, stepped into them, and with a so-there! look in his direction, shuffled determinedly toward the bathroom.

Accepting defeat, he snatched her shoes off the floor with one hand and stopped her halfway to the bathroom. He caught her hand, held it palm up and slapped the shoes into it.

"I'm remembering," he said irascibly, "that things usually had to end up your way."

She closed her eyes a moment, her expression darkly amused. "Yeah, well, that stopped right after you left. Thank you for getting my shoes." She stepped out of his and headed for the bathroom.

Jackie, Hank thought, made space travel seem simple.

"WHY DON'T YOU join us for breakfast?" Adam Fortin asked Hank. He and Jackie and Hank stood under the inn's red- and gray-striped awning.

Jackie smiled in Hank's direction, hoping her father would interpret the look as seconding his invitation, but that Hank would understand she didn't want him to come. She hadn't liked the hopeful look in her father's eyes when Hank pulled into the inn's parking lot with Jackie in the passenger seat.

"Thanks, but I have to get to the office." Hank shook her father's hand.

"It's Saturday," Adam protested.

Hank grinned. "Electrical and plumbing emergencies on Saturday mean overtime. You two have fun."

Grateful that she was about to escape an embarrassing explanation, Jackie offered Hank a cheerful goodbye. Her wish that he have a good day never left her lips.

He cupped the back of her head in one hand and covered her mouth with his in a firm, lengthy kiss. Then he freed her, gave her a look that told her she couldn't expect everything to go her way, and climbed into his van.

Jackie was both indignant and delighted and wasn't sure which emotion deserved free rein. Adam chuckled, put an arm around her shoulders and led her to the sporty little Cadillac Catera he'd rented. "I'd better get you some food," he teased, "to put into that open mouth."

The Breakfast Barn was a favorite hangout of locals, huge amounts of simple but delicious food served at a reasonable price. A nineteenth-century dairy barn housed dozens of tables, a long counter with bright red stools and a banquet room at the back where Kiwanis, Rotary and The Revolutionary Dames held their weekly meetings.

Brick-red walls were decorated with old farming tools, photos of patrons and the city league teams the restaurant sponsored. Each booth and table had a bud vase of flowers appropriate to the season. This morning, sprigs of hawthorn and pine filled the vases.

"God, I love this place!" Adam slipped into a booth opposite Jackie and closed his eyes as he inhaled the aroma of bacon and spicy Portuguese sausage frying, the smells of coffee, of citrus and melon and the perfumes and aftershaves of the men and women beginning their day at the Barn. "The only thing that comes close to the down-home sincerity is the small-town pubs in England."

"I'd wager you didn't meet Sabrina in a pub," Jackie said, pulling off her jacket and letting it fall to the seat. When she looked up again, her father studied her with a frown.

"What kind of a welcome-home remark is that?" he asked, then was distracted by the waitress, who brought menus and poured coffee.

"Well, Adam Fortin, as I live and breathe!" The short plump woman had a curly up-do colored an unconventional shade of burgundy. She was a good friend of Adeline Whitcomb. "Heard you were home. Hi, Jackie."

"Rita, how've you been?" he asked genially. "I got

in last night. And you keep forgetting this is no longer home for me. I live in Miami now.''

'''Cause of the decorator?'' Rita interrogated him with the ease of long friendship.

''What decorator?'' he asked, clearly convinced she couldn't possibly mean the one he'd brought to town with him just the night before. He'd apparently lived in Miami long enough to have forgotten the Maple Hill information pipeline.

''The princess you brought with you.''

Jackie couldn't help enjoying his stammering while he tried to decide whether to be offended by the remark or astonished that someone across town already knew—a mere ten hours after the fact—that he'd brought a woman home with him.

Curiosity won over sensitivity. ''How could you possibly know about her?''

Rita Robidoux smiled and leaned an elbow on the back of Jackie's side of the booth. ''Adeline was already in this morning. The board of Revolutionary Dames meets at 7:00 a.m.''

That failed to clarify things for him. ''And how did she know?''

''John Granger's mother is our secretary. I waited on them.'' She shook her head pityingly. ''I heard all about the heat lamp in the bathroom. Sounds like a bit of a prima donna to me.''

Jackie saw her father's eyebrows beetle and decided it was time she intervened. ''I'll have a Denver omelette with egg substitute,'' she said quickly, ''and fruit instead of potatoes and toast. Daddy?''

"The usual," he said with a frown, handing back his menu.

Rita took it from him. "How can you say you live in Miami," she asked with a provincial tilt of her chin, "when you can walk into a restaurant in Maple Hill and order 'the usual?'"

She walked away before he could attempt to answer, knowing Adam's "usual" was bacon and eggs over hard, hashbrowns and whole wheat toast.

Adam looked at Jackie in affronted disbelief. "Is there no civility left in this world?"

Jackie shrugged. "Not judging by Sabrina." Since the subject had already been opened for review—with a sledgehammer—she felt safe continuing the discussion. "What are you doing with her, Dad?"

He took a sip of coffee, probably counting, she guessed.

"I like her," he replied with strained patience. "I met her on the cruise, we had a good time together, and she enjoys being with me." When she looked skeptical, he asked stiffly, "You don't think that's possible?"

"Of course I do." It occurred to her that at this point in time she was the last one to question who took up with whom, but she put that reasonable thought aside, more comfortable with her filial disapproval. "I love your company. Your granddaughters love your company. All the inn's employees love it when you come home. And it is home, Daddy. You just don't like to think of it that way anymore because Mom's no longer here. Well, guess what? The rest of your family still is, and after two years of your quest for whatever it is you're searching for to prove your desirability or your virility or to come to terms with the fact that you're still alive when Mom isn't, you're…you're making everyone wonder when you'll come to your senses.''

"Oh, really." He leaned toward her on his forearms. "Well, let me tell you something, missy. I have never lived my life to conform to Maple Hill's expectations. I love everyone here, but you know they'll gossip about anything and everything.''

He fixed her with a steady look and she met it unflinchingly. "Yes, I know that. But what about your granddaughters' expectations? They haven't had you for any length of time in two years, and then you come home with a woman a third your age and a snob to boot.''

"My granddaughters and I understand each other very well. You don't have to…'' He paused abruptly when Rita brought a twelve-ounce glass of orange juice to the table—part of his "usual.''

"You don't have to remind me of my duties as a grandfather,'' he said more quietly. "And you should be the last one to rake me over the coals. At least I'm trying to keep my heart alive. You haven't cared about your emotional life since you realized what a tragic mistake you made with Ricky. Judging by the surprised look on your face when Hank kissed you, you haven't a clue what's going on between the two of you.''

She sighed patiently. "Daddy, how would you know what's going on between us. You haven't even been here.''

"John likes to talk as much as his mother does," he replied. "And I'm not the only one in the family this town is worried about. You should have gone with Hank when you graduated."

She stared at him openmouthed. "You knew what I was up against. And he wouldn't even let me explain!"

"If you hadn't chickened out at the last minute," he said mercilessly, "you'd have made him listen."

"Dad...!" she gasped.

He put a hand to his forehead, took a sip of juice, then sat back in the booth and shook his head regretfully. "I'm not saying you didn't live bravely with your decision and do the absolute best you could in an impossible situation, but damn it, Jackie. Now's your chance to fix it."

She'd have loved to believe that, but she knew better. "Some things can't be fixed, Daddy."

He sighed deeply. "Everything can be fixed—just not easily. And if he's moved back here and apparently still in love with you, you're going to have to either move to Miami with me so you don't have to see him every day..." He studied her face and seemed to see that that very thing was already taking its toll on her. "Or...fix it," he added softly, reaching across the table to take her hand.

She knew he was right, but she felt fairly sure that an attempt to "fix it" would end it. And the love that had evaded her all those years ago and now offered itself so generously a second time would be lost to her forever.

She couldn't think about that, so she turned the discussion back on him. "Are you expecting Sabrina to fix things for you?"

He shrugged. "Right now, I'm not sure. We like a lot of the same things, she's smart and funny and she thinks I am, too. She had two weeks between jobs, so I invited her to meet my family. I know she can be a little demanding, but she owns a business with twenty-three branches. She has to be forceful and in charge, or everything would fall apart. Don't take it personally."

He was right. At least he was willing to take a step out in faith and see what happened. As his daughter, she had to honor that.

"When can the two of you come for dinner?" she asked, leaning back as Rita arrived with their food. "Unfortunately, the girls are gone until Sunday night. A church group outing with Addy Whitcomb."

He rolled his eyes. "How is Addy? Still supervising the world?"

"Now that we have a space station," she laughed, "she's going interplanetary."

He nodded. "That's our Addy. So you're alone for the weekend?"

She was afraid to reply on the chance he intended to invite her to join them and become better acquainted with Sabrina. "Alone with mountains of laundry, payroll for the inn and city paperwork. I should get a lot done in the peace and quiet." That barrier erected, she asked amiably, "What are you two doing?"

"Sabrina has a friend at Amherst she wants to see

this afternoon,'' he replied, ''and tomorrow she wants to just drive and see the Berkshires.''

The Berkshires were magnificent. Sabrina did show good taste there. ''Shall I serve as concierge and make reservations for you to have lunch at De Marco's?''

He looked pleasantly surprised by the offer. ''Thank you. I'd appreciate that.''

''Sure.'' She grinned as she passed him the pepper. ''In exchange you have to promise me that you won't make her my stepmother.''

Teasingly, he yanked the pepper away. ''How about if I just flaunt our May-December romance to the Revolutionary Dames and get the whole town talking?''

Rita had reappeared unnoticed and sloshed coffee into his almost empty cup. ''The ship's sailed on that one, Fortin. We already are.''

THE WEEKEND was painfully short. Jackie did get the laundry done and prepared the inn's payroll. She had lied about having to do paperwork for the city, but was tempted to go into the office on Sunday anyway to catch up on correspondence.

But that might mean running into John Brockton, and she didn't want that to spoil her solitude. Monday would be plenty of time to learn the details of his impeachment plans.

So she sat alone in her living room Sunday afternoon and tried to absorb the quiet. The moment the girls got home, it would be gone. She'd adjust immediately; she loved the sound of their voices. But when she was stressed, she longed for the precious gift of having the house to herself.

She didn't seem to be able to enjoy the last few hours of her day, however. She found herself wondering why Hank hadn't called—and hating that it worried her.

She told herself she hadn't expected him to call. She'd told him that nothing could come of their fragile relationship and she sincerely believed that. But somehow the possibility that he finally did, too, was upsetting.

Would he just give up on her now and find another woman to pursue? There were certainly enough single women in town wanting to pursue him, according to Haley. Maybe now he'd want to meet that niece of Addy's friend.

She went into the kitchen to bake cookies and put the subject out of her mind. Instead, she got a clear mental picture of enjoying her plate of sweet treats with him at the tea shop. And she remembered the perfect BLT he'd made her, and the bag of Oreos they'd shared.

She was about to paint the inside of her eyelids black in the hope that images couldn't form there when the front door burst open and Addy appeared with Erica and Rachel. Everyone spoke at once, souvenirs were shoved in Jackie's face, and she found the madness of the moment a delicious relief from the constant image of Hank's face.

As the girls carried their bags upstairs, Addy gave Jackie a hug. "We had a wonderful time," she reported, ''and you'll be pleased to know that they were cooperative and well-mannered every single moment.''

Jackie narrowed her eyes in teasing suspicion. ''You wouldn't be trying to kid me.''

Addy laughed. ''Not at all. They're great fun to be with. You have every right to be proud. So, when are we going to decide on colors?''

Jackie blinked. ''Colors?''

''Wedding colors,'' Addy replied.

Jackie laughed. ''You took my daughters off for a weekend and now one of them is getting married?''

Addy swatted Jackie's arm. ''*Your* wedding. Rachel insists there's going to be one. Erica thinks you'll fold and won't be able to commit to Hank. Which do you think it's going to be? If I'm going to be mother of the groom, I'll need a little time to shop, to…''

Jackie wasn't sure which opinion was more upsetting. She swatted Addy back. ''Ha, ha. I've seen him several times, we do enjoy each other's company, but I promise you there's no need to run out shopping.''

Addy made a face. ''You're sure? The girls and I were planning a shower and everything.''

''I'm sure, Addy.'' Jackie hugged her then opened the door. ''But if anything changes, you'll be the first to know.''

''I look good in blue,'' Addy said as Jackie walked her out onto the porch. ''And green. Yellow makes me look jaundiced, and pink just isn't me. Lavender, though, is…''

''Addy!''

''I could buy an Easter outfit that'd do double duty.''

Jackie decided the only way to turn her off was to pretend she wasn't talking. "Thank you. The girls seem to have really enjoyed the weekend." She walked Addy down the steps and to her car. "Poor things never see anything but school and me."

Addy opened the driver's door. "A man in their lives would be a nice addition. You should see Hank in a tux."

"I have," Jackie reminded her. "Our senior dance was formal."

Addy made a dismissive sound. "That was before he had shoulders."

"Good night, Addy," Jackie said firmly.

Addy sighed. "Good night, Jackie."

It took the girls an hour of talking on top of each other over milk and cookies to settle down. They'd bathed and changed into pajamas, but still looked wide-awake.

"What did you do while we were gone?" Erica asked. She leaned both elbows on the table and propped her chin in her hands. Not precisely the good manners Addy had just praised her for, Jackie thought, but while they were eager to share their experiences was not the time to quibble. "Did you have a date?"

Rachel seemed excited at the possibility, but Erica looked as though she already knew the answer. She wondered why her oldest child felt sure her mother couldn't commit.

"I did, as a matter of fact," Jackie replied, putting her coffee cup casually to her lips. "Hank took me out for a sandwich after my shift at the inn on Friday."

Both girls sat up and stared at her in astonishment. "He did?" they asked simultaneously.

She nodded, deciding to withhold the part about going to his place and staying the night.

"We had a very good time."

Erica continued to stare, then asked, eyes widening, "Did he kiss you?"

Jackie wasn't sure what she was doing here. She shouldn't be encouraging them to think he could become a part of their lives, but she couldn't pretend he'd simply disappear, either. Something had to be done. And soon.

Erica pointed to Jackie's face. "He did kiss you!" she exclaimed. "Your cheeks are pink!"

"Yes, he did." There was little point in denying it when she'd been seen through like a window. "But just once."

"Was it nice?"

"Nice. Yes."

"Did he take your clothes off?" Rachel wanted to know.

Erica turned to her impatiently. "Don't be stupid! Mom's pregnant."

Rachel looked surprised by her sister's angry reaction. "On TV whenever they kiss, they start taking each other's clothes off."

Jackie focused on Erica. "What have you two been watching? I thought I told you to stick to Disney and Nickelodeon."

"Ashley Browning told me," Rachel explained. "She gets to watch whatever her parents are watching.'' She frowned at Jackie in sudden worry. ''It hurts to have a baby, you know. There's a lot of yelling and screaming, 'cause the baby has to come through your belly button.''

Erica collapsed on her folded arms, laughing hysterically.

Jackie wasn't sure she could deal with this tonight, though she had a little difficulty suppressing her own smile. She knew right where she'd put the children's book on childbirth she'd bought, certain that such questions would come up as delivery approached.

She urged the girls to put their dishes on the counter, then ushered them upstairs. ''That part isn't quite right,'' she said gently, snatching the book out of the case in the hall. ''It does hurt, but the doctor has medicines that take away the pain and help the baby come safely. Climb into bed and I'll read to you about how it happens.''

Rachel scrambled eagerly under the covers. Jackie noticed that Erica, who'd laughed knowingly at her sister's misinterpretation of the facts, hung by the door.

Jackie patted the edge of the mattress beside Rachel. ''Would you like to join us?''

Erica wandered unhurriedly toward them. ''I know what happens, but some stuff is…you know…blurry.''

Jackie nodded, covering her as she climbed in beside her sister. ''Right. Well, maybe this will clarify it.'' She opened the book and began to read.

JACKIE AWOKE Monday morning feeling huge and heavy and very depressed. According to Haley, John

Brockton and Russ Benedict would file charges against Jackie today. And while she didn't think Brockton had a leg to stand on, simply raising the issue would plant doubts in some people's minds and was bound to make everything she did as mayor just a little more difficult. She had to watch her every step.

She'd been through worse, she told herself as she woke the girls cheerfully and made pancake batter. Of course, the whole world hadn't known then that her husband never loved her enough to be faithful, and she hadn't been carrying an anvil in her stomach, either.

And she'd managed to forget what she'd done to Hank sixteen years ago. Well, she'd never forgotten, but she'd been able to bury it by reminding herself of her pure intentions.

While the girls ate, she checked the kitchen calendar, her mind too cluttered with her own problems to allow her to remember if Erica or Rachel had anything going on after school. A quick look told her the girls' schedules were open, but she had an ultrasound right after lunch. She'd had one scheduled at four months, then gotten a cold and canceled the appointment. She'd been unable to find a spare moment since then to reschedule, and a normal pregnancy had removed any urgency to do so. But her doctor insisted she have one as she approached her ninth month.

She grabbed an energy bar and a commuter mug filled with milk and drank and ate on her way from the school to City Hall.

John, Russ and a tall, slender man they introduced as the impeachment committee's attorney handed

Jackie a thick sheaf of papers before she'd crossed the lobby to the stairs. They'd invited Haley and a representative from the radio station, apparently making a media event out of filing charges.

City employees stood in the doorways of all the open offices with varying degrees of anger or approval on their faces. Some watched from the second-floor railing, and she noticed Addy and Parker in the basement doorway.

A light flashed from the direction of the stairway, and Jackie looked up to see Haley lower her camera with a rueful wave.

"You can't do this!" Evelyn, Jackie's secretary, appeared from behind her, her lunch and her briefcase still in hand. "It's wrong, and you know it!"

Jackie pulled herself out of her depression and smiled at Evelyn, then at John Brockton. "No, it isn't, Evelyn. It's what the whole process is about, and many of our Maple Hill ancestors fought for that very thing— the right to expect honesty in our government." She held up the sheaf of papers toward Haley, giving her a moment to get another shot, then smiled confidently at her audience. "The recall hearing will give me the opportunity to prove that I'm the honest one, and that John Brockton and Russ Benedict are—" she paused to consider all the things she'd like to say about what she thought they were, then remembered that she was trying to prove herself fit to govern "—not," she finished pleasantly. "Back to work, everyone. Maple Hill doesn't run itself."

"May I have a word with you, Ms. Mayor?" Haley

asked at the bottom of the stairs. Her polite, professional expression hid an uncertainty Jackie identified and understood immediately. Haley was just doing her job.

"Please," Jackie said. "We'll talk in my office."

Evelyn held up a paper bag from the bakery. "I thought we might need sugar today. I'll make the coffee."

Jackie led the way upstairs. "Bless you, Ev." To Haley, she said, "You can't teach that kind of clever crunch-time thinking."

"So, what's your strategy?" Haley asked as she and Jackie sat at the small sofa in her office. "I know you think you can beat this because everyone loves you and your family, but I want to make sure you're covering all the bases here."

Jackie nodded. "Of course. I want to read this through first, then when I know what I'm up against, I'll get a lawyer and be prepared."

Haley took notes. "Bart says he'll volunteer his services. You deny any suggestion of impropriety in your administration?"

"Unequivocally," Jackie replied firmly.

"Without reading the charges?"

"I have never at any point in my service done anything even remotely illegal or self-serving. I don't have to read the charges to know that."

Haley nodded. "Good. Perfect pull quote." She put down her pen. "Can I have another maple bar? Or should I be thinking about fitting into a bridesmaid's dress?"

Jackie picked delicately at a giant apple fritter. She'd hate herself later, she knew, but this was now. She took a long pull of decaf coffee, thinking that even a long pull didn't equate to a short sip of the real stuff. "Have you been talking to your mother? Or my girls?"

Haley shook her head. "Rita at the Breakfast Barn. She said Hank, Bart and a couple of the guys in Hank's office had pie and coffee there after basketball practice last night. He picked up the tab, then forgot to pay it. Apparently everyone was teasing him about being in love. Said he'd performed very poorly during practice. Couldn't focus. He's usually their high scorer. And Friday night, I couldn't reach him and I couldn't reach you. Simple coincidence, or two loonies finally coming to their senses?"

Jackie leaned back against the sofa cushions, balancing her coffee on the padded arm. Life was too complicated today to try to lie about anything. She told Haley about Hank picking her up Friday night, and her staying until morning.

"I was stressed, he can be very comforting," she said, as though there was no other way to explain it. "I had the first good night's sleep I've had in years. But…that's all."

"Jackie." Haley touched her arm. "When it's right, it's right. I had a tough time coming to terms with that, too, because I didn't want to put my faith in anyone after what Paul Abbott did to me. I'm sure you feel that way because of all that Ricky put you through. But Hank isn't like that. You know he isn't."

"I know." Then she expressed the concern that had

been bothering her since Saturday morning. "But he hasn't called me since."

"There's some kind of power crisis at the senior housing complex. He was supposed to come for dinner last night and canceled."

"Oh."

"Why don't you call him?"

"It's just not that simple."

"Ha! Because you're in politics, you think everything has to be complicated and intricate, but it doesn't. You love him, he loves you…"

Jackie looked at her watch. "Don't you have ads to sell or pages to paste up or something?"

"Ads are sold," Haley said, "and the computer does the paste-up now. But I can take a hint." She put her cup down on the coffee table and picked up her large briefcase-purse.

"Can you have lunch today?"

Jackie shook her head regretfully. "Thanks, but I have a doctor's appointment this afternoon."

"Everything okay?" Haley asked, her brow furrowing.

"Everything's fine. Just an ultrasound. Maybe tomorrow?"

"Sure. You and the girls are coming to Mom's birthday celebration Sunday, right? I ran into your dad and invited him, too." She grinned wickedly. "I met Frosty Fanny."

Jackie laughed aloud at Haley's assessment of Sabrina. "Is she invited, too?"

Haley hunched her shoulders apologetically. "It was only polite."

"Of course it was." They stood, Haley helping Jackie up. "We'd love to come."

"Two o'clock?"

"We'll be there."

Jackie had Evelyn hold her calls and spent the rest of the morning reading the charges filed against her and the copy of the charter the committee had provided, the section on Impeachment highlighted.

Most of the accusations were transparently vindictive, and served more to indict Brockton's motive than to prove guilt on Jackie's part.

He cited her absence at several meetings, all of which had occurred because her children were ill or she was—and the council had been notified the day before so that Paul Balducci chaired the meeting in her place and with her notes on matters on the agenda.

He termed her efforts for Perk Avenue "influence peddling," and asked that the situation be investigated.

He asked for an audit of the funds for the project for the homeless, suggesting there was ten thousand dollars less in the account than had been given them. But that money had been paid to the builder and she felt certain John knew that.

Only the suggestion that she was improperly funneling work Hank's way had any possibility of sticking.

They had been high-school sweethearts, and she was now offering him work in her capacity as mayor. But she was sure she could prove one had nothing to do with the other.

If only she didn't look into anyone's eyes, she thought as she fell back dispiritedly in her chair. Because she did feel like Hank's lover—probably because she wanted to be. They hadn't been lovers in seventeen years, but she'd change that tomorrow if she could.

She decided she'd better phone Bart.

CHAPTER ELEVEN

PETE MARCOTT, Maple Hill's radiologist, spread gel on the mound of Jackie's stomach and gave a long, low whistle as he wiped his hands. "That baby must be lying stretched out, like on a lawn chair. Either that, or there are three other babies in there hiding behind him and evading our womb-spying technology."

Jackie raised her head to glower playfully at the tall young man who looked more like a Chicago Bears quarterback than a kind and gentle doctor. "Don't even tease about that, Paul. I have enough turmoil in my life right now."

He frowned as he put the convex probe to her stomach. "I heard about this impeachment foolishness over breakfast this morning. What's going on, anyway?"

She felt Pete guide the probe over her stomach. She explained about John Brockton's resentment of her when she was just a councilwoman, his shock and disapproval when she was named mayor, then his eagerness to thwart or subvert her every move ever since.

"Then I encouraged Bridget and Cecilia to get that spot on the square for the tearoom when he'd promised his brother-in-law he'd be able to put a Cha-Cha Chicken franchise there. Unfortunately, his brother didn't have the financing together in time, and lost out to Perk Avenue. He blames me.'' She sighed. ''Now he's really out for blood. You would think that since everyone knows he…''

Pete shushed her abruptly.

''What?'' she asked, all senses suddenly focused on the procedure. ''Something wrong?''

He held up a hand for silence, his eyes on the viewing screen.

Her heartbeat accelerating, Jackie followed his gaze and saw the swirling stuff she always had difficulty identifying as anything on other proud mothers' ultrasound prints. She looked up at Pete, really beginning to worry about that frown of concentration.

''Pete, what it is?'' she demanded, worry turning almost instantly to fear. This was her third child, and though the last thing she needed to worry about after what had happened with Ricky was another life, this baby was part of the family. She'd lived with it for eight months, her girls nuzzled it and felt it kick. She wouldn't let anything be wrong. ''Tell me!'' she said firmly. ''What is it?''

He gave her a quick, apologetic glance before turning back to the screen. ''Nothing's wrong, Jackie. It's just that…'' His long index finger pointed to the screen and a small, pulsing spot of light. ''See that?''

''Yes.''

''That's his heartbeat.''

''Oh!'' She felt excitement blunted by concern. ''Is there something wrong with it?''

His finger moved across the screen to another pulsing light. "Here's another one. My joke about three other babies hiding behind the first one wasn't so far wrong. Except that it's only one. You're carrying twins, kiddo."

In view of the morning she'd had, the chaos that was her life and the potential for disaster that was her growing relationship with Hank, all she could do was put a hand over her face and swear. And hope that he was wrong and it was possible to give birth to one healthy baby with two hearts!

"I know," Pete said apologetically, pushing a button to print the image. "I'm sorry. It's a shock. But both babies appear to be perfect. You want to know the sex?"

Oh, God. She couldn't unscramble her thoughts, couldn't find words, couldn't…couldn't… "Ah… okay."

"Boys. Both boys. And you're probably looking at an earlier delivery date, here," he said. "At the size of these guys, there's no way you're going to go full term. I'll call your OB-Gyn and see if he can see you right now."

Her appointment with Sam Duncan was a blur. He was sympathetic, trying to buoy her with the assurance that the twins were in perfect health so far. "You'll have to ease up a little, delegate more at the office, make the girls help you at home."

She was still too stunned to give him the look that suggestion deserved. Her co-workers were overworked as it was, and her girls meant well, but they were children. Their good intentions were forgotten in a minute when the invitation to play or a favorite television show intervened.

"I want to see you next Tuesday," he said as she walked out of his office. "Before, if you have any problems at all. Call me anytime."

She walked halfway around the lake. She was going to have two babies instead of one, four children instead of three. One whole extra life would depend upon her, Jackie Fortin Bourgeois, who'd so irretrievably screwed up her life that there was probably no saving it. What was God thinking?

By the time she was on her way back to City Hall, the shock and confusion had turned to fear and panic.

She couldn't breathe. She tried stopping in the middle of the parking lot at the back of the building, hoping to drag in a deep breath. But it didn't seem to be there.

She tried to fight off the panic. This was silly. There was breath in her lungs. She knew there was. She just had to calm down and breathe. Faith Hill had a song about it. Breathe. Just breathe. It was early afternoon, lunch breaks over, and the parking lot was almost empty. She judged the distance to the back door against her absence of air and emitted a little squeak of dismay.

Then she noticed Hank's van behind the big, bare oak, the sliding side door open as he seemed to be inventorying supplies and making notes on a clipboard. He leaned away from the van in her direction, apparently searching for the source of that sound.

He caught sight of her and asked in puzzlement, "Jackie?"

She had no air to speak, so she stretched out a hand toward him.

He tossed the clipboard into the truck and ran toward her, his eyes concerned as they looked into hers.

Even had she been able to speak, she could not have told him how glad she was to see him. It was curious, she thought, that he was a source of part of her problems, yet that didn't seem to matter now. She'd be fine if he would just wrap his arms around her.

As though he read her mind, he did just that. "What is it?" he asked, one arm tightening on her while the other tipped her chin up so that he could explore her face. "Are you having contractions?"

She shook her head, gasping for air. There was a scary, rasping sound when she tried to breathe.

"Can't breathe?" he asked, putting a hand to the baby as though that would somehow help.

She nodded, trying again and feeling a whisper of air come through. Encouraged, she breathed in again and felt her lungs expand. She held on to Hank as he led her toward the van.

"I'll take you to the hospital," he said, opening the passenger door and lifting her into his arms. He put her into the front seat.

She shook her head desperately.

"No time to argue," he said, trying to back out of the van and close her door.

She grabbed his hand and held on. "I'm...I'm fine now," she said, her voice soft and raspy between more gulps of air. Her chest rose and fell and she continued to breathe deeply so that he could see she could do it. "I'm…breathing."

He looked somewhat relieved, though still concerned. "Well, that's good, but I think we should know why you almost stopped."

"I can tell you," she said. "Can you just…get in?"

He closed her door and the sliding door, then ran around to the driver's side and climbed in behind the wheel. "Jackie, I'm taking you…"

She grabbed a fistful of the front of his jacket and pulled him toward her until he was kneeling between the seats. "Hold on to me," she pleaded.

"But you're…" he protested, clearly confused by her behavior.

"Please," she whispered breathlessly. Tears filled her eyes and she had the most awful feeling sobs were going to be the next step in this weird mood progression.

He noted her brimming eyes, and with a frown of consternation wrapped her in his embrace. "All right, take it easy," he said, rubbing gently up and down her spine. "Whatever it is, we can fix it. Just relax. I'm right here."

She held on and wept for what felt like an hour but was probably only moments. She allowed herself the luxury of sinking into the comfort and security of his arms and forgot about all the really difficult elements in her life. For the space of time he held her, she let herself believe they could be fixed, that the impeachment hearing would prove Brockton didn't have a case, that she could explain to Hank what had happened seventeen years ago and he'd understand. He might even forgive her.

She raised her head from his shoulder and looked into his face, trying to gauge if that was possible. But beneath the kindness and concern of the moment, she saw the strength, the toughness that made him who he was, and couldn't decide if those qualities would work in her favor or not.

In the interest of getting through the next few weeks, she allowed herself to believe that they would. Then, after the babies were born, she'd try to explain.

One superhuman effort at a time.

HANK WASN'T SURE what was going on, except that the longer he held her, the more even her breathing became, and for the moment that was all he needed to know.

She drew slightly out of his arms and looked at him, her eyes a little frantic. They seemed to be trying to read his, and for a moment it looked as though they didn't like what they saw. He wondered if his love for her was visible. It troubled her that he continued to care, though she considered their relationship hopeless.

Yet she'd come to him. She'd asked him to hold her—even demanded it. So what did that mean? That he couldn't trust what she told him, obviously.

Then she seemed to relax and come to some sort of decision. She hugged him fiercely for a moment, then smoothed his hair in a gesture that just about unraveled him. "You must think I'm crazy," she said.

He levered himself into the driver's seat. "I've

thought so ever since the day you told me you were staying in Maple Hill. But what's going on today?''

She drew another deep breath that seemed to go through her without obstruction. ''Just a panic attack, I think,'' she said calmly, a weird serenity taking over.

''Over the impeachment?''

''Partly.'' She smiled grimly. ''And partly because I just learned I'm carrying twins.''

Twins. Two for one. That sounded like a deal to him rather than a worry, but then he didn't have to give birth to them. Keep them healthy and happy and raise them to be good and honest citizens along with two other children.

He used to think raising children would be scary, but he didn't anymore. Growing children with her had real appeal. But she probably wouldn't want to know that now. He scanned his mind for something positive to say that wouldn't sound patronizing. Concrete help, he realized, was probably the best thing.

''We'll get you some help,'' he said, putting a hand out to touch her shoulder across the gap between the seats. ''My mother's already mobilizing her ladies for you. I'll…I'll do whatever you need me to do—drive the girls to school and pick them up, do your shopping, run errands.''

She put a hand to his forearm and rubbed gently— another gesture that turned his spine to noodle. ''Thank you. Unfortunately, that'll only substantiate Brockton's accusations.''

''Do we care about that?''

''Technically, no. But if I'm going to have to defend

myself against them, we'll have to be more…
circumspect.''

"I'm your friend.'' He hated having to settle for that.
"That allows me to help, despite whatever spin Brockton might put on it. For starters, I'm taking you home.''

"I have…'' she tried to protest.

"Evelyn can cancel whatever was on your calendar,'' he insisted, pulling the seat belt gently around
her, having to expand it to its farthest reaches to make
it fit. "You can call her from home.''

"I have to pick up the girls…''

"I'll do that.''

"Hank…''

"You need to rest and get your bearings. I'll make
you a cup of tea, you can put your feet up and try to
restore yourself before we make plans for the next few
months.''

She frowned at him. "You haven't heard a thing I've
said about being careful.''

"Yes, I have,'' he corrected, then indicated the
empty lot. "Do you see anyone around?''

"No.''

"Then what are you worried about? Just sit back and
relax.''

SHE HAD TO ADMIT that it was nice to have him put-
tering around her house. He'd put her in her favorite
chair, pulled off her shoes, covered her with a knitted
throw then disappeared into the kitchen to make tea.
She liked the sound of drawers opening and doors clos-

ing—the knowledge that he was occupying her space, touching her things.

Twins, she thought with fatalistic amusement. Two babies. She put a hand to her stomach, where she'd often thought a tiny contortionist was growing—there'd been kicks in so many directions at once. But she had two babies in there.

She wasn't sure why laughter bubbled up, but it did. And it was somehow liberating and soothing to let it free.

"Now, that's more like it," Hank said, carrying in a tray with a pot and two cups. "Are you thinking about how delighted the girls are going to be? They seemed so excited about one baby. Imagine when they learn they'll each have a baby to fuss over."

Jackie was feeling less desperate, but she couldn't help a groan over the reality of what she faced. "Oh, Hank." She took the tea he offered and smiled grimly. "One baby keeps you up for months in the beginning. Two babies will be awful. I'm sure they won't be co-operative enough to sleep at the same time, to not wake each other up, to respect the fact that I often have 8:00 a.m. meetings. Addy's lining up her friends to help me, but you can't expect volunteers to stay the night and get up with screaming babies."

He placed the tray on the coffee table and took the loveseat opposite her. He seemed to be giving the matter thought. "You need a husband," he said. "Someone with the right and the responsibility to stay the night and get up with screaming babies."

She shook her head. "I've had one. They don't do that."

"I'd be happy to prove you wrong about that."

Jackie put her cup down to her lap and let several seconds tick away. The house was quiet; she knew she hadn't misheard him. And he didn't look as though he was teasing.

"Hank," she said finally. "That would never work."

He seemed unimpressed by her rebuttal. "You always say that, yet when you needed help, you came to me."

"You were in the City Hall parking lot."

He shook his head. "You were glad I was there. You needed me, and you came to me."

She looked down at her cup, afraid he'd see how true that was. "You can't propose to me out of some misguided wish to set the past right," she said, her voice faint and stiff.

"That's not it and you know it," he objected, placing his cup on the tray with a small bang. "And if either of us has to set the past right, it's you."

She looked up at him then in mild panic, wondering if his remark suggested that he knew.

He met her eyes, and though they studied hers, she saw no evidence there that he referred to anything other than their last argument.

"I'm asking," he said, "because I love you. I've always loved you. I loved you the whole time we were apart. And you love me. You might deny it, but it's always in your eyes, in your touch."

She fought for calm. "I do love you," she admitted, expecting to see triumph in his eyes. But all she saw was a sort of awed wonder. "But I don't think we should do this to save me from sleeplessness." When he would have protested that that wasn't the reason, she shook her head to stop him. She couldn't believe he was offering what she'd wanted all her life, and she had to refuse. "After the babies are born and I get my life organized, maybe we can...talk about it?" *And maybe by then I'll have the courage to explain—and you'll have the generosity to understand.*

But it wasn't something she could simply confess on the spur of the moment. She needed the right place, the right time.

He leaned toward her, his elbows on his knees. "You think time will make it easier to accept how stupid we were as kids?"

"No," she said with a pleading smile. "You can't imagine how many times I've wished we'd handled that differently. But it'll help me get to an even place where I can think clearly, and deal with only one life-altering decision at a time."

"All right," he agreed finally. "Later. But I'm not going to just disappear until then. Brockton will have to—"

The sound of the doorbell pealed through the house. Jackie lowered her feet off the hassock, but Hank stopped her with a raised hand and went to answer the door. She leaned against the back of her chair with great relief that he'd been distracted from the subject of marriage.

Her father walked into the living room, his brow knit with worry, Sabrina following in his footsteps.

"What happened?" he asked, coming to sit on the hassock near her feet. "I called at your office to talk to you about dinner, and your secretary said you decided to come home after your doctor's appointment. Is everything all right?"

Dinner! She'd completely forgotten about having invited her father and Sabrina. She smiled apologetically at Sabrina, who seemed to be trying to pretend concern for Jackie while looking around the old house with the same greedy expression she'd worn when surveying the inn. She was probably thinking about painting everything white, laying down carpet, reupholstering.

Jackie turned her attention back to her father. "I'm fine," she said, squeezing his hands. "Just a little stunned. I'm having twins, Dad."

"Twins!" He grinned broadly, the reaction the word seemed to engender in everyone. Then he appeared to reconsider from her point of view and asked anxiously, "How do you feel about that?"

"Worried," she replied. "Overwhelmed. Fortunately Hank was around to make me a cup of tea and keep me sane. I'm calmer now and maybe, almost, cautiously...excited."

He kissed her hand. "The girls will be ecstatic."

"I know." That thought did give her pleasure. "About dinner, what say we all go—" She'd intended to suggest they all have dinner at the Old Post Road Inn, but her father interrupted her.

"Actually, I was calling to tell you that Sabrina had

accepted an invitation from the McGoverns at the same time that I accepted your invitation.''

"Before, actually,'' Sabrina put in apologetically as she settled on the loveseat. "I thought you'd understand if we rescheduled for tomorrow. Our treat, of course. And not that the Old Post Road Inn isn't…charming, but I thought we'd go to Springfield to the Firelight.''

If there were any pretentious people in down-to-earth Maple Hill, it was the McGoverns. He was a retired stockbroker who'd made millions for some of his clients, and she behaved as though all his success were hers. And if there was any restaurant Jackie didn't like because it carried elegance to an uncomfortable level, it was the Firelight. Her father looked embarrassed. She forgave him for not standing up his family. She had a new understanding of what it was like to have your life proceed almost without your control.

She patted her father's hand. "Tomorrow will be fine, but I'm not sure the girls have the right frame of mind for the Firelight.''

He nodded. "I'd prefer the Breakfast Barn myself.''

Over her father's head, Jackie saw Sabrina force a frail smile that she strengthened when Adam turned her way. "Sure,'' she said. "Whatever everyone else wants.''

"Now, since I can't visit with my granddaughters tonight,'' Adam said, "what about if Sabrina and I pick them up at school and take them for ice cream?''

"Uh…okay.'' Jackie was eager to share her news

about the twins, but knew they'd be thrilled to see their grandfather. The news could wait until dinner.

Hank returned from the kitchen with the coffee carafe, cups, and cream and sugar. It was the old plastic set Jackie kept on the kitchen table, and she saw Sabrina look it over with distaste.

They visited for half an hour, Sabrina rhapsodizing about the Berkshires and how it was ripe for some stylish touches.

Jackie caught Hank's eye across the room and noted the amusement there. She also caught Sabrina glancing at him often, making remarks about the provincial qualities of Maple Hill. She confessed relief at finding intellectual life in Amherst, presuming, Jackie supposed, that since Hank had just moved home from Florida, he'd share her sophisticated views.

He was polite, but generally silent.

Just before three, Jackie called the school to tell them the girls' grandfather would be picking them up. Then Adam and Sabrina left on their mission.

"Is she horrid?" Jackie asked as Hank gathered up cups. "Or is it me?"

"She's horrid," he confirmed.

"What do you suppose my father sees in her?"

"What's missing in his life since your mother died," he replied without pause.

"But my mother was nothing like that."

He carried the tray to the kitchen, then came back to sit opposite her again. "It's not that, it's just she makes him feel something—excitement, sexual eagerness, whatever—and that's getting him over the awful feeling of being dead himself. When I moved to Florida, I dated a scuba-diving, beach-bunny surfer in her early thirties who was as different from me as it was possible to be. But she was attractive and she liked me and that brought me out of the sinkhole I fell into when I had to leave Maple Hill alone. It lasted about a month and we finally parted by mutual consent.''

She smiled. ''I can't imagine you on a surfboard.''

He laughed. ''Well, that's because I didn't spend much time on it. Usually I was under it, or chasing it, or trying to outswim it after I fell off so it didn't decapitate me.'' He sobered slightly. ''You spent a couple of years in Boston right after that. Did you finish school, or were you looking for something, too?''

The smile froze on her face.

HANK WONDERED about that look. It crossed her face often now—a sort of horrified guilt whenever he talked about their relationship growing more serious.

''Did you love someone there?'' he asked gently, quietly. He hated the thought that there'd been more than just Ricky in her life since the two of them had been lovers, but he had to be realistic. She was beautiful and smart, and scores of men must have found her appealing.

He wasn't sure what to do when her eyes brimmed suddenly with tears. They seemed to surprise her as much as him. She closed her eyes and drew a breath.

He went to sit on the side of her chair and wrapped his arms around her. ''It's all right,'' he said. ''You don't have to tell me about it. But I can see there's something unresolved from that time."

She leaned into him with a vulnerability she seldom displayed. He could feel a tremor in her.

"Is it anything I can take care of for you?" he asked, concerned by her abject misery.

She held tightly to him and shook her head. "No," she said finally, drawing another breath. "It's something I have to do."

He framed her face in his hands and looked into her eyes. "But it involves me, I can see it when you look at me. So why don't you let me help?"

That expression reappeared, stared him in the face, then slipped away when she lowered her lashes and looked up again. "I'll explain it all," she said in a half whisper, "as soon as I can think clearly again. I promise."

"Okay," he said, seeing that she needed out of the discussion. As much as he wanted to understand the problem, he didn't want to torture her with it. Whatever it was, he wasn't going to let it get in his way. "Why don't I take you and the girls to dinner if your father and Sabrina have other plans? As a celebration of the news about twins." Then it occurred to him that she might like to tell the girls in private. "Or would you prefer that to be just a family moment?"

She gave him a look that melted something inside him—one that surprised him after the misery he'd seen in her only moments ago. It was filled with warmth and affection and something deeper she seemed able to acknowledge even if she didn't know what to do with it. It said he belonged.

"What about the Breakfast Barn?" she asked. "The girls love strawberry waffles, and an omelette sounds really good to me."

He tried to act as casually as she did. "Sounds good to me, too. I'll haul some wood in for you while we're waiting for the girls." He indicated the almost empty brass wood box.

"Actually," she said, scooting toward the front of the chair, preparing to push herself to her feet. It seemed such an ordeal for her. "I wanted to talk to you about adding outlets in the girls' rooms."

He stood in front of her and offered his hands. She pulled herself up with a sigh and a groan. "There's only one in each room in these old homes, and while we've modernized the rest of the house, their rooms need a little work. Their clocks and bedside lamps take up the outlet, but I was thinking if we put one across the room, I could get them each a disc player to help numb the fact that they'll have a lot less of my attention while I'm adjusting to the twins. Want to have a look?"

She led the way upstairs. She explained what she had in mind, and Hank offered options. Darkness had fallen and they were still discussing it when there was a great commotion downstairs.

"They're home," Jackie said.

Hank laughed. "You're sure? It sounds more like bumper cars going through."

She caught his hand to pull him along with her as she headed toward the hallway to greet them.

The girls rounded the landing and were heading up to the second floor, their eyes alight, their cheeks flushed.

"Twins!" Erica squealed. "We're having twins!" She wrapped her arms around her mother, who'd stopped in the middle of the hallway, clearly disappointed she hadn't been able to tell the girls herself.

"Sabrina says she could tell even before the doctor told you," Rachel reported, getting in on the hug, "because one baby doesn't usually make you so big."

Hank put a hand to Jackie's shoulder, trying to massage away the strain he could see stiffening her back.

Adam appeared on the landing, out of breath. "I'm sorry, Jackie," he said. "Sabrina was excited and spilled the beans without thinking. Hello, Hank."

Hank returned her father's greeting and rubbed a little harder on her shoulder, knowing she was struggling with a careful response. "I doubt she does anything without thinking," she said finally. "But it's all right. Enjoy your dinner tonight."

Adam shook his head. "I'm sure she didn't mean…"

Jackie cut him off with a wave of her hand. "It's okay, Dad. Have fun."

He studied her another moment, then waved and went back downstairs to let himself out.

Erica seemed to understand the mild tension. "Grandpa was mad at her for telling us," she said, then smiled brightly. "But I don't see what difference it makes. We're going to have two babies! Two!"

"One for Erica," Rachel said, "and one for me."

Jackie kissed each head. "Don't I get one of them?"

"Just for diapering," Erica teased. "We get to play with them."

"And get up with them for midnight feedings?"

"Casey Carlisle's mom has a nanny for Casey's little sister," Erica said, "and the nanny lives there."

"Can guys be nannies?" Rachel asked. "'Cause we could have Hank be the twins' nanny, then he could live here. He's not getting to be your boyfriend fast enough."

"He can't be a nanny," Erica pointed out reasonably, "because he has his own business already. If he's going to move in here it has to be because he marries Mom."

"Is that gonna happen?" Rachel asked hopefully.

"They have to fall in love."

"How long does that take?"

Jackie gave Hank an apologetic glance. "Don't you love having your life dissected in the upstairs hallway? It takes longer than we have right now. Hank's taking us to dinner." She shooed the girls toward the bathroom. "Go wash your hands, and Rachel, change your shirt for one that doesn't have ice cream on it."

Giggling and pushing, the girls went to do as they'd been asked.

Jackie led the way downstairs. "Sabrina is trying to separate Dad from his family," she said, giving rein to her anger now that the girls were out of hearing.

"She's done everything she can to annoy me and thwart my efforts to get us all together. She's hoping I'll stay out of their way and she can have him to herself."

He stopped her at the bottom and caught her shoulders. "She can't do that and you know it. Your father's very devoted to you and the girls."

"Then why is he going to the McGoverns with her, when he was invited to dinner here? She said she'd accepted that invitation first, but I'll bet she didn't. She probably sought it out rather than come here. And there was a day when nothing would have kept him from putting us first."

"He'll catch on to her," he insisted. "You just have to let him discover her tricks for himself."

She subsided slightly and folded her arms. "I hope he does that before I'm forced to kill her."

He wrapped her in a hug. "I hope so, too. I'd hate for you to do life in maximum security just when you're falling in love with me again."

She wrapped her arms around his neck, her large belly pressing into his groin. "I don't recall saying that exactly," she taunted.

He kissed her quickly, gently. "I don't either. Why don't you just say it clearly so we can both remember."

To his complete shock, she looked into his eyes and said with grave conviction, "I love you, Hank."

"I love you, Jackie," he replied, kissing her again. Less gently this time—less quickly.

A corner of his mind not occupied with the miracle of her admission heard giggles on the stairs.

CHAPTER TWELVE

"ALEX AND AUSTIN!" Erica suggested. They'd finished dinner and dessert and Erica made a list of twin names on her napkin while Jackie and Hank lingered over second cups of decaf.

"Do the names have to match?" Rachel asked.

Interpreting that to mean did they have to start with the same letter, Jackie shook her head. "They don't have to. But twins names often sound alike or start with the same letter."

Rachel sat up brightly, all her inherent verve glistening in her eyes. "What about Barney and Baby Bop?"

Erica looked at her as though she were a bunch of broccoli. "Baby Bop is a girl!" she said in complete exasperation. "And that's a stupid idea."

Jackie fixed Erica with a firm look. "It's not stupid. They're names that are familiar to her."

Erica looked horrified by her mother's tolerance. "I'm not going to the same school with a kid called Baby Bop."

Jackie laughed. "You won't have to." She patted Rachel's hand. "Keep trying," she encouraged. "Something a little more...special."

"Justin and Joey," Erica said. "Or Justin and JC."

Hank raised an eyebrow in question.

"Singers with 'N Sync," Jackie explained.

"Ah, well, how about Scottie and Bonzi?" Hank contributed.

It was Erica's turn to look confused.

"Portland Trailblazers," he explained. "I'm just trying to get into the spirit of the thing."

Rachel frowned and rested her chin in her hands. "It's too bad they're not girls. Girls' names are better."

"What about Adam and Alex?" Hank suggested.

"After Grandpa!" Erica said, writing it down. "That's a good idea, Mom. And Alex is a good name."

"Do you like them?" Jackie asked Rachel.

She yawned widely. "Yeah. But I want mine to be Adam."

Erica rolled her eyes. "You don't get to just pick one."

"I can if I want!"

"That's stupid."

"You're stupid!"

Jackie smiled wryly at Hank. "Civility's breaking down. Time to go home."

Hank paid the bill and they walked out of the restaurant, he and Jackie between the girls to prevent bloodshed. Hank wrapped an arm around Jackie's shoulders as they started across the parking lot toward his van.

They were intercepted almost immediately by John Brockton and Russ Benedict. Before anyone could react, John Brockton raised a camera to his eye and light flashed in their faces.

"You still maintain there's nothing going on between you two?" he asked with a smug smile.

Hank grabbed John's shirt front in a fist and yanked the camera from him.

"No!" Jackie shouted, putting her hand on Hank's where his knuckles dug into John's throat.

Hank ignored her. He gave John a shake. "You look pretty prepared here, Brockton," he said, holding up the camera in his free hand. "Are you stalking us?"

John was perspiring, but he seemed to know he had an advantage. "You still maintain…" he said again, "that there's nothing going on?"

A crowd had begun to gather around them.

Jackie tugged on Hank's arms. "Hank, the girls," she whispered urgently.

Hank hesitated a moment, then flung John from him so that the man staggered backward into the hood of a truck.

Jackie drew Hank back, holding his arm with both of hers. She then wrestled the camera from him and handed it to Ross Benedict, unashamed of whatever it immortalized. "Let's just go," she said quietly, seeing her career dissolve in disgrace.

"Hank's going to be our dad!" Erica said vehemently, stepping up to John Brockton, her manner aggressive and fearless. Jackie watched in astonishment. It was Hank who caught her arm and pulled her back. "He can be with us if he wants to be," she continued, resisting Hank. "And you leave my mother alone!"

"Yeah!" Rachel stepped forward to put her two cents in. "We're going to get married 'cause they were kissing."

Jackie withheld a groan.

Hank scooped Rachel up in one arm, holding firmly to Erica with the other.

Jackie decided it was time *she* did something. She couldn't leave her defense to her children. The only thing she could think of was probably foolish and maybe even dangerous, but it was a solution.

"Hank and I are engaged, John," she said with icy courtesy, not even considering the repercussions of her statement.

Complete silence greeted the words. Erica and Hank turned to look at her.

And then it hit her. Her heart began to thud. She'd just told a parking lot filled with her friends and neighbors that she was engaged to Hank Whitcomb. She couldn't decide if she felt horrified or exhilarated.

"And if you still consider that that makes his work for us a kind of business nepotism," she went on, angling her chin, "you might remember that he's rewiring City Hall for no charge. I don't think you have a leg to stand on."

"Really." Haley appeared beside them, taking notes. Bart took Rachel from Hank and glowered suspiciously at John.

"What's going on?" he asked Hank. "We just got here. You need a lawyer?"

The two councilmen stalked off to the restaurant.

"Have you set a date for the wedding?" Haley asked

with a detached interest that belied the twinkle in her eye.

Jackie turned to her with a quelling look. "Don't you ever cook?"

She held up her cell phone. "Mom called. Her car was broken down at the market. We picked her up and took her home and thought we deserved a cup of coffee. So. A wedding?"

John Brockton was gone, but the need to carry on with her story remained, Jackie realized, as the audience they'd collected lingered. She was sure they didn't know whether to believe her or not. Suspicion once cast on a public figure or a celebrity would attach itself to that person until they were cleared without a doubt, or the whole thing simply blew over.

But impeachment proceedings would not blow over.

"After the babies are born," Hank said for her when she hesitated too long. "Too much to do before they come."

Haley blinked. "Did you say ba-*bies?* Plural?"

"Yeah!" Erica smiled broadly and wrapped her arms around Jackie.

Rachel clapped. "We're going to be flower girls!" she told Bart and Haley. "And Mommy's having twins!"

Haley squealed and hugged Jackie and the girls. Then she giggled and she embraced her brother. "You're in for it, Hank."

Hank laughed. "Thanks to you, I'm accustomed to dealing with challenges."

Bart grinned at him. "I presume I'm in line for best man? And baby-sitting?"

Hank shook his hand happily. "Yes, on both counts."

Jackie felt another panic attack coming on.

With a glance at her face, Hank reclaimed Rachel and started moving toward the van.

"You do realize you're front page news," Haley warned them, "and there's nothing I can do about that."

Jackie frowned and nodded.

"Good. Then two o'clock Sunday." Haley reminded them of Addy's birthday dinner. "Can you bring fruit salad?"

Jackie nodded. Conversation bubbled around her as they drove home, but her mind was too cluttered to allow her to participate. While Hank fielded the girls' questions about John Brockton and reassured them that the man could do nothing to hurt them, Jackie prayed that was true. The girls had been through so much with their father's death, and Erica had suffered especially with the rumors about Ricky's involvement with other women.

When they got home, Jackie put the kettle on while the girls milled around Hank, clearly delighted at the prospect of him becoming a part of their lives.

Jackie carefully avoided his eyes while she bustled around the kitchen with cups, cocoa, tea and coffee.

"Can I get a new dress for the wedding?" Rachel wanted to know as she climbed onto Hank's knee.

"We'll all get new dresses for the wedding." Erica

stood beside him, leaning an arm on his shoulder. "What color, Mom?"

Jackie was losing her ability to breathe. The harmless deceit had seemed like such a good idea. Actually, when she watched her children with Hank, the whole thing seemed like such a good idea.

Of course, it was all likely to blow up in her face, but she didn't know how to apply the brakes. And in the deepest places in her heart, she could admit to herself that she didn't want to.

"What color do you like?" Hank asked Erica.

"I like yellow," she replied. "Like daisies."

"I want a purple dress," Rachel said excitedly. "Like Barney!"

Erica groaned. "See? We'll never be able to agree."

Hank smoothed the hair out of Erica's face. "Well, do you have to wear the same color? Can't you wear yellow and let Rachel wear purple?"

Even Rachel winced. "That'd be ugly."

Hank turned to Jackie with a laugh. "Help me out here. Our wedding's about to be thwarted by a fashion crisis."

"What color are you going to wear?" Rachel asked him.

"I have to wear a suit," he replied gravely, "and I have only one. It's gray."

"What'll you wear, Mom?" Erica came to take the plate of cookies while Jackie carried the tray of mugs to the table. "Will any of your stuff fit you after the twins are born?"

Jackie let her mind linger longingly on the time

when she would not be bearing this weight. Comfort and a wardrobe would be hers again. She couldn't resist a little shudder of delight.

She caught Hank's eye and saw a watchfulness there that concerned her—and served to bring her back to reality.

"Can we decide on a color tomorrow?" she asked, handing them their cups. "I'm pooped right now. And *Castaway Kids* is on."

The girls scrambled off, cups held carefully, to watch their favorite program.

Jackie sat at a right angle to Hank and drew a breath, wondering how she could explain what she'd done.

"The engagement was a ploy to save us from the suggestion of an affair," he said, leaning across the table toward her, reading her mind with alarming clarity. "But it's developing into a plan you can support, isn't it?"

"Yes." It would have been pointless to deny it. "But we have a million details...issues...to work out."

One really big one, she thought with burgeoning panic.

THERE IT WAS AGAIN, Hank thought. That pleading look that told him nothing about what troubled her, only that she needed him to understand.

"All right," he said, taking a sip of his coffee. "We'll talk about it when you're ready. But I'm moving in tomorrow. You're starting to look pale and more stressed than usual."

"Hank," she said worriedly. "Brockton's out to get us! If you move in…"

"It'll prove we're serious," he interrupted. "I'm not leaving you alone at this point. So I'll take over the home duties so you can concentrate on whatever you need to do to fight the impeachment and set up things with the city so it doesn't fall apart while you're on leave. Now that we know you'll deliver early, we'd better make sure nothing happens to endanger your pregnancy. If he sees us acting like a family, making wedding plans, it'll destroy his ability to make you look like a reckless, loose-living city official."

"But we'll be *living* together!"

"Yes, but the scandal in that is having sex." He lowered his voice in deference to the miss-nothing little girls. "And that isn't safe in your condition."

Her first reaction was a smile, as though she liked that idea. Then she bit her bottom lip, apparently deciding that his solution came with its own problems.

"What about your business?" she asked.

"You handle both," he replied. "I'm sure I can do the same."

"There'll be two lively children," she reminded him, "and two little babies in this house."

He nodded. "I can count. The girls and I do fine together, and I don't have much experience with babies, but I'm sure I'll learn."

She gave him a sweet smile and reached along the table to cover his hand with hers. "You *did* admit to coming home to get a life, but a thriving business, a wife and four children makes you a bit of an over-achiever.''

He caught her hand in his and assumed a teasingly superior air. ''Story of my life.'' Then he felt regretful of the strained circumstances. ''I'm sorry the situation is so lacking in romance.''

She clutched his hand more tightly and uttered a little sound like a laugh with a sob in it. ''When you're this huge and tired,'' she said, ''and this much under siege, it's terribly romantic to have someone insist on taking care of you.''

He brought her hand to his lips and kissed her knuckles. ''When life settles down—'' he waggled his eyebrows wickedly ''—I'll want a few things in return.''

She came to wrap her arms around his neck and kiss the top of his head. ''I hope so,'' she said.

He thought that a curious answer. But then he felt the twins move strongly against his shoulder as she leaned over him, as though they'd tumbled over each other.

She gasped and put a hand to her belly.

Hank stood quickly and pushed her gently into his chair. ''Are you all right? That felt like more than a simple kick.''

She expelled a sigh and smiled tiredly, rubbing where the action had been. ''They're very busy lately. Tidying up, maybe, and getting ready to move.''

He reached over and pulled her teacup toward her. ''Maybe I should move in tonight,'' he suggested.

She shook her head. ''I'll be fine. The activity probably just seems more extreme to me because I know there're two of them in there. They've settled down now.''

He hated the thought of leaving her, but he, too, was going to have to put a few things in order at home if he was going to spend the next few months here. And if his mother was having car trouble, he'd probably have to pick her up in the morning and take her to his office before he moved his things.

"I'll pick up the girls for school in the morning," he said, "so you can have a little extra time to sleep."

She made a face at him. "Thank you, but that's not necessary. I'm fine, and as soon as I get a good night's sleep, forget about Brockton and just concentrate on my children and my job, I'll be even better. Go home, Hank.

"There's a key under the pot of geraniums on the porch. Erica's always losing hers, so I keep an extra. Bring your things in whenever it's convenient."

He leaned over her and looked into her eyes. She framed his face in her hands and brought it down to kiss him chastely. "I can't believe I let you go," she said, a catch in her voice.

He cupped her head in his hand and kissed her soundly, lengthily. "I can't believe I went," he said. "I'll see you tomorrow."

He went to say goodbye to the girls, who offered their cheeks for kisses without moving their eyes from the television. Fatherhood, he decided as he let himself out, was going to be a revelation.

JACKIE WAS A LITTLE SURPRISED that business at City Hall could go on as usual despite the fact that her entire life was about to undergo enormous change—twins, marriage and the threat of professional destruction.

Haley stopped by to take her for a mocha at Perk Avenue.

"Do you know how many calories there are in a mocha?" Jackie asked her as they sat at a small table with mismatched chairs. "I think the twins are going to come out carrying free weights."

Haley settled in across the table and smiled apologetically. "I thought the chocolate would steady your nerves when I tell you that you're front page news this issue."

Jackie rolled her eyes. "The impeachment?"

"That, and your confrontation with Brockton in the Breakfast Barn's parking lot. I'm sorry. It embarrasses you, but it shows Brockton for what he is, which is important as you fight the impeachment. I talked to Rosie Benedict—they're splitting the sheets, you know—and she told me Brockton has been following you, waiting to see you and Hank looking cozy."

Jackie's mind was too turbulent to decide if this was good or bad for her cause.

"Brockton dared me to use his photo of you and Hank," Haley went on, "so I'm going to."

"Haley…"

Haley raised a hand to interrupt her protest. "But I'm using it with a sidebar about your engagement with a little background about your high-school romance and our families' long friendship so that people understand your relationship isn't just a flaming affair."

Jackie put a hand to her forehead, feeling as though stress had tightened everything from her head to her toes. "And this is considered hard news?"

Haley leaned toward her, her eyes grave. "The only real issue Brockton has with you is your relationship with my brother. So we have to prove that it's not a tawdry thing. And the fact that Hank's doing the work gratis takes any threat out of the suggestion of nepotism. We have to make that clear." Haley sighed, snapped her biscotti in two and offered half to Jackie. "I'm sorry it puts you in the spotlight, but ultimately, it's the best thing for you."

"How did I change from the woman people seldom noticed—including my husband—to the center of a public scandal?" Jackie bit into the thick cookie.

"Brockton's trying to make it into a scandal, but it isn't one. That's why we have to be aboveboard about everything."

"Then maybe you'll want to include that Hank's moving into my house today." She chewed and swallowed, everything so beyond her control she wondered why she was worried. There seemed to be little she could do to affect the course of events.

Haley grinned broadly. "No kidding. So, you really are engaged?"

Jackie nodded. "We really are. The girls are thrilled."

"And you?"

Jackie avoided Haley's probing gaze. "I've loved him most of my life."

"Then everything should be fine. Cheer up. Don't worry about the impeachment. None of the charges will stand." She reached across the table to pat Jackie's hand. "Things are looking up for you at last, woman! Jackie Fortin's going to win one!"

Jackie returned her friend's smile, wanting to believe that. If she were to balance the blessings against the hard knocks in her life, the blessings would far out-weigh the problems she'd faced. She had the girls, the house, her work, good friends.

And now, it seemed, she had Hank, and while she knew she should tell him the truth about their shared past before they got married, she didn't have to do it yet. She could just enjoy this time together, pretend there was nothing between them until the twins were born. Build up to the truth. Then, maybe, he'd be so much a part of her little family that he'd consider that his blessings outweighed her truth.

She could only hope.

HE'D PICKED UP THE GIRLS and was fixing dinner when Jackie got home. He smiled and waved a spatula at her over the counter. "Hi!" he called. "Lasagna and green beans with bacon. You'd better have an appetite."

Erica poured milk into two glasses while Rachel set the table.

The girls stopped to greet her with hugs and a giggly ebullience.

"Your sister bought me a mocha in the middle of

the afternoon.'' Still holding the girls to her, she walked around the counter to watch him toss the beans in a bacon-and-onions mixture. ''It's a plot to make me look as though I'm carrying triplets, isn't it?''

He leaned down to give her a quick kiss on the cheek. ''Not at all. I just want those boys to be born big and strong so they can pull their weight around here as soon as possible.''

Jackie looked into Hank's smile and was suddenly overwhelmed by the sweetness of having him here when she came home after a grueling day, and seeing the girls cheerful and apparently happy. That situation had never existed with Ricky. He usually wasn't home for dinner, or if he was, she was fixing dinner, he was watching television and the girls were in their rooms or playing outside. Dinner had never been an eagerly awaited family time.

With her arms still around the girls, she leaned into Hank with a grateful sigh. And he did just what she hoped he'd do. He dropped the spatula and turned to her, wrapping the three of them in his embrace.

''Thank you,'' she breathed into his ear as his cheek rested against hers.

''My pleasure,'' he whispered back.

''Can we have a tickle fight?'' Rachel asked, crooking her index finger and threatening Jackie with it. ''Glory says her family always had tickle fights when she was little. They're really fun. Everybody ends up on the carpet.''

Jackie drew away from Hank with a lingering glance that punctuated her thank-you. Then she turned her attention to Rachel. "Honey, if I got on the carpet, it would take heavy equipment to get me up again."

Rachel made a face. "What's that?"

"You know, those big yellow trucks that haul heavy things around. Like tractors and cranes."

She looked disappointed. "You mean we have to wait until after the babies are born?"

Jackie nodded. "I'm afraid so."

Rachel turned to Hank, who'd gone back to the green beans. "Now that you're the dad, you can say we can have a tickle fight."

"I'm not ticklish," he said with unconvincing nonchalance.

With a child's acute perception of adult weakness, she attacked him. "You are, too!" she cried victoriously. "You are, too!"

He dropped the spatula and backed into a corner, his arms pressed to his side as he tried to fend her off, already laughing. Erica joined the attack.

Jackie left them, Hank's phoney shouts for help mingling with the girls' high-pitched squeals of delight, and went upstairs to change out of her binding clothes and into her robe.

She found Hank's shirts and jeans in her closet, and an unfamiliar shaving kit on the counter in the bathroom. She felt a little thrill at the knowledge that he was sharing her room.

Dinner was delicious. The girls talked nonstop and Hank didn't seem at all bored by their childish tales and observations. He asked questions, learned about their teachers and their friends, then Jackie joined in when the conversation worked its way around to the wedding.

Guilt pinched her viciously, but she ignored it. As though there was nothing in the world to steal away her happiness, she agreed that pink would be a nice color for her and the girls to wear—a decision the girls had come to after Hank said he liked to see women in pink.

"Not a chauvinist opinion," he said when Jackie arched an eyebrow. "Just an aesthetic one. Seems no matter what a woman's coloring, when you put pink on her, her cheeks become a darker shade and her eyes brighten."

"And how many women have you put in the pink?" she teased when the girls went to dish up ice cream.

He grinned. "You're the only one I'm counting. How do you feel?"

She stopped to analyze the afterglow of their delicious meal, her new and exhilarating sense of well-being, the inexplicable mother-high of knowing her children were happy, and admitted without reserve, "In the pink. Definitely."

She helped him clean up while Erica did her homework and Rachel bathed, then curled up with him on the sofa to watch the news.

They tucked the girls in.

"Where are you gonna go on your honeymoon?" Erica asked, leaning up on an elbow.

"We'll have the twins," Jackie said, pushing her down again and tucking the blankets in around her.

"There won't be time for a honeymoon. They're going to keep all of us very busy until they're about three."

Erica frowned. "I think you're *supposed* to have one. So you kind of get to know each other when you're all by yourselves."

"Hank and I have known each other for a long time, remember?"

"Yeah." Erica was up on her elbow again. "But that was as friends. Won't it be different to be married? I mean, don't you have to get to know each other like a husband and a wife?"

For an instant, Jackie wondered if she was talking about lovemaking. Then Erica clarified her question. "I mean, you'll have to balance the checkbook and share the van. Daddy never liked that stuff, remember?" To Hank she added, "Mom forgets to write things down in the checkbook, and sometimes she forgets to put gas in the van. Daddy used to get mad about that." She fell grimly quiet.

Hank came up behind Jackie and wrapped his arms around her. "I love everything about your mom. That doesn't mean we won't sometimes annoy each other and even quarrel, but you can disagree without getting angry, and she's the only woman I ever want to be with. We'll see about the honeymoon. Maybe after the twins are a couple of months old."

Then Hank released Jackie and eased Erica back to her pillows, pulling the blankets up under her chin. "I don't want you to worry about things anymore," he said, leaning down to kiss her cheek. "I'm here to take care of you. Everything's going to be fine. This is going to be a good family.''

Erica wrapped her arms around his neck and squeezed. "I know. Good night."

"Good night, Erica."

"I'm still awake!" Rachel called from her room.

"A good family except for her," Erica grumbled as Jackie and Hank crossed the hall.

Jackie stopped on the threshold of Rachel's room and looked in. "You've already been tucked in," she said gently but firmly. "And you've had your water and you've got your bear."

Rachel sat up, clutching the bear, the soft glow of a nearby night light putting her in shadow. "But I haven't been tucked in by a daddy in a long time," she said. "Can I do it again?"

Before Jackie could reply, Hank pushed her gently aside and went to Rachel's bedside. She hunkered down with her bear and Hank pulled the covers up over her shoulders and tucked them in. He leaned over her to kiss her hair.

"Good night, Rachel," he said.

"When can I call you Daddy?" she asked.

Jackie felt a stab of emotion in her chest. Hank smoothed Rachel's hair. "I won't officially be your dad until your mom and I get married."

Rachel sighed. "Is it okay…if it's not officially?"

There was a moment's pause, then Hank cleared his throat. "It's okay with me. Is it okay with you?"

"Yeah," she replied. "Good night, Daddy."

Another pause. Another throat clearing. "Good

night, baby.'' Hank kissed her again, then pulled the door partially closed behind him.

Jackie opened her arms to him and he wrapped his around her, having to tuck her into his side, around the obstruction of the twins. "Okay, whatever paternal sternness I might have had is dissolved into a puddle of adoration. I hope you're not going to count on me for discipline.''

In a moment, she'd be able to laugh about that with him, but for now, she, too, was a puddle of adoration— for him. Her heart had ached for years over the casual and often minimal effort Ricky made with the girls, and how they'd clung to every little show of affection.

Things would be different with Hank.

"Usually, all they need is a little direction,'' she said, leading him toward the stairs. "But you'll have to toughen up or they'll learn quickly to use your easy-going ways against you.''

He held her arm as they walked down the stairs. "I never thought of myself as easygoing.''

"Their father was often tense and preoccupied. You do lighten the atmosphere. Another cup of decaf while we watch TV?''

"Sounds good to me. You sit down, I'll get the coffee.''

THE HOUSE WAS QUIET when they went to bed shortly after ten.

Giving Jackie a few moments to adjust to the fact that her room was no longer her own, Hank looked in on the girls, pulled the blankets over Rachel's protruding feet, then pushed Jackie's door open to find her standing at the foot of the bed, contemplating a length of black lace.

She looked up a little guiltily. "I could wear this," she said, color in her cheeks, "but frankly, it's itchy. My skin is so dry." She rubbed her belly unconsciously as she spoke.

"Or you could wear nothing," he bargained, taking the negligee from her and tossing it at a chair, "and make me and your itchy skin happy."

She made a face. "This body's pretty ugly," she said, crossing her arms over the big chenille robe she'd put on. "I put the lights out even when I'm alone in here."

He scolded her with a look and went into the bathroom for a bottle of moisturizing cream he'd noticed earlier, when he'd been putting his things away.

He emerged and held up the bottle. "Wouldn't this help?"

She shrugged. "I forget to use it. Or I'm too tired."

He took her hand and drew her gently toward the bed. "Let me do it for you," he suggested softly.

SHE DIDN'T WANT him to see her veiny and bulbous belly and breasts. But he'd already tossed the blankets aside, was plumping pillows up against the headboard, then helping her off with the robe. His touch was gentle, almost clinically detached as he left her socks on and pulled the blankets up to her hipbones.

He sat on the edge of the bed beside her, straightened her nearest arm and put her hand on his shoulder. He took cream in his hands and worked them up and down her arm from shoulder to elbow, then elbow to wrist. He used his fingertips and the heel of his hand, up and down, then up again. She began to feel as though that side of her body had been sedated.

She tried not to think about his hands as he worked on her other arm. But her mind refused to budge from the delicious sensation of him massaging her.

Even as a boy, he'd had a delicate but powerful touch. He used it now, pulling her toward him, leaning her into his shoulder as he applied a dollop of cream to the middle of her shoulder blades. He rubbed up and down her spine, across her shoulders, up one side and down the other, skimming the cleft of her buttocks.

Sensation ricocheted inside her.

He eased her back to her robe, which protected the sheets, and worked on the point of her shoulders. Gently, almost studiously, he applied cream to the dry skin of her breasts, then over her enormous belly.

He shifted focus for an instant to smile at her. "You okay? I can't feel you breathing."

She nodded briefly in response, certain her lungs weren't working. Nothing was working but her nerve endings. She felt a curious edginess that seemed out of place in a massage.

Then his fingertips traced the curve of her belly, and some emotional knot inside was suddenly and dramatically undone.

Oh…my! She thought. *This can't be hap—oh, God!*

IT TOOK HANK A MOMENT to understand what was happening. While trying to pretend a detachment he didn't feel at all, he noticed a mild quiver wherever he touched, a little gasp in her breath as his fingertips smoothed cream into the chapped skin between her belly and her thigh.

She moved suddenly and he thought he'd hurt her.

He stopped to look up at her, saw a flush in her cheeks, a furrow on her forehead, and a sudden, desperate movement of her hand reaching for him.

He caught it in his cream-slick fingers just as she uttered a soft little cry he remembered from long ago.

He experienced relief and a touch of arrogance. Jackie was having an orgasm. He ran his free hand over her belly, doing what he could to prolong it.

JACKIE FELT THE MOVEMENT throughout her body, the languid warmth, the little waves of sensation, the exquisite freedom from the fear that she'd never know that feeling again.

She emerged from the sudden and unexpected fulfillment in astonishment. She hadn't experienced it in the last three or four years of her marriage—even when the twins had been conceived. Yet Hank hadn't even touched her intimately.

She was elated, embarrassed, shaken.

"How…did that happen?" she breathed.

Their hands still joined, he leaned over her to plant a light kiss on her lips.

"Nuclear power," he replied. "We've always had it."

When she could think again, she felt a glow of happiness, a blossoming sense that this was all too good to go bad on her. She wanted to give it a couple of days, to let Hank settle in, to let herself adjust to the wonder of having him within reach, then she would tell him everything.

He would understand. She was growing more confident of that. And then nothing would stand in the way of her and her daughters' happiness. Or Hank's. She would love him as no other woman had ever loved a man.

CHAPTER THIRTEEN

JACKIE HAD four delicious days before Addy's birthday party at Haley and Bart's. The family routine was quiet and sweet and the girls seemed to thrive under it.

Hank got the girls up, made breakfast, managed to find all the critical items that managed to get lost in the morning rush—shoes, homework, field trip permission slip. He drove the girls to school while Jackie got up, took a shower and dressed with the promising smell of fresh coffee in her nostrils.

She made breakfast for herself and Hank, and they ate it together when he returned. Then he drove her to work. He walked her up the stairs to her office, kissed her with the tantalizing promise of what awaited them when there was no longer thirty pounds of babies between them, then went down to the basement to his office.

Glory picked up the girls in the afternoon and stayed with them until Hank and Jackie got home. Glory had started dinner several times. "I've got to learn something about cooking," she explained with an embarrassed smile. "I really like Jimmy and he can't even make coffee."

Her spaghetti sauce was delicious, but her meat loaf

the following night had the consistency of a brick. Fortunately, Addy arrived with a pork and noodle casserole.

"Do not buy me anything for my birthday," she said firmly, placing it in the middle of the set table. "All I want is to be surrounded by my family." She smiled beatifically at Hank. "Now that they've finally come to their senses."

"We already have your present!" Rachel said, "It's…!"

Erica covered her mouth. "You're not supposed to tell."

Addy looked dismayed.

"Come on, Mom," Hank teased, trying to take her coat. "You know you always say that the day before your party, knowing your gift will already be bought. Pretty transparent ploy."

She held on to her coat and frowned at him. "All right, but it would have showed more delicacy if you hadn't pointed it out. Especially since I just brought you your favorite casserole and prevented you from having to eat hardened clay."

Glory, shrugging into her jacket, stared mournfully at the black lump. "I don't know what I did wrong."

Erica patted her arm. "You tried. That's what counts."

Addy hooked her arm in Glory's and led her toward the door. "Oven was too hot, that's my guess. Sometimes the wrong pan can do that to you, too. I hear you're dating Jimmy Elliott."

"Yes."

"Now, that's a nice boy. Likes my brownies."

"Really? I didn't know he liked brownies."

"He does. Without nuts. I have a great recipe…"

Addy opened the door. "See you Sunday, Addy," Jackie called. "Have a good weekend, Glory."

The women, their attention focused on brownie recipes, ignored her.

"If she's your mom," Erica asked Hank when they gathered around the table, "then we can call her Grandma."

Hank nodded. "She won't care that it's still unofficial."

After the girls were tucked in for bed, Hank and Jackie followed their routine of a last cup of decaf while watching an hour or two of television, then went upstairs to bed.

Under the covers and flannel sheet, Hank wrapped his arms around Jackie, her back to his chest. She felt as though she sank into him, physically, emotionally, even spiritually. She let herself be overtaken by the security he represented in her turbulent life, the steadiness that was such a part of him and the generosity he offered every time she turned to him.

The only heartache was the knowledge that she might have had this for the past seventeen years as well. But she didn't dwell on that because everything had been different then. She had him now, though. She had him now.

She reached a hand back to touch his face. "I love you, Henry Jedediah Whitcomb," she whispered.

He kissed her neck. "I love you, Jacqueline Denise Fortin Bourgeois Whitcomb."

"Not officially Whitcomb," she reminded him.

He nuzzled into her hair. "Officially doesn't seem to count around here."

HANK COULDN'T QUITE BELIEVE how much he enjoyed family life. True, it had been less than a week and the girls were being particularly sweet and helpful, and Jackie's usual tendency to resist his every suggestion was blunted by the growing weight she carried and an exhaustion clearly visible in her face. He was also very much aware of his value to the group.

The girls seemed fascinated by his presence and were always nearby, either to ask permission for something or to tell him where the seldom-used melon-baller was in the kitchen and advise him against using the hot cycle on the dryer because it didn't work.

If he settled in the big chair to watch the news or a ball game, Rachel sat in his lap and Erica curled up on the arm of his chair.

Jackie seemed to love those moments, even though it meant she couldn't get near him. She gave him a smile that said she absorbed his love through her children. It surprised him that he understood that.

Yes. He was going to love married life, he thought. Even though two new babies would complicate their schedules and no doubt shred everyone's nerves for a while, they would adjust and the love would expand to encompass all of them. He'd never understood before how flexible love was—or how inexhaustible. He found himself wishing his father were around to see the successful man he'd become, personally and professionally. But he dismissed the thought, realizing that personal demons prevented the man from enjoying his own life. He'd probably be unimpressed by Hank's successes—or unaware of them.

He and Jackie had made a fruit salad for the party that he packed into a cooler with a frozen ice pack. "Where would you go on a honeymoon?" Erica asked, handing him the can of whipped cream to top the fruit with when they arrived.

Rachel knelt on a chair and watched the proceedings.

He put the back of his wrist to his forehead in a theatrical gesture and replied in the voice he remembered Erica mimicking, "A month in Bermuda, I think!"

Erica laughed.

"When I get a honeymoon," Rachel announced. "I'm going to Disney World!"

Erica shook her head pityingly. "That's where little kids go. You're supposed to go someplace romantic."

"What's romantic?"

"Where you can kiss and hug."

Rachel looked confused. "Can't you kiss and hug on the teacups?"

"You can hug and kiss anywhere," Jackie said, walking hurriedly into the kitchen, the girls' coats over her arm. "But we don't have time right now. We're going to be late." She handed Erica her coat and helped Rachel with hers.

Hank caught her as she shooed the girls toward the

door and showed her that you could also hug and kiss anytime—even when late for a birthday party.

Haley and Bart's house was filled with family and friends—Addy, the guest of honor, Haley and Bart's fifteen-year-old foster son, Mike, Adam and Sabrina, Jackie and Hank and the girls and several of Addy's friends. After a potluck lunch, everyone gathered around the dining room table where an enormous birthday cake decorated with pink flowers and a telephone receiver to signify Addy's work with Hank held a place of honor in the middle of a lace tablecloth.

Mike, who seemed very fond of Addy, teased her about the large number of candles and the possibility of the fire department responding to the smoke.

Addy took it all good-naturedly and blew out the candles, her friends helping so that she would get her wish.

"What did you wish for?" Haley asked.

"She can't tell," Rachel intervened, "or her wish won't come true."

Haley leaned down to kiss the top of Rachel's head. "Well, what if we try to guess. Is that okay?"

Rachel turned to Erica for a ruling.

Erica turned to Jackie. "Is it?"

"Um...I think the you-can't-tell rule only applies until you're fifty," she said, then grinned slyly at Addy. "And Addy's way, *waaay* over that."

The decision was met with laughter from the group and the threat of a throttling from Addy.

"Because if you wished for grandchildren," Haley said, "it comes with a guarantee."

Addy patted Jackie's stomach. "I know. Four of them! Do you believe it?"

"Five," Haley corrected.

For a moment, Addy didn't understand. Then Haley and Bart exchanged a look of utter ecstasy, Jackie shrieked and the room exploded with sound.

Hank found Bart in the melee as the women surrounded Haley. He wrapped his arms around him, because now that he had a glimpse of what having children was like, a handshake simply wasn't enough. "Congratulations," he said, clapping him on the back. "When's this going to happen?"

"Middle of October," Bart replied.

Bart had lost his pregnant wife several years ago, and Hank studied his face for any sign of remembered grief. But he seemed completely happy.

"I'm good with it." Bart nodded, apparently reading Hank's mind. "What you lose stays with you always, but you find you're able to go on and things can still be wonderful. Better than you deserve, even."

"Yeah." Hank could agree with that. Of course, he hadn't experienced the same degree of loss Bart had. Jackie hadn't died, just gone out of reach. But he'd reclaimed her after all so he hadn't lost anything— simply gained four children in the process. A pretty good deal all in all.

The women surrounded Bart and drew him into the circle, and Hank noticed that the only one not part of the weeping, laughing knot of guests was Sabrina. She had pasted on a smile, but she looked completely bored with the goings-on. She drifted toward the high-backed settee where Hank stood.

"Loud group," she observed, swiping the back of the settee with a hand before she leaned against it in her white woollen dress.

"Babies are cause for excitement around here," he answered.

"Seems there're a lot already."

"Some believe there are never too many."

She turned slightly toward him and said more quietly, "I'll bet there weren't many at NASA."

He nodded. "That's why I came home."

Obviously finding him as dull as the children, she wandered away toward a window that looked out onto the garden.

Haley suddenly flew into his arms. "Did you ever think you'd be this happy?" she demanded. "You getting Jackie and four beautiful children, and me getting pregnant?"

He loved seeing her so happy. "No, I didn't. But we've both always been pretty good at getting what we wanted."

She hugged him again. "But for a long time, I didn't even know I wanted this."

He held her close. "I know. Fortunately, Bart did. Jackie didn't know she wanted me, either, but I straightened her out. You women don't know how lucky you are."

She squeezed him tightly, then stood back to smile into his face. "Any other day I might dispute that, but today I think you're right. Can you imagine how wonderful next Christmas is going to be around here with Mom acquiring five grandchildren in one year?''

He nodded seriously. ''I hope she appreciates what we've done for her.''

The cake was cut and chairs were carried in from the kitchen so that everyone sat in a large, irregular circle eating cake and ice cream. Hank was helping Rachel with a scoop of ice cream that had fallen off her plate and onto her jumper when he heard a small commotion at the other end of the room. Jackie, who'd been helping Haley serve, looked pale and in pain. She fell into a chair her father quickly vacated, and Hank went immediately to her side.

She breathed through her mouth, her eyes closed.

''Nobody panic,'' she said, puffing. ''I'm okay. Just…just the babies turning around, I think.'' She put a hand out. ''Hank?''

He laced his fingers in hers. ''Right here. You're sure that's all it is?''

Her puffing breaths slowed and she opened her eyes, obviously analyzing how she felt.

''I think you should call your doctor to be sure,'' Adam said. He leaned over her from behind, his face tight with concern.

''No, I think I'm okay,'' she insisted with a small smile for Hank. ''This has happened a couple of times. I think they just forget they're in a cramped space and stretch out.''

''You're sure?'' Hank asked. ''It'd just take a couple of minutes to run you to the hospital and check for sure.''

"No." She was adamant. "It didn't feel like a contraction, just a…"

"Hank's right," Adam insisted. "Remember when you carried Henry, you had to spend the last three weeks in bed."

The room fell silent. Hank, focused on his concern for Jackie, failed to realize for a moment what was wrong with that simple sentence.

Then he saw panic take over Jackie's expression, saw the same panic in Adam's face when she turned to him. Then both of them looked at Hank, and somewhere behind him, his mother's voice asked in confusion, "Who's Henry?"

And that was when Hank felt the sky fall on his head. Henry. Jackie had carried a child named Henry. After him. That was the secret she couldn't share, the truth that brought guilt to her face so often when she looked at him. Probably the reason she'd decided not to leave with him that fateful day seventeen years ago. She'd been pregnant! With *his* baby.

Adam's lips worked as though he intended to say something, but couldn't quite form the words. He turned to Jackie again. She was ashen now.

Hank's mind churned with all the details that didn't make sense. If Jackie had had his baby, his mother would have told him. Haley would have told him.

But Jackie had gone to Boston, he remembered. Was it possible that she'd gone before it had been obvious to anyone?

But she'd come back just two years later.

Without a baby.

Confusion was morphing into anger, and anger was quickly becoming rage. Jackie had given away his baby!

"Jackie," Adam whispered, his face contorting with apparent horror, "I'm sorry!"

Jackie wrapped her arms around his neck and hugged him. "It's all right," she said quietly. "It's all right, Daddy."

Everyone looked at everyone else, frozen in a startled tableau. Then Haley began ushering everyone into the kitchen. "Come on," she said briskly. "Let's finish our cake in there."

"But…what's wrong?" Erica wanted to know, coming toward her mother. Then tension was so palpable, her child's radar had picked it up.

Bart caught her arm and led her toward the retreating group. "She's fine," he said, "because Hank's going to take good care of her." With that he gave Hank a speaking look that Hank noticed but ignored.

"Mommy?" Rachel asked worriedly.

"It's all right," Jackie said in a strangled voice. "Go ahead with Uncle Bart. I'll come and get you in a minute."

Adam tried to begin to explain, but Jackie stood and urged him toward the kitchen. "I have to tell him, Dad."

"But, I want to ex—"

"No," she said. "I have to."

Clearly torn between honoring her wishes and doing what he thought best, Adam finally settled for standing in front of Hank and telling him firmly, "I'm sure your years with NASA have taught you to get all the facts, then think them through before you make a decision on something. I'll consider you less of a man if you don't do that now.''

"Daddy," Jackie pleaded.

With a last worried look in her direction, Adam pushed his way through the swinging door into the kitchen.

The moment they were alone, Hank turned to Jackie, feeling as though an inferno raged inside him. "You had my child!" he accused.

JACKIE WANTED TO DIE. She knew people used that expression all the time to exaggerate their desperation, but at the moment, if it hadn't been that her children needed her, she'd have happily fled the earth.

She'd planned to tell Hank carefully, to remind him of how much they now had together and how much they could have if he would only understand. But the news that he'd had a child no one had told him about had been announced in front of his astonished family and friends—and not even by Jackie herself.

She'd known it didn't pay to be selfish, but she'd so hoped she'd be able to preserve her little bit of heaven by waiting until the moment was right.

She wanted to bawl, to sob, but he'd only think she was playing on his sympathies, so she swallowed against the burning sensation in her throat and held his gaze with cussed determination.

"Yes," she replied. "I did. I tried to tell you...."

"When?" he demanded, taking several paces away

from her as though he found her distasteful. "When did you try to tell me? I don't remember once in seventeen years—"

"That day," she said, struggling to maintain control. Everything inside her shook with emotion and old pain.

And new pain.

"I tried to explain why I couldn't go with you," she went on, "but you—"

"You said you thought it'd be better if you stayed behind," he said, taking several angry steps back to her. "You never once mentioned a baby."

"You talked over me," she returned quietly. "You didn't give me a chance. Then you stormed away."

"Well, what about the seventeen years since?" he roared at her. "Why didn't you call or write?"

Oh, God, she thought, steeling herself. Anguish squeezed her lungs and made air escape in a painful sound. She had to pull herself together. The hard part was coming.

"And where the hell is he?" he asked, both arms spread out to indicate the child's absence. "Where is Henry?"

"I..."

"Did you hate me so much for not listening to your explanation that you couldn't even raise him yourself?"

"Hank, I..."

"What? What! Did you give him away to someone you thought could give him the things your struggling engineer couldn't? Did you find him some high-society family on Beacon Hill?"

"No!" she shouted back at him, her meager composure evaporating as the horror of that time came back in vivid detail. "I had him for five months and I would never have given him to anybody! He's dead! He isn't here because he's dead!"

When Henry died, she used to make herself say the word—*dead*. Not passed away, or gone, but dead. She knew it was the only way she'd accept it. She'd thought herself so strong to be able to do that, so she was surprised to discover that saying the word now could hurt even more than it had then. She didn't know if it was because his father was hearing it for the first time, or because she now had growing children and was forced to confront the real depths of Henry's potential and therefore the real magnitude of her loss.

Hank fell silent, pain a dull force in his eyes. "Dead," he said finally, as though he, too, needed to hear the word again to believe it.

"He had glycogen enzyme deficiency," she said, holding on to the back of a straight chair before lowering herself into it. Her back ached abominably. "He was weak from the very beginning, but he was diagnosed at about a month. They told me there was no cure, and that he wouldn't survive very long." Her mouth began to quiver as she remembered looking into Henry's eyes and seeing Hank there, knowing that the part of him that was his father made him fight to survive. But in the end, nature was stronger than the baby's will. "He fought to stay with me for...for five months. Then...he couldn't...fight anymore."

HANK COULD NOT REMEMBER anything in his life hurting this much. Shock, anguish, loss, all beat through him from head to toe and limb to limb, making him feel as though he had burrs in his bloodstream, hooks in his lungs. His heart throbbed against his ribs, feeling like the claw end of a hammer.

He found that he, too, had to sit. "What…what was it again?"

"Glycogen enzyme deficiency," she repeated. "Glycogen is produced in the tissues, particularly the liver and the muscles, and it's changed into a simple sugar as the body needs it. I guess in simplest terms, his body couldn't feed itself."

His brain had a mental image of an infant struggling to survive—*his* infant—and anguish and anger tumbled over themselves to take control of him. The anguish was too painful, so he gave the anger free rein.

"Why didn't you tell me you were pregnant?" he demanded.

"Because you had big plans," she replied, sniffing and dabbing at her eyes with a tissue. "I wanted you to have your dreams."

He bolted out of his chair, energized by his fury. "The dream that came first with me," he raged at her, "was you and the life we'd make together."

She didn't want to hurt him anymore, but her own anguish was beyond control. "That must be why you shouted me down and took off without looking back when I tried to explain why I couldn't go with you."

"That's not fair," he said with quiet vehemence.

She shook her head at him and replied in the same tone. "None of it was fair."

He paced away from her, hands in his pockets, then stopped at the sofa and turned back to her. "I can't believe you didn't even call me to tell me he'd been born."

A sob swelled inside her. "I knew there was something wrong from the beginning."

"Did you think I couldn't deal with that?" he shouted. "That I'd somehow require he be perfect before I claimed him?"

"No!" she screamed at him. "It was because it hurt so much! It seemed futile to subject you to that when nothing could be done." As Jackie heard herself speak the words, they sounded hollow and absurd, though they'd made sense in her abject misery at the time.

But judging by Hank's expression, he accepted them at their current value. "How can you look at me and say that?" he asked in angry disbelief. "I was his father. I should have known him. He should have known me. You deprived me of five whole months of having a son and him of having a father!"

He was absolutely right. Her parents had pleaded with her at the time to call Hank. But she'd been so destroyed herself, she hated the thought of doing that to him when his mother reported that his letters said he was doing well. Jackie had lived with the guilt ever since.

"I told him his father loved him," she whispered.

"I should have told him myself! How could you have prevented me from doing that?"

"Is loving you an excuse?" she asked, knowing his answer even before he roared it.

"No!" He came back to her to look down into her face, his own tortured with pain. "Because I don't believe you did. How can a mother keep her son from his father and claim she did it for love?"

She wondered how she could make him understand that her own grief and pain had warped her thinking. But he didn't wait for an answer. He stormed out of the house, and an instant later, she heard the van drive away with a screech of tires.

The door to the kitchen burst open and her father rushed out, sitting beside her and wrapping her in his arms. "Jackie, I'm so, so sorry," he groaned. "I can't believe that after all these years of keeping it from everyone, I blurt it out in front of Hank. You'd just gone so pale and I was worried that something would go wrong with..."

"Daddy, it's okay," she reassured him, though tears began to fall in earnest. "It's okay. I should have told him long ago. It's my fault."

"I wanted to come out here and make him understand, but Addy thought..."

"Addy thought that he'd be hurt and angry," Addy said, coming to stand over them, placing a hand on each shoulder, "but that he'd understand. Seems I was wrong."

"No, you weren't." Haley appeared with a cup of coffee, which she handed to Jackie. "He just needs a little time. You can understand that it was a shock. He's a planner, an organizer. He feels vulnerable when he's surprised by things. And most men get angry when they feel vulnerable. Drink this, Jackie. It's decaf, but it's hot.''

Jackie obliged her with a sip, then decided it did feel good going down, warming her chest where a cold rock seemed to have formed. She rubbed at it, needing to make contact with her babies. ''Where are my girls?'' she asked, suddenly horrified by what they must have thought when they heard her and Hank screaming at each other.

''Bart took them out in the back yard when the shouting started,'' Haley replied.

Remembering how angry Hank had been, Jackie was sure they must have heard something—even outdoors.

She clung to her father's hand and, putting her coffee down, caught Haley's in her free one. ''I'm so sorry your party was spoiled.''

''Oh, please.'' Haley held Jackie's hand in both of hers. ''Don't be silly. I'm just sorry…it all happened.''

''And it was a wonderful birthday,'' Addy said. ''Thank you for the beautiful sweater.''

Jackie was suddenly exhausted beyond bearing. ''You'll understand if I excuse myself,'' she pleaded to Haley.

''Of course. Why don't I take you home?''

''I'll take her home,'' Adam said. ''I'll go get the girls and put them in the car, then I'll come back for you.''

''I'm okay, Dad.''

''Just wait here for me,'' he ordered.

''Adam,'' Sabrina said, ''we're supposed to meet the

McGoverns for a drink at their place before the theater.''

Jackie looked up at her in surprise, having completely forgotten she was there.

Adam, too, seemed taken aback by her presence. ''Get Jackie's coat, will you please?'' he asked her, ignoring her agenda alert. He then went through the kitchen for the girls.

Head in the air, Sabrina headed for the study, where Haley had put coats.

The ride home seemed eternal. Jackie sat in the back of her father's Cadillac, the girls pressed in on each side of her, exceptionally quiet. She wondered if her father had asked them not to talk about what had happened.

She waited until they reached the house, then went upstairs with the girls while her father and Sabrina stayed in the kitchen. She had no idea how to explain all that had happened to Erica and Rachel, but knew she had to try.

The three of them sat on the bed in the room she'd shared for the past few days with Hank. The jeans and flannel shirt he'd changed out of for the party were thrown over a chair, and the smell of his aftershave clung to the bedclothes still disturbed from the nap she'd taken just before they left.

Erica seemed to understand that she needed help. ''You had a baby named Henry,'' she said.

Jackie nodded.

''But not with Daddy.'' When Jackie drew a breath,

Erica added gently, "Uncle Bart took us outside, but we could still hear you."

"No. Hank was my boyfriend then. Way before you were born. Way before I married your dad."

Rachel leaned into her. "But if Hank was just your boyfriend, you couldn't have a baby. You have to be married to have a baby."

"No, you don't have to be married," Jackie corrected. "But it certainly makes things simpler for everybody if you are. Hank and I were planning to move away together, but when I found out I was going to have the baby, I didn't tell Hank because I was afraid he'd want to stay here and wouldn't go to school, and I didn't think that would be good for him."

Erica looked confused. "But then Henry didn't have a dad."

Jackie nodded, pain swelling in her all over again. "I did the wrong thing. I thought it was the right thing to do at the time, but it wasn't."

"And Henry got sick and died."

"Yes."

Rachel wrapped her arms around Jackie's stomach as far as they would go. "Were you sad?"

"I was very sad."

"Did you cry?"

"For a long time."

"Now Hank's mad at you," Erica observed, "because he never got to see Henry."

Jackie nodded, the affirmative catching in her throat.

There was a long silence while they all sat together in the quiet room.

"Is he coming back?" Erica finally asked.

Jackie tried never to give the girls a noncommittal answer to any question, but this time it was the only one she had. "I don't know," she said.

HANK DROVE TO GLOUCESTER at the opposite end of the state. He hadn't intended to, he just kept driving and looked up at some point in the darkness and saw the monument to the New England fisherman.

He stopped at a small diner for a cup of coffee, filled up the gas tank at a neighboring station, then headed for Boston.

He tried to think as he drove, but his mind was so completely occupied with pain that all he could do was control the car. His brain wouldn't allow for anything else.

Once he reached Logan International Airport, he turned around and headed west. He stopped for coffee again, and when the waitress pointed out that his hands were shaking and he should probably eat something, he ordered bacon and eggs. His stomach refused the bacon and the hash browns, but he ate the eggs and the toast.

As he drove west on Interstate 90, his brain began to look for something to occupy it. He saw a picture in his mind of Jackie with a baby in her arms and quickly pushed it away. Work. He could think about work. And all he could think was that he'd have to move Whitcomb's Wonders to another town. He couldn't stay in Maple Hill now. He couldn't look at

Jackie every day and remember that she'd deprived him of his child.

Then he remembered that he'd promised the Maple Hill Manor Private School outside of Maple Hill that he'd see what was wrong with the illuminated marquee, and he was supposed to meet with Holden Construction to talk about doing the wiring on a development up the hill from the Old Post Road Inn. And all his "wonders" lived in and around Maple Hill. How could he leave?

Well. He'd have to move out of his office at City Hall at the very least. He couldn't stand the thought of running into Jackie every day.

Then he remembered that he'd promised to rewire the building, and that his promise was part of the city council minutes. Doing the job from an office outside of the building to make the next month or so easier on himself when he had everything he needed right in the basement would be foolish.

All right, then. He'd stay in the building. But there was no question now that he had to move out of Jackie's house. He wouldn't be able to be that close to her every day and not want to berate her for what she'd done, and he couldn't do that in front of her children.

Yes. He was moving out first thing in the morning.

He was in Auburn, about fifty miles from Maple Hill, when he remembered that he'd promised Rachel he'd put lights in her dollhouse, and Erica that he'd help her with her science project. And he'd promised Jackie that he'd add that outlet to their rooms. Not that he cared about his promise to her, but she thought the disc players the outlets would accommodate would help the girls feel less neglected when the babies arrived, so he wanted to do it. He'd stay until the twins were born because he'd promised the girls he'd take care of them, then he was out of Jackie's house, and the moment he'd finished rewiring City Hall, he was out of there, too.

But he was moving into Jackie's spare bedroom the moment he got back to Maple Hill.

He heard the plan collapse around him.

CHAPTER FOURTEEN

JACKIE AWOKE to the aroma of coffee brewing and something sweet in the oven. She sat up, her heart thumping in excitement. Hank was back! Then she remembered that her father and Sabrina had stayed the night in the spare bedroom, insisting she shouldn't be alone after the emotional upheaval and the unexplained contraction. Sabrina had smiled bravely when he canceled their theater date with the McGoverns.

The vicious headache and generally foggy feeling reminded Jackie just how horrid yesterday had been. She'd lain awake for hours during the night, too grief-stricken to cry, knowing that she'd probably never see Hank again.

At the thought, she sank back against her pillows. She would have given anything to be able to spend the day in bed, but this was a teachers' in-service day at school and she had to figure out what to do with the girls. She had City Hall business to conduct, an impeachment proceeding to fight and babies to prepare to deliver. There was no downtime in her immediate future.

She allowed herself to sob in the shower, to indulge herself with the memory of the last week and how stupid she'd been to let things play out as they had, then dried herself off, blew her hair dry into a somewhat messy, flyaway style that was mercifully fashionable these days and pulled on a khaki jumper over a white blouse. It made her look like a Humvee, but it was comfortable. She put a hand to her aching back and headed to Erica's room. It was empty. As was Rachel's.

She went downstairs and spotted the girls at the table, chatting happily as they ate waffles with strawberries and whipped cream.

"Dad," she exclaimed as she walked into the kitchen, "thanks for cooking, but you don't have to…"

She stopped short at the sight of Hank working at the stove.

Her heart rocketed in her chest. He'd come back! They could talk. Perhaps she could make him…

No. He pulled a plate out of the oven and carried it to her place along with a bowl of berries. When he gave her a cursory glance and a polite "Good morning," she knew he was there simply for the benefit of her children.

Her heart fell like a dropped bowling ball.

Actually, the bowling ball was an interesting metaphor, she thought with gallows humor as she returned his terse greeting and took her place at the table. She did look as though she'd swallowed several.

Well, she'd have a talk with him when the girls went upstairs to get their school things. If he was here because he thought he owed her something because of the impeachment hearing, she would set him straight. If he was here for the girls, that was noble of him, but if she and Hank had no future together, it would be easier on the girls in the long run to make that clear now.

"When did you get back?" she asked Hank civilly, ignoring the fact that he probably didn't care to speak to her.

"About four-thirty this morning," he said, pouring a cup of coffee, which he brought to her. "Your dad and Sabrina were in the spare room, so I sacked out on the sofa."

"Grandpa's going to take us for a ride today." Erica pushed the napkin holder her way. "He went to get gas for the car."

Hank avoided her eyes and went back to the counter to replace the coffee carafe.

Jackie glanced at the clock. "Did Grandpa just leave?"

"A few minutes ago," Erica replied. "Sabrina wants to go shopping, but Grandpa wants to go hiking. He says we need to burn off some steam."

"We can call Hank Daddy now." Her waffle gone, Rachel ate the rest of her strawberries with a spoon, lost in a world of her own where they were a perfect family, unaware that her mother had fixed things so that the dream was dashed forever.

Erica gave Jackie a knowing glance. She understood what had happened, but with the optimism Jackie had taught her to indulge, probably believed that things would work out. Hank was back, wasn't he?

She wished she had the innocence to believe that, too.

Ten minutes later her father returned.

"Are we ready?" he said, handing the girls their jackets from the hallway. "Thanks for spelling me, Hank."

Hank nodded. "No problem, Adam. Where you guys off to?"

"Some unknown destination." Adam leaned over Jackie to give her a hug. "I'll call you if we're going to be later than 2:00. I've got an appointment with the dentist at 2:30. Sabrina!"

Sabrina stumbled into the kitchen, elegantly turned out in bright pink fleece, but an air of martyrdom hovered about her. With a cursory good morning to Jackie and Hank, she went out to the car, clearly unhappy at the prospect of spending the day with children.

Unaware, the girls shrugged into their jackets. "Want me to fix dinner tonight?" Adam asked Jackie, then turned to Hank with a neutral expression. "Or are you going to be here? In which case I don't want to intrude."

"I'll be here," Hank replied, "so I'll fix dinner. Why don't you join us?"

"Great. We'll bring dessert."

"Six o'clock."

"Perfect."

As her father hurried off with her children, Jackie braced herself to confront Hank about his presence here.

But the kitchen door opened again and Rachel raced back in, bear-shaped backpack slapping against her blue coat. Jackie turned away from the table, prepared to answer a question or find some misplaced treasure.

Her services weren't required, however, as Rachel ran to Hank. He dried his hands on a tea towel, then braced them on his knees to look into her face. "Hey, Snooks," he said with a smile. "You forget something?"

"I forgot to kiss you goodbye," she said, reaching up to loop her arms around his neck.

He circled her small body with his two hands and kissed her cheek as she smacked him noisily. Then she looked into his eyes with a big grin. "Bye, Daddy," she said.

That was why she'd really come back, Jackie knew. She wanted to be able to say the word.

For an instant, the man who handled most emergencies with skill and calm looked defeated. Then he swallowed, cleared his throat and pinched her chin. "Bye, baby," he said. "Have a good day."

"You, too!" she sang as she raced toward the door. "You, too, Mommy!"

The door closed behind her with a bang that vibrated for several seconds.

Hank came to the table and sat at a right angle to Jackie, his eyes just as turbulent as they'd been yesterday afternoon, though now a glaze of exhaustion lay over them. He pointed to the closed door. "Rachel and Erica are the only reasons I'm back," he said coolly, "and only until the twins are born. Between now and then you have to find a way to explain to them that I'm not staying."

He was well within his rights to be angry with her, but she didn't think she could stand it if he'd returned simply to make that point over and over again until she delivered.

"I did explain to them yesterday that you might not come back," she said quietly, but without the penitence she'd previously shown. "Maybe you should be the one to make them understand why you did. Because if it's just for the opportunity of beating me over the head with what happened, I don't think it'll help them in the long run because I'm the one who's going to have to deal with them when you're gone. I'll do a better job if I'm emotionally intact."

"Why should you be?" he asked, looking her in the eye. "I'm not."

"Hank, I can't change it." She pushed her half-eaten breakfast away and leaned toward him, desperate to make him understand, or at least try. "I was wrong. I take full responsibility, even though you walked away from me when I tried to tell you I had to stay because I was pregnant. I never called you, but you never called me either. I can't tell you how I regret doing that to you, and no matter how I try, it won't change how you feel. So why don't you go now? I'll make the girls understand."

He shook his head mercilessly. "You took away my prerogative to assume my responsibilities when Henry was born. You're not going to do it again. These aren't my children, but I made them a promise to take care of them and I'm going to do it."

"For a while," she reminded him with the same brutality. "Your promise to them wasn't conditional as I recall."

"Don't try to blame this on me," he said coldly.

"Why not?" she shrieked at him, finally unable to take another moment. "I know this is awful for you, but can you think for a minute what that time was like for me? An eighteen-year-old girl in a strange city with a dying baby, the man she loved gone to follow his dreams? You can't forgive me, but I think God has. I died a thousand times myself during those five months. I think I've expiated my sins."

HANK DIDN'T WANT to think about her with a dying baby in her arms. She'd been a warm and wonderful friend and lover in those days, and he could only imagine the intensity of her pain at losing her child. But he'd lost Henry too, and thanks to her, he hadn't even known it. He'd been at school, studying, partying, completely oblivious to the fact that a thousand miles away his son was born and died.

He could see the agony in her eyes, but somehow that served only to deepen his own.

Yet his fury didn't negate his need to stay. His work was here—several major projects underway—and he'd promised the girls. But something else kept him—grief for what Jackie must have endured, an empathy he didn't want to admit to but felt strongly all the same. He felt her pain. He loved her.

He just didn't think he could forgive her.

"I'll take you to work when you're ready," he said,

and left the kitchen to take a quick shower and change his clothes.

When he came back downstairs, the kitchen was empty, and he hadn't heard her upstairs. He looked out the kitchen window and found her using his stool and trying to climb in behind the wheel of his van. He knew she could no longer climb into hers. Seems she didn't fit behind his wheel, either.

He helped her off the running board, where she'd stranded herself, unable to sit behind the wheel and unable to step back down to the pavement because the stool had overturned. Then he reclaimed the keys he'd given her last week. He walked her around to the passenger side and helped her in, expanding the seat belt and handing it to her.

Her face was blotchy and tear-stained, her eyes puffy, her nose red. He felt like a heel. He had to remind himself that his position was justified. They drove to City Hall in silence.

In the parking lot, Jackie tried to climb down without his help, but her belt was looped through the strap of her purse and she appeared close to a meltdown when he came around to help her. The purse freed, he offered her his hand, but he could see as she tried to turn toward him that trusting her to step onto the narrow running board, then down to the pavement without mishap was tempting fate. So he scooped her out, then set her on her feet. She hit him with her purse and walked awkwardly toward the door, a tragicomic figure whose being was now so allied to his that he finally understood in that moment that half his rage and pain over

Henry was because she hadn't allowed him to share her pain.

He left the van in the lot and strode toward the street and the French Maid Bakery. He ordered an Americano and a maple bar to go, then turned to leave with it and spotted Bart and Cameron in a booth in the back. Bart waved him over. The last thing he wanted at the moment was company—particularly company privy to what had happened yesterday—but if he went to work he'd have to face his mother, and that would be worse. Bart moved farther into the booth to make room for him. He looked natty in a pin-striped suit.

"You're back!" Bart observed.

Hank nodded. "Obviously. You got court today?"

Bart frowned at him, hesitated, then said, "Yeah. I take it you two haven't made up yet?" Bart handed him a napkin from a dispenser on the table.

Hank shook his head and took a deep sip of coffee. Then he ripped his maple bar in half. "I don't think we're going to."

"Why not?"

With an apologetic glance at Cameron, Hank turned to Bart and said impatiently, "Because I won't be able to forget that because of her I never saw my son. Come on. Cameron doesn't want to hear this."

Cameron rolled his eyes. "My father's a drunk and my mother's in jail. Other people's problems don't embarrass me. And that puts me in no position to criticize, so feel free to talk. Is her honor the mayor being difficult?"

Hank absorbed Cameron's information with surprise,

then drank more coffee. "It's what she does best," he said finally.

"And you're going to let this be it," Bart asked, "because she tried to save you from the pain she endured?"

Hank turned to his friend in disbelief. "It was a baby, Bart, not a common cold. I lost my son without ever seeing his face."

Bart was silent for a moment, then he said grimly, "So did I. I understand what you feel."

Engrossed in his own misery, Hank had momentarily forgotten that Bart had lost two unborn babies when his pregnant wife died in a plane crash. Hank had sat with him for hours on end, day after day to prevent him from slipping into the darkness yawning at his feet—similar to the one that beckoned Hank at the moment.

"I'm sorry," Hank said, offering him half his maple bar. He suddenly wasn't very hungry. "I'm not usually this self-indulgent, but damn it! I had a son!"

Bart was silent. Hank wondered if it was because he really had nothing more to say, or because Hank had reminded him of his own loss.

"Hard to find fault with a woman who wants to protect you from anything," Cameron weighed in with quiet detachment. "So many of them either want what you've got or want to blame you for what they haven't got. I mean, she was wrong, but she was thinking of you."

Hank finished off his coffee. "You don't have kids."

"No," Cameron admitted.

"Then I'm not sure you could understand."

Cameron shrugged. "I know what it's like to be alone. I thought that gave me the right to tell you to think twice if that's how you're going to end up."

Hank really liked Cameron Trent. He hadn't known him very long, but that didn't seem to matter. He was genuine, willing to put himself out for the job and never complained about the pay or the conditions. It was hard to fault a man like that.

"Thank you," he said simply, though gratitude wasn't precisely what he felt.

Cameron chuckled. "And get the hell out of your face, right?"

"Right."

"Okay." Cameron glanced at his watch. "I'm due at Perk Avenue in ten minutes anyway. Hot water pipes are whining. I'll call in when I'm finished." He slid out of the booth and strode away.

Hank moved to the free side of the table.

"Where'd you go last night?" Bart asked. "Addy and Haley were frantic."

"Gloucester," Hank replied, taking a bite of maple bar.

Bart raised an eyebrow in surprise, then went to the coffeepot on the counter, brought it to their table and refilled their cups.

Hank swallowed the hot brew gratefully.

"You love her," Bart offered, resuming his place.

"Yes," Hank replied, feeling his own grimness settle inside him as though it had plans to stay, "but I can't forgive her."

Bart leaned back in the booth and pinned him with a look. "You're sure it isn't yourself you're having trouble forgiving?"

Hank grew immediately defensive. "What do you mean?"

"If you'd listened to her when she tried to tell you she was pregnant," Bart said, "you'd have known your son." He explained that he knew that detail of their relationship by adding, "Haley went to Jackie's last night and stayed with her for a couple of hours. They talked."

Hank raised both hands in disbelief, then brought them down to the table with a crash that shook the napkin holder and sloshed the coffee. "I don't understand how I get to be the villain in this! I've got to leave before I ram a silk carnation down your throat."

Bart nodded. "Just remember what you were always telling me when Marianne died. 'It's not going to stop hurting if you don't stop focusing on the pain.'"

"Put a sock in it." Hank slipped out of the booth.

"Did you forget that the impeachment hearing's today?" Bart called after him as he headed for the door.

Hank stopped in his tracks, sure there was a stunned look on his face. He had forgotten. And she hadn't mentioned it. Well, he thought, pushing his way outside, they weren't each other's problem anymore. Only the children mattered.

"But, Your Honor," Brockton said as the judge for the impeachment's preliminary hearing refuted the claim that Jackie had advanced her own interests when she'd encouraged the addition of Perk Avenue on Maple Hill Square. "Those women are friends of hers. They…"

The judge, a middle-aged man from Springfield, had made short shrift of most of Brockton's claims. "This is a small town, Mr. Brockton. Everyone knows everyone. And I understand the only other claim on the spot was one…" He consulted his notes. "A Cha-Cha Chicken franchise that wasn't prepared to purchase the building." The judge looked up pleasantly. "The interested party was related to you, I understand."

John squared his shoulders. "That's right, Your Honor, but he was going to put in a restaurant that would have offered more jobs and brought in more revenue. I had nothing to gain from my brother's business."

The judge frowned at him. "I've examined the records, Mr. Brockton, and found nothing to prove that Mrs. Bourgeois profited from Perk Avenue in any way. Mr. Megrath, however, has provided me with a statement from Mr. Benedict's wife that says in part that you're a silent partner in Mr. Benedict's construction company, and had your brother purchased the building, you'd have profited in the renovation for which your brother intended to hire Mr. Benedict."

Jackie turned to Bart in astonishment. He winked at her and returned his attention to the judge.

"Let's move on to your last claim, Mr. Brockton," the judge said.

Jackie shifted nervously—or tried to. She felt so

enormous this morning, so weighted down that the best she could manage was a small fidget.

John cast a dark glance in Jackie's direction and faced the judge. "Everyone in town is aware that Mrs. Bourgeois and Hank Whitcomb had a relationship when they were teenagers."

"And how is that relevant now, Mr. Brockton?"

He pointed to the judge's bench. "You'll notice the photographs included with the Committee for Impeachment's report. The mayor is seen in several instances in intimate circumstances with Mr. Whitcomb. We believe that the relationship is once again active, and that the presence of Mr. Whitcomb's office in City Hall, and the fact that Mr. Whitcomb was hired by the city to…"

"He's rewiring City Hall at no cost, I understand," the judge put in.

"But Mr. Dancer hired him to replace the light fixtures, and I know he's being considered for the homeless project."

Bart stood. "Your Honor, Mr. Whitcomb and Mrs. Bourgeois do have a relationship…"

Did have a relationship… Jackie amended to herself, noting Hank's absence in the room.

"But his employment by the city," Bart went on, "has nothing to do with Mrs. Bourgeois. The city manager is empowered to hire on his own for jobs under a certain amount, as this one was. Those over that amount require the approval of the council. Further, Mr. Whitcomb was hired because of his excellent reputation. Mr. Brockton has done everything within his power to make City hall a hostile environment for Mrs. Bourgeois. He was a confidant of our former mayor, who is now serving time for fraud. Mr. Brockton had hoped to be appointed mayor in his place, but Mrs. Bourgeois—a relative newcomer to city politics, but a longtime resident of Maple Hill with its best interests at heart—received the appointment instead. We believe that simple jealousy and ill will are at the bottom of this impeachment effort.''

''This is pretty flimsy evidence, Mr. Brockton.'' The judge looked through his notes. ''My copy of the invoice for the lights shows that Mr. Whitcomb charged the city three dollars an hour less than standard. And another part of Mrs. Benedict's statement says that you and her husband stalked Mrs. Bourgeois and Mr. Whitcomb.''

John Brockton gaped. ''We…conducted a surveillance.''

''Without legal backup, Mr. Brockton, that's stalking.''

''We're an impeachment committee!''

The judge banged his gavel. ''You're not anymore. I find no cause for impeachment, but due cause for an investigation of your behavior, Mr. Brockton, and that of Mr. Benedict. Go back to work, Mrs. Bourgeois.''

Bart helped Jackie stand as the judge left the courtroom.

And right there, in front of a courtroom packed with citizens who'd come to support their mayor and now applauded her victory, Jackie's water broke.

CHAPTER FIFTEEN

HANK SAT AT HIS DESK, working on Whitcomb's Wonders' accounts receivable. He'd chosen to do paperwork today so that he didn't botch anything electrical. He was too distracted to think clearly. Not very professional on his part, but true all the same.

His mother hadn't spoken to him since he'd arrived that morning. She'd asked him how Jackie's court appointment had gone and he'd told her he'd been repairing a bad connection in the radiology lab at the hospital.

His mother had glowered at him. "I know this has been shocking and painful for you, Hank, but you weren't the only one involved. She was wrong but she acted out of love for you, not because she was being selfish. You should have been at court with her. I'm sure the hospital could have waited." Then she'd gone to work on her quilt. "If you're going to be around the office, you can answer your own phone."

He wasn't sure the hospital could have waited, but he had to admit he'd been grateful for the excuse. All he could think about this morning was babies and children and the horrible injustice of having to lose them before they reached adulthood.

He'd been staring at the Maple Hill Manor Private School's account on the computer screen without seeing it for five minutes now. He tried to refocus and get something done. He'd sent Cameron to the campus, which was two miles out of town, the previous week to give them an estimate on replumbing the kitchen in a minor renovation.

He hit a function key to access Cameron's estimate. He was just making notes for himself when the telephone rang. His mother pulled up a stitch and pretended not to hear. He hated office work, he thought as he picked up the receiver. It was impossible to concentrate on one task for any length of time.

"Whitcomb's Wonders," he said, still making notes. "This is Hank."

"Hank, it's Bart."

Something in his voice made Hank push the notes away and concentrate on the call. "Yeah? They aren't going ahead with the impeachment, are they?"

"No, the judge denied the petition." Bart didn't sound as pleased about that as he should. "If you cared about the result, you could have shown up."

"Look, the hospital had a power problem," he said defensively. "Don't make judgments when you haven't got the facts. Anyway, Jackie didn't even mention it to me this morning."

"Big surprise. You're not easy to talk to suddenly."

Hank swallowed an angry retort. "Did you want something?"

"Yes," Bart replied. "Jackie's in the hospital."

Hank was on his feet. "What happened?" he demanded.

"Nothing," Bart replied. "She's delivering. She asked me to call your mom and ask her to come down, and to tell you that Haley and I'll keep the girls until she comes home. You can go."

Go? Hurt feelings kept Hank silent for a moment.

"Hank?" Bart prompted.

But there was something else wrong here. "Uh…" Hank was thinking. The girls. Where were the girls? "Adam's got the girls. They went hiking. He was supposed to be back at two."

"Jackie asked me to let him know, but neither he nor Sabrina is at the inn. Where would he be?"

"Jackie's?"

"I just called there."

"He had a dentist's appointment at 2:30." Hank looked at the clock. It was 4:15. "Maybe he took the girls with him."

"Who's his dentist?"

"Heck if I know. Bart, I don't know what's going on, but I'm going to the hospital. You find out, all right? Find out if he made the appointment. We've only got three or four dentists in town."

"Jackie'd know."

"Yeah, but I don't want her to think we don't know where her father and her children are while she's having the babies. It may be nothing, but she doesn't need that added worry now. I'll be there in five minutes." He hung up the phone. "Mom, Jackie's having the twins," he said as he handed her his key to Jackie's house. "Will you go to her place and wait there? Adam and the girls are overdue from their trip. If they call or show up, call me on my cell, okay?"

She stuck her needle in the fabric and was hurrying to get her things together as he walked out the door.

To Hank's complete surprise, he arrived at Jackie's room to find Parker with her, massaging her back. Jackie lay on her side, her back rounded, her hair already matted to her head.

When he blinked at Parker's presence, she explained, "Well, I was in the courtroom along with many of her other friends," she said, and Hank couldn't tell if there was mild censure in her tone or not. "Massage can help a lot in childbirth. If you're taking over," she said, pulling him beside the bed and putting Jackie's hand in his, "she's having a lot of back pain, so press with your knuckles and the heel of your hand, adding pressure with your other hand. They're going to be taking her to the delivery room soon. According to the nurse, twins progress more quickly than single babies. Are you okay?"

He was probably pale. He felt pale. He didn't know what to do, or even why he felt he had to be here, but he did. So he was going to have to be useful. And in the back of his mind was a nagging worry about Adam and the girls.

"I'm fine. I'm staying if you have things you need to do."

She glanced at her watch. "I do have a 5:30 appointment."

"Go, Parker," Jackie said. "Thanks so much."

"Sure. You've got a free massage coming your first day back to work. Bye. Good luck."

When the door closed behind her, Jackie asked wearily, "Where's Addy?"

"Out shopping," he replied, pressing the heel of his hand to her back and rubbing. "I left her a message. How's that?"

"Good. Thank you." She gasped suddenly and rolled onto her back, catching his hand and grinding his knuckles. He turned his hand in hers and held it tightly.

The pain seemed to subside after a moment, but she was panting heavily. When she could speak again, she said with a weak shake of her head, "You don't have to be here, you know. You didn't promise the girls you'd see me through labor."

He kept a grip on her hand when she would have drawn it away. "I wasn't there for Henry," he said. "But I'm here now."

PAIN HELD A TIGHT RED WRAPPER over everything in her mind, and Jackie couldn't decide if his words were intended as a promise of support or a condemnation. Did he mean she hadn't let him be there for Henry, so this would somehow make up for that? Or did he mean that he regretted not being there to help her deliver Henry, so he wanted to help her deliver the twins?

She couldn't analyze, couldn't decide. Another contraction rolled over her, and whether he wanted to go or not, she dedicated all her strength to holding on to him.

She had no idea what was really on his mind. He was obviously determined to honor his promise to the girls to take care of them, but he'd already warned her that it didn't extend beyond her getting the twins safely home.

So this time with him would be over in a day or two at the most. She felt a horrible sadness at that realization, then tried to focus on something else. She didn't want her babies to leave her body in an aura of impending doom. She wanted them to move from womb to world in a state of serenity.

"I wouldn't trade this time for anything," she said, instinctively curling up against the back pain. She felt his knuckles rub into her back. "I like knowing what we'd have been like as adults had we stayed together. I think we'd have been happy, even though we couldn't have saved Henry."

"We'll talk about Henry later," he said, working his knuckles up her spine then down again, concentrating on the spot where a head probably pushed, preparing to make an exit. "Right now you should be concentrating on the twins."

"I want you…to understand about Henry." Another contraction racked her and she rolled back again. He held her hand. It felt like a lifeline as pain seemed to submerge her in a well of blackness. She surfaced again in a few seconds, the pain only slightly relieved. "I want you to…understand," she whispered.

"I do," he said, taking the cup of ice chips from the bedside table and putting it to her mouth. He didn't look her in the eye, she noticed, but concentrated instead on the cup of ice. He was fibbing to appease her. "Want some of this?"

"Don't lie to me, Hank," she scolded gently.

He smoothed her hair. His cool hand felt heavenly against her hot forehead. "Can we deal with that later," he asked, "and focus now on the twins?"

She sighed anxiously. "I don't want them to come into a world where you hate me."

"I don't hate you," he denied.

"You can't forgive me," she reminded. "Same thing."

He took issue with that, putting the cup aside and shaking his head. "It isn't at all."

"People say that all the time," she complained. "I love you, but I can't forgive you. But I don't think that can be. If you love, you're openhearted. And if you're openhearted, you can forgive." Pain rolled over her again and she gripped his hand. She felt herself sink once more into the black well of pain, but only part of it was the fault of the contraction. When it was over, she panted, "You should go."

He grinned and indicated the hand she held. "I'd have to leave without my hand. You don't seem to be willing to let it go."

Jackie smiled sadly and freed him. "I know. Isn't it ironic. All that time I couldn't believe in us, you were so patient and let me lean on you. Now that I've established the habit—it's over."

Energy surged up in him. He didn't know where it came from and couldn't quite define it, but it was strong. "It isn't over," he insisted.

"You can't stay because of…" She was interrupted by pain. Even his grip seemed to provide little relief this time. "Because…" she continued breathlessly, struggling to remain rational, "you feel obligated."

He was analyzing why he *was* there when a nurse came in, pushed him gently aside, and made adjustments to the bed. Then she began to roll the bed out into the hall and toward the delivery room.

"You coming?" the nurse asked Hank.

"Can I?"

"Sure. We'll gown you up and you can keep coaching."

He took Jackie's hand and walked beside the gurney until they reached the delivery room's double doors.

It all happened with amazing rapidity. The nurse had warned him to expect a twenty-minute pause between babies, but Adam was born at 6:07 and Alex at 6:16. Born a month early, they seemed alarmingly tiny to Hank, but the doctor assured him after he'd removed them for tests that they were fine.

The births were more amazing and more deeply moving than Hank had anticipated. He'd gone to work for NASA because he longed for the excitement, the thrills, the sense of accomplishment offered by the exploration of the unknown. Yet when he saw Adam and Alex screaming their arrival to the world, he realized that the most profound emotion came with the most familiar gift—life.

He'd known that on some level, because he'd come home in search of personal connection. He just hadn't expected that the connection he'd made years ago would still be open—almost waiting for him—and that he'd find his life wrapped up in Jackie's.

Jackie held the boys, one in each arm, her face devoid of makeup but absolutely radiant. They bellowed and she made comforting sounds.

"Your sisters are going to love you," she crooned. "You're going to be so spoiled, and so adored."

Hank didn't know how to repair what they'd done to each other, but knew only that he wouldn't be left out of this. Henry would understand.

He scooped up one of the babies and held him close, studying the pruney little face, the tiny eyes screwed shut as the infant screamed in agitated waves.

"Who've I got?" he asked.

"First one out," the nurse replied. "Adam, wasn't it?"

"Hank, would you call Dad again?" Jackie asked.

"Mr. Whitcomb!" Another nurse pushed open the room's double doors. "Phone call for you."

He tucked the baby back into Jackie's arm. "That's probably him," he said, kissing her forehead. "I'll be right back."

Hank was pointed to the nurse's station, where an aide handed him a receiver.

"Hank, I don't know what the hell happened," Bart said. "Adam never made the dentist appointment, and I got his cell phone number from the inn, but it doesn't pick up."

Hank could see down the corridor to the revolving doors leading outside. Night had fallen and rain came down in a torrent. Adam and the girls were now five hours overdue.

"Oh, God," Hank said, trying not to even consider the possibility they'd been involved in an accident.

"Maybe they got lost and there's no service where they are," Bart suggested. "Haley's on her way down. She's bringing Jackie a change of clothes and blankets your mom made to take the twins home in." There was a moment's hesitation. "I think I'd better call the police."

He was right. "Thanks, Bart," he said. "I appreciate it. The boys are here."

"All right!" Bart's voice lightened. "Congratulations!" There was another hesitation, as though he wasn't sure he'd made the right response, then apparently decided to leave it at that.

Hank hung up the phone and headed back to Jackie's room. He was surprised to hear shouting coming from it as he reached the door. He went in to find Haley trying to calm a clearly agitated Jackie. She brushed at Jackie's hair, which was sticking up in curly spikes.

Jackie caught her wrist to stop her. "If my girls and my father are missing," she shouted, "I don't give a rip how I look!"

Hank went toward the bed, eyes locking with Haley's.

"I'm sorry," Haley said sympathetically. "I wanted to reassure her that Bart was looking everywhere, that she wasn't to worry…I didn't realize you hadn't told her."

He absolved her with a shake of his head. "It's not

your fault." It would have been comforting to be able to blame someone else, but not fair.

The focus of Jackie's anger turned from Haley to Hank. She did not look like a woman who'd just exhausted her last efforts giving birth. Haley glanced from one to the other, then excused herself and left the room.

"How dare you not tell me my family is missing!" Jackie accused.

"You were a little busy," he began, reaching for her hand, "I didn't want to endanger..."

"If my children haven't been heard from in five hours," she shouted, "I don't mind being interrupted! It's not as though having the twins means I get to give up the girls!"

"Jackie, be reasonable," he coaxed gently, alarmed that she'd so misunderstood his intentions. "You were in labor. We might have compromised the safety of your—"

"That doesn't matter!"

"How could it *not* matter?" he demanded. "We don't know the whole story and you were bringing new life into the world. I was trying to protect you from—"

"They're my girls!" she shrieked at him, her eyes brimming. "My babies! My father! How I dealt with the news while in labor should have been my—"

She stopped abruptly midtirade and stared at him as though he'd turned to stone. Or she had.

OH, GOD, Jackie thought, the sudden silence in the room a very loud thing. So this was how it felt to be deprived of knowledge you had every right to know. The reason didn't seem to matter, only the feeling of alienation the withholding of knowledge created. The situations were different, but she finally understood with blinding clarity why Hank couldn't forgive her.

"I WAS TRYING to protect you!" Hank heard himself say, then stopped abruptly. What was it Jackie had said about Henry's birth and death. *It hurt so much, and I couldn't imagine inflicting that on you when there was nothing you could do.*

He grasped suddenly why she'd thought that such a valid excuse. She'd loved him. However misguided her decision—and his—they'd been made with the most sincere and loving intentions.

JACKIE FELT HERSELF dissolve into a puddle of anguish. "I'm sorry!" she said, reaching blindly for Hank. She felt him sit beside her and wrap her in his arms, and she clung to the warmth and strength he provided.

"Bart's called the police," he said. "There's probably some good reason your father hasn't checked in, but just in case..."

"I know you had my best interests at heart. The news may very well have affected the babies' birth. And I'm so sorry about Henry."

"It's all right." He kissed her cheek and pressed her head to his shoulder. "I understand how you feel. I'm sorry, too."

"I don't know what I'll do," she said in a strangled voice, "if...something's happened."

"Let's not even consider that until there are no other options left."

Hank's cell phone rang.

Jackie's heart pounded. She thanked God for the safe arrival of the twins and begged for the safety of the girls and her father.

Hank's broad grin made her take in a hopeful breath.

"They just called your house from the airport," he said as he closed and pocketed the phone.

She blinked. "The airport?"

"I don't know. They'll explain when they get here. They're on their way. And so's my mother."

Jackie fell back against her pillows, relief flooding through her. "Thank God!" She put both hands to her face, sure she was too spent to cry, but residual hormones made it possible anyway.

She felt Hank's hand in her hair. "It's all right," he said. "Considering you've faced impeachment, given birth to twins, and lost and found your family in the space of one afternoon, I think you're entitled to cry."

She wanted to ask, "And what about us?" But a nurse arrived to wheel her back to her room, and Hank left her to telephone Bart and find a cup of coffee.

As the nurse turned the gurney one way, Jackie watched Hank walk off in the other direction and wondered if this was a metaphor for her future. They'd had an epiphany about each other's feelings a few minutes ago, but was that sufficient for him to want to go back to the way things were when they were planning a pink wedding?

Or would he remember only that he'd put himself out to help her through the birth of her twins while selflessly withholding the news of her missing family, only to have her scream at him like an ungrateful banshee. How many times could he let her hurt him before he said, "Enough!"

CHAPTER SIXTEEN

JACKIE'S ROOM overflowed with family. Thanks to her rather public onset of labor, everyone in town knew the twins had arrived. Flowers crowded every surface and helium-filled balloons bumped the ceiling and danced around the room.

Erica and Rachel stared at their new brothers in the hospital bassinet that had been moved into Jackie's room. The boys shared a single one, apparently feeling no distress at the tight quarters, accustomed as they were to sharing the even tighter space under Jackie's heart.

"We'd driven into the hills," Adam said, "and Bree wanted me to turn around and head back to civilization so she could go shopping, but I thought the girls could use some fresh air and conversation. So I promised we'd hit the mall in Springfield before we came home." He rolled his eyes. "Well, I went down a side road to explore, got turned around, blew a tire and took out my cell phone to let you know I'd be late, and she just lost it."

"She grabbed the phone out of Grandpa's hand!" Rachel contributed excitedly. Erica shushed her, reminding her of the babies. Rachel moved closer to the bed and lowered her voice. "Then she threw it! She told Grandpa all he ever thought about was you and me and Erica, and what she wanted didn't matter at all!"

Erica wandered over, too. "Then Grandpa told her she was being selfish, and she told him he was being an old coot." She smiled apologetically at Adam. "Sorry, Grandpa. That's what she said."

Adam nodded with a laugh. "I heard her. They probably heard her in Boston. Anyway, it took me a while to change the tire—not as young as I used to be—then to find my way back. By the time we were on our way home, Bree was livid, told me she was not staying in Maple Hill a moment longer, and wanted to be taken directly to the airport."

"She didn't want to stop for her clothes or anything," Rachel said. "We have to mail them to her."

"That's why we called from the airport," Adam concluded. He checked his watch. "Her flight left an hour ago. Whew! I thought I wanted the excitement of a younger woman." He chuckled. "Turns out our hearts make their own connections, and no matter what we do, they'll nag us till they get what they want. I want Maple Hill, grandchildren and maybe the occasional date at the movies with a woman I have some hope of understanding." He winked at Addy.

Addy, on a chair in the corner, smiled wryly. "Oh, really. And what makes you think I'd want that, too?"

He shrugged humbly. "I can only hope."

"Well," she said, her hauteur deflated, "so happens

I like the movies, too. But what about your place in Miami?''

"I like it there," he said. "It's a great place to spend January and February. You might like it, too."

Hank stared in stupefaction as his mother blushed.

Bart and Haley reappeared after carrying a load of flowers out to their car. Haley studied Addy's pink cheeks. "Mom?" she asked. "You okay?"

Addy grinned a little sheepishly. "I'm fine."

"Want to come home with us?" Haley asked.

Before she could reply, Adam said, "She's coming home with us to help out with the twins. I'll drive her."

Haley met Hank's eyes and he saw that she'd detected the subtle change in chemistry between their mother and Adam.

"Okay, then." Haley went to hug Jackie, then the girls. "We're off. If you need us for anything, call." Then she hugged Hank, her grip a little more fierce than usual. He could see that she wanted to ask questions and didn't dare.

She and Bart left with a bouquet of balloons.

Adam went to one last, very large flower arrangement. "I'll take this out to the car," he said, "then I'll take Addy and the girls home and you can have a peaceful night's sleep before Hank brings you home."

"Thanks, Daddy," she said as he walked off with the flowers.

"Our little brothers are so cute," Erica whispered. She and Rachel had wandered back to the bassinet.

"I wish I could have both of them," Rachel said,

looking from one to the other as though trying to select the more beautiful baby and unable to.

In a rare moment of sisterly understanding, Erica wrapped an arm around her shoulder. "We have both of them. They're our brothers."

Addy stood and put an arm around both girls, then beamed at their mother. "You can thank their Sunday School teacher for that insightful observation. We're studying families."

Rachel looked up at Hank, who stood on the other side of the bassinet feeling overwhelmingly possessive. "The whole world is our family," she observed seriously. "Did you know that?"

"Uh...sort of," he replied. "Yes."

"And everybody, even the people who are dead, are all one big circle. They're part of us, and we're part of them."

He liked that notion, was amazed that she seemed to understand it. His mother must be powerful stuff in the church basement on Sunday mornings.

"So...Henry's here, too," Erica said, reaching across the twins for his hand. "You'll always have five children. Well, maybe more, you know, if you and Mom..." Unable to decide on the right words to express herself, she concluded, "Anyway, our family starts with five kids. Right?"

Though his throat was tightening and his eyes blurred, Hank swore he could feel his heart mending. "Right," he said with certainty.

Adam returned a moment later, stopping in the doorway at the sight of Addy and Jackie in tears. He turned to Hank in question. The fact that Hank had to clear his throat and draw a breath deepened Adam's concern as he walked into the room.

"It's all right," Hank assured him. "Despite a lot of smart talk, my mother's very emotional. That's something you should know about her. And it's been an emotional day all around."

"Then we'll say good night. Job well done, Jackie." Adam leaned over her bed to hug her.

The girls kissed her, Addy wrapped her arms around her, then embraced Hank. "You did a pretty good job, too, I hear from the nurses. You were a good coach."

He shrugged. "Launching rockets, birthing babies. Big projects are all pretty much the same. You go into it with purpose and determination, and it usually works out."

"Are we forgetting that I was the launchpad?" Jackie teased.

Adam and Addy left arm in arm, the girls dancing off ahead of them.

Hank went to Jackie's bedside. She looked pale, tired and uncertain. He had to fix that.

HANK SAT BESIDE JACKIE, leaning back against her pillows and wrapping an arm around her. She nestled into him gratefully, not sure if this was simply the victorious moment shared by two people who'd endured a long and difficult day, or the coming together of partners determined to share the future.

She felt as though she stood on the tip of a spear, a fall one way promising heaven, the other...

"I understand you have a longing to vacation in Bermuda," he said lazily.

Her heart fluttered. "How did you know?"

"Erica told me. She does a great imitation of you under stress. I thought we'd go in June."

Afraid to presume too much, she asked simply, "Who?"

"You," he replied, "me, the kids, and Glory to help out with them. You think she'd want to come?"

She pushed a hand against his chest to sit up in the circle of his arm and gaze down on him. It occurred to her that she'd looked upon that face in some of her most desperate moments today, and it now felt like her heart's focal point. Did he mean the wedding was still on?

"Are you talking about…a honeymoon?" she asked breathlessly.

"No." Her fragile hope crashed with the simple, forceful reply. Then he added with a smile, "A honeymoon is something we should do alone. Maybe a week in the fall when the boys are able to be without you. We can find a quiet little inn somewhere and never come out of our room. I'm talking about a family vacation in Bermuda. I'm sure the next couple of months will be harrowing. We'll probably all need sun and sand by then."

She stared at him, her heart erupting inside her. Love flowed everywhere, finding every corner in every part of her being. She wrapped her arms around his neck and squeezed with new strength. Life had been such a long, dark haul the last few years that sharing love made her feel as though the Bermuda sun was already beating down on her.

"I love you," she whispered, a sudden and surprisingly virulent sense of heartbreak washing over her because Henry wasn't here. She opened her mouth to express that thought, but he shushed her, putting a hand to his heart and tapping it.

"I've got him right here," he said in a broken whisper. "We'll always have him. Erica said so. All connected. One big circle. And look at the richness of our family now. We're going to be so happy." He cupped her head in his hand and brought her closer to him. "I love you, too. We can get married next weekend."

She hugged him fiercely again, heartbreak dissolving in her overwhelming happiness. "Good. I'm getting tired of you being unofficial."

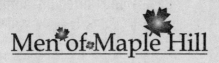

Men of Maple Hill

Muriel Jensen's new trilogy

Meet the men of the small Massachusetts town of Maple Hill—and the women in their lives:

Hank Whitcomb, who's back in Maple Hill, determined to make a new life for himself. It doesn't take long before he discovers he wants his old high school flame, Jackie Bouregois, to be a part of it—until her long-held secret concerning the two of them gets in the way!

Cameron Trent, who's despaired of ever having the family he's wanted, until he meets Mariah Shannon, and love and two lonely children turn their worlds upside down!

Evan Braga, who comes to Beazie Dedham's rescue when a former employer threatens her life. Then Beazie learns the secrets of Evan's past, and now the question is—who's saving whom?

Heartwarming stories with a sense of humor, genuine charm and emotion and lots of family!

On sale starting January 2002

Available wherever Harlequin books are sold.

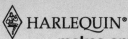